Burden of innocence

Months after their affair had ended, Alex Bennet was still obsessed with the beautiful, enigmatic Christa. So, when out of the blue she peremptorily demanded to see him, he went immediately, only to find her dead. Yet fear of incriminating himself prevented Alex from 'phoning the police. Instead, he contacted Christa's closest friend, Ruth Page, and together they cooked up a story which involved Christa's new lover . . .

DCI Jack Finch's shrewd, intuitive probing finally untangled a web of deceit, suspicion and jealousy – and a deadly resolve to kill.

BURDEN OF INNOCENCE

June Thomson

Constable · London

First published in Great Britain 1996 by Constable & Company Ltd
3 The Lanchesters, 162 Fulham Palace Road, London W6 9ER
Copyright © 1996 by June Thomson
The right of June Thomson to be identified as the author
of this work has been asserted by her in accordance with
the Copyright, Designs and Patents Act 1988
ISBN 0 09 475870 0
Set in Palatino 11pt by Pure Tech India Ltd, Pondicherry
Printed and bound in Great Britain by Hartnolls Ltd, Bodmin

A CIP catalogue record for this book ia available from the British Library

1

When the phone rang that July evening at about quarter-past eight, two days before the end of the school term, Alex Bennet was inclined to ignore it. It was probably Nick Duffield asking him out for a drink, an excuse to talk about his divorce, and Alex wasn't in the mood. He was in the middle of marking a set of ninth-year essays which were due to be returned the following day. But it went on ringing and at last, exasperated by its persistence, he leaned across the desk and picked up the receiver.

'Yes?' he said impatiently.

To his astonishment, Christa's voice cut across his own.

'Alex? I want to see you.'

'When?' he asked, trying to speak naturally despite the shock of hearing her again after so long a time.

'Straight away, at my place. I assume you can make it?'

'Yes, yes. Of course.'

He was about to ask why she wanted to meet him so urgently but she had already hung up. All the same, he went on foolishly holding the receiver to his ear, still dumbfounded by the unexpectedness of the call, coming like that out of the blue, and by the abruptness of her summons.

What had prompted it? He had no idea. He had been trying for weeks to get in touch with her but had reached only her answerphone. None of the calls had been returned nor his letters answered. He preferred not to think of those other occasions when he had sat in his car, keeping watch on her house, nor that evening when he had followed her to Buckleigh Green and had seen Robert Murray, her new lover, get into her Renault and be driven away.

He was still ashamed of the jealousy which had overwhelmed him at the time; and frightened by it, as well. He had never experienced such feelings before. In the past, it was he who had usually put an end to a relationship, hardly ever the woman.

He would go to see Christa, of course. There was no question of not turning up although, as he found his keys and let himself out of his flat, he thought what a fool he was. She had only to pull on his string and he went running back to her. Not that he was under any illusions about her motive for wanting to see him again. It wasn't because she was thinking of resuming their affair. She was angry with him; why, he had no idea. Her voice had sounded cold, peremptory; contemptuous even. And there had been some other quality about it which he couldn't for the moment define.

So the meeting was going to be a confrontation of some kind. And yet, knowing that, there he was taking the familiar route down Parkway as he had done so many times in the past, as buoyed up as ever by just the thought of seeing her again. Like some bloody love-sick adolescent, he told himself angrily.

The turning where she lived, Clifford Street, off London Road, was crammed with cars as usual and he had difficulty finding somewhere to park. He had to drive almost the length of it before he found a space.

Getting out and locking the car, he set out to walk back, his jacket over his arm. It was too hot to wear it. The air was stifling with the stored heat of the day and heavy with the threat of a storm which had been predicted earlier on the weather forecast. The light was already going, sucked down into the thunderous gloom. Only a dull cindery glow remained in the sky, like the after-glow of a great bonfire, throwing into silhouette the squat chimney-pots and the skeletal outlines of television aerials, bristling above the roof-tops.

The street was deserted apart from an elderly man who was coming towards him with a dog on a lead, both plodding slowly as if weighed down with the heat. As they drew level, the dog stopped to cock its leg at a gatepost while the man waited patiently, shifting from one foot to the other. Later, Alex was to recall that scene with particular vividness – the black and white terrier with its back leg raised and the grey-haired man staring into the middle distance, deliberately avoiding Alex's glance as the dog relieved itself.

At the time, though, he thought nothing more about it. He had almost reached Christa's house. In that street of red-brick Victorian villas, hers was different. The last in the road, it was one of a pair, set back from the pavement at the end of a garden which was enclosed at the front by a tall gate and railings of black-painted wrought iron. The house itself had the same formal simplicity. Built of grey gault brick with white stone facings round the windows and the front door, its only decoration was a triangular pediment of the same white stone and grey brick surmounting the roof, and a

6

semicircular fanlight over the door shaped like a shell. Light came streaming out through this fanlight and a yellowish glow filtered through the lowered bamboo blind over the sitting-room window on the right of the porch.

In contrast, the house next door, which was an architect's office, was in darkness as usual, apart from a security light shining down on to the steps. Alex registered these details automatically, not aware then of their significance.

Pushing open the gate, he went up the red and black tiled path and pressed the bell, hearing it ring inside the hall and bracing himself for the moment when she would answer it. He imagined her coming out of the sitting-room to open the door and standing there with the light behind her, gleaming on her hair. But no one came.

He rang again but there was still no answer and, as the seconds passed, he experienced again that same sense of loss like a hollow ache under the ribs when, after she had broken off their affair, he had tried phoning her and had reached only her recorded voice.

She wasn't going to come, he realised, and suddenly the thought roused in him a new and unexpected reaction. Not loss, not grief, not jealousy this time but a clear, uncomplicated anger. And why not? She was obviously at home. The lights were on in the house and there was her Renault parked by the gate. So what the hell was she playing at? It was she who had phoned him and he was damned if he was going to walk tamely away just because she had changed her mind at the last minute about seeing him.

There was a side entrance to the back garden round the corner in Henrietta Street. Although it was probably bolted, it might be worth trying it before he gave up and went home. Striding back down the path, he turned to the left, walking along the side of the house to where a wooden door was set in the high boundary wall. To his suprise, it was unlocked although he thought little of it, only relief that he wouldn't, after all, have to leave without seeing her. Turning the handle, he pushed it open and stepped into the garden.

It was hotter and darker in there, the high brick walls and the trees which surrounded it trapping the heat and shutting out the last of the light. Through the gloom, he could just make out the pale glimmer of the white garden furniture and further off still the vague outline of the head of the Greek goddess, Artemis, which stood on a pedestal at the far end. At closer view, the lighted downstairs windows at the back of the house threw a subdued glow across the flagstones from behind closed curtains or blinds.

7

Of course she was in. She wouldn't have gone out leaving all those lights on, including those in the kitchen and her upstairs studio, the one room in the house he had never been allowed to enter. And she certainly wouldn't have left the french doors to the sitting-room wide open.

He fumbled with the curtains, pushing them aside on their rings and stepping over the low sill into the room. It ran the length of the house, the nearer end furnished as a dining-room in the simple style Christa preferred, the furniture nothing more than an old pine table and rush-bottomed chairs similar to those in some of Van Gogh's paintings, the walls plain white, the polished floorboards left bare.

The far end, which was reached through an arched opening in the dividing wall, served as a sitting-room and here there was greater concession to comfort, although the furniture, which Christa had picked up cheap at auctions and second-hand shops, was shabby and unconventional. There was a bentwood rocker, a heavily carved high-backed chair, oriental in style, and an old chesterfield over which she had thrown a white silk shawl, embroidered with pink peonies, in order to hide some of its worn red velvet cover.

Both rooms were empty as he saw immediately on entering and yet had the air of having only recently been vacated. All the lamps were switched on and the cushions on the rocking chair and the sofa were crumpled as if someone had sat there only a short time before. He assumed Christa was upstairs in the studio which might explain why she had not answered the door even though it occurred to him that it was not much of an excuse. She would have heard the bell; it was loud enough.

But what struck him most was the silence. It was as oppressive as the heat and seemed to stop him from calling out Christa's name. To do so would have been like taking a hammer to a sheet of plate glass.

Instead, he crossed to the sitting-room where the door leading into the hall was set ajar, walking as softly as he could on the bare boards and feeling a ridiculous sense of relief when he reached the large, faded rug which covered them on the farther side and which deadened his footsteps. Reaching the door into the hall, he pulled it open, intending to look for her upstairs.

He saw her at once. She was lying on the floor almost immediately opposite the door and close to the little rosewood table on which the telephone stood. Above it hung a mirror in a battered gilt

8

frame and, as he stood in the doorway, he caught sight of his own reflection in the glass.

It was like confronting a stranger. He saw briefly a face he hardly recognised as his own; dark hair, dark eyes, high cheekbones above an open-necked blue shirt. But the expression it was wearing was oddly familiar even if the features were not. He had seen it on the face of a boy at the school where he taught who had fallen down some steps and broken his hip. It was that same look of shock, rigid, staring, the eyes wide but registering nothing.

Christa was dead. There was no doubt in his mind. Later, he would try to analyse why he had been so certain that she hadn't merely fainted. She was lying face down, her head turned so that he could see only her profile, the chin raised and one eye visible. It was open and, like the boy's eyes and the eyes he had glimpsed in the mirror, it was expressionless, its gaze fixed in a blue stare at the skirting board which ran along the bottom of the wall. But this was different. There was an opaqueness about it which he knew wasn't a sign of unconsciousness.

And there was something else as well. It may have been then that he first noticed the odd lift to her chin and the piece of fabric – a belt, was it, or a scarf? – which was twisted tight about her throat, forcing up her jaw at that unnatural angle. Or had he registered it as soon as he saw her which was why he had known she was dead? He could not remember.

Nor could he recall backing away. He was only aware that he had moved when he found himself standing in the sitting-room. He was still facing the open door into the hall but the angle of view had shifted. Christa's face was no longer visible, only the lower part of her body. She was wearing a cream cotton kaftan, the type of long, loose robe she often wore in the evenings, and a pair of little, heelless slippers, one of which had come loose, leaving her foot bare. It was small, with a high arched instep, and reminded him so poignantly of the living Christa that he could bear it no longer. He had to get out. Turning abruptly, he crossed the room, thrusting aside the curtain in his haste to leave.

On one level he knew he ought to phone the police although he couldn't yet bring himself to form the word 'murder' in his mind. Christa was dead. That was as far as he could go in admitting to the reality of what he had seen. And yet, his mind must have been working on a more instinctive level. Why else should he have walked straight on when he reached the corner of Clifford Street instead of turning right towards his car? Was it an innate sense of

9

self-preservation which made him reluctant to walk back along the road the way he had come in case he should be seen? A fear of witnesses?

It had begun to rain, big, heavy drops which left marks like dark stars on the dry pavement and slithered down the leaves of the trees which lined the road. Within seconds, it had turned into a downpour but he walked on, barely conscious of it, turning left at the next crossing, more concerned with distancing himself from Christa's house and what it contained. Christa dead. The lifted chin. The one naked foot beneath the hem of her robe. He remembered other details as well which he hadn't realised he had registered until that moment. Her hair had come loose from the big tortoiseshell clip she wore on the top of her head and had spread out across the polished boards in fine, shining strands. The first time he had met her in the White Swan at Elmsfield, she had worn the same clip to catch her hair up into a coil, leaving the nape of her neck exposed. But he thrust aside that other image of the tight band about her throat, biting into the flesh, and the blank, fixed look in her eye.

He quickened his step as if to outpace the memory as well as the guilt of leaving her there alone, however irrational that reaction might be. There was nothing he could have done for her. She was beyond help, his or anyone else's. But at the same time, he realised that this was merely a rationalisation to cover another and deeper level of guilt which wasn't so easy to justify. Quite simply, he was afraid.

The road down which he was walking seemed vaguely familiar. He supposed he must have driven along it in the past when he and Christa were still lovers and he used to call on her. He remembered the houses, smaller than those in Clifford Street; terraced cottages opening straight on to the pavements, some of them prettied up with window-boxes and fake Georgian front doors. He recalled, too, the shop on the corner, a sub-post office with a pillar box and a telephone kiosk standing on the tiny forecourt.

Alex felt ridiculous relief at the sight of the phone box. It seemed to lift some of the guilt. Perhaps that was why he had walked in this direction when he left the house, he told himself. Subconsciously, he may have remembered it and been drawn instinctively towards it. He couldn't have phoned from the house, not with Christa lying in the hall. It would have meant leaning over her body to reach the receiver or stepping over it to go upstairs to use the extension in her bedroom.

10

Now that he could think more clearly about his actions, that part at least made sense. But he still couldn't shake off the feeling that his decision to walk away from the house had been motivated by the fear of being seen; a coward's reaction.

He had already shut himself up in the kiosk and was lifting up the receiver ready to dial 999 when this last thought struck him. It was hot in there and the air stank of stale cigarette smoke and human sweat. The rank odour in that confined space seemed to reek of fear itself. The kiosk was claustrophobic, like a cell, totally enclosed, the small panes of glass so misted over that he could see nothing of the street outside, and he felt panic rise in him as he stood there clutching the receiver. The weight of it in his hand and the sight of the round, perforated mouthpiece into which he would have to speak jolted him into a sudden awareness of the reality of the situation.

Christa had been murdered. It was he who had found her. He had no witnesses to prove she was already dead by the time he reached the house. He couldn't even prove that it was she who had phoned him, asking him to call and see her.

The police weren't likely to believe him. Why should they? As he went over the account in his own mind, it seemed implausible even to him. They were bound to ask questions, not just of him but of anyone else who knew about his relationship with Christa. Ruth Page, for example. Or Nick Duffield. Even if he didn't tell the police himself, sooner or later they'd find out that the affair had ended two months earlier.

Why then had she phoned him? Even he couldn't answer that. And why had he agreed to see her? He could hardly tell them the truth – that he was still obsessed with her.

And it wouldn't end there either. There was the rest of it – the letters he had written to her, pleading letters, angry letters, letters in which he had poured out all his misery and frustration. God knows if she had kept them. And then there was the time he had borrowed Nick's car in order to tail her. How was he going to explain that away? Or the evenings he had kept watch on her house when he had been seen by someone on at least one occasion. Or the time he had talked to Ruth Page, Christa's friend, about her after she had thrown him over without any warning and when he had needed someone who knew her and who he felt might understand.

Ruth had understood what he was going through at the time. In fact, she had helped him out of the black pit of despair which had threatened to overwhelm him.

He would phone her first before ringing the police, he decided.

11

Ruth would accept his innocence without question and he felt a desperate need for that reassurance. She was also someone who would grieve with him over Christa's death, the only person who would feel her loss as keenly as himself. Besides, she had a right to know. He couldn't bear the thought of her finding out through a policeman arriving on her doorstep to tell her Christa had been murdered.

He had enough change in his pocket to make the call and, pushing the coins into the slot, he dialled her number. The phone rang several times and he was on the point of hanging up when he heard her voice; not recorded, thank God, but speaking to him directly. She sounded as if she had run to the phone.

'Ruth,' he said quickly. 'It's Alex.'

'Alex? Sorry if I kept you waiting. I was in the shower –' she began but he cut in, anxious to tell her about Christa before the money ran out although he had no idea how he was going to express what he had to say. How in God's name did you tell someone her best friend had been strangled? When he at last spoke, the words came out too fast, too brutally.

Like an eavesdropper on someone else's conversation, he listened to himself saying, 'It's about Christa. She's been murdered.'

He heard Ruth's harsh intake of breath before he hurried on.

'I found her about ten minutes ago. She was lying in the hall. Someone's strangled her. Ruth, I didn't kill her.'

'No, no; of course not!' Ruth's voice sounded strong, reassuring in its certainty. There was a moment's pause in which he could hear her struggling to control her breathing and then she added, 'Have you told the police?'

'Not yet. I wanted to speak to you first. What the hell am I going to do? They'll think I killed her.'

'Listen, Alex,' Ruth said. 'Where are you calling from?'

'A phone box.'

He wondered why she wanted to know this. It seemed so bloody irrelevant.

'Near Christa's house?'

'Yes.'

'Have you got your car?'

'Yes.'

'Then come straight to my house. Don't phone the police yet until we've . . .'

He lost the rest of the sentence. The money had run out and the line had gone dead apart from the dialling tone.

Replacing the receiver, he pushed open the door, gla[...] into the open air. He would follow Ruth's advice, he d[...] drive over to her house before phoning the police. He h[...] her judgement before after Christa had broken off th[...] had talked sense then although God alone knew what she coul[...] or say to help this time.

It was still raining heavily as he walked back to the car but it seemed to have loosened some of the tension in the atmosphere. The air was lighter, fresher. Alex, too, felt a lifting of oppression. His mind seemed to work more coherently. For the first time, it occurred to him to ask himself: Who did kill Christa?

It was not an intruder. He was quite certain about that. There was no sign that anything had been disturbed. So it had to be someone who knew her.

He hesitated to give the man a name, preferring to let him remain anonymous. Identifying him would put him into too clear a focus. But before he could suppress the memory, the image of Robert Murray's face rose clearly in his mind and with it his own shame and anger at that first encounter with him. For a few seconds, Alex saw Murray walking towards him and felt again that surge of jealousy and hatred which had left him shaken by its primitive and irrational force.

He had no proof, of course, that Murray was guilty. But supposing she had ended her affair with him as well? Christa had the capacity to arouse deep emotions. He knew that from his own experience. If Murray had also called on her earlier in the evening to plead with her and she had been cool and dismissive as she had been with him, Murray might well have lost control and strangled her.

Having seen Murray at close quarters on only that one occasion, Alex knew too little about him to judge his reactions in such a situation. And at the time, he had been more concerned with Murray's physical appearance. But he remembered there had been an air of sexual energy about the man which might suggest someone of strong passions.

To avoid walking back past Christa's house, he had taken the long way round and, by the time he reached the top of Clifford Street where his car was parked, his hair and shirt were wet through. The air was cooler, too, and he shivered as he climbed into the driver's seat. Starting the engine and switching on the heater, he sat there for a few moments, trying to control the spasms of shuddering which ran through every muscle, even those in his face.

As he stared out through the streaming windscreen, he repeated to himself over and over: Christa is dead. Christa is dead. Christa is dead.

Something about the rhythm of the words recalled a quotation although he could not remember where it came from.

All passion spent.

The phrase seemed to calm him a little although, as he leaned forward to turn on the windscreen wipers, he realised that none of it was really over. In a sense, it was only just beginning.

2

The rain had stopped by the time he reached Ruth Page's house which was on the other side of town in Bishop's Close, a cul-de-sac off Springfield Road. It was one of a small development of detached chalet-type houses of red brick and white-painted cladding built in the sixties in what had been the grounds of a much larger residence, demolished to make way for them. Mature trees and hedges separated the houses from each other and from the road.

Ruth must have been looking out for him for, as soon as he parked and got out of the car, she opened the front door and came out on to the porch to meet him. Without a word, she stretched up to kiss him on the cheek, gripping him tightly by the upper arms and then, leaning against him, laid her head against the front of his jacket. For a few moments, they stood together in silence. Alex was surprised and also comforted by this physical closeness. Ruth Page had never shown him such intimacy before. She had always been friendly but in a brisk, matter-of-fact manner, almost sisterly in its informal acceptance of him. Now, as she embraced him, he felt she was expressing more than just her own grief at Christa's death. She was also acknowledging his loss as well as her total belief in his innocence. He found it unexpectedly reassuring, as if some bond had been sealed between them.

Then, as suddenly, she released him and, still without a word, drew him into the house.

Neither spoke until they were seated in the sitting-room, Alex in an armchair, Ruth on the sofa, her feet tucked under her. Although she was dressed in jeans and a loose T-shirt, her short dark hair was still damp and spiky from the shower. Without make-up, her face

14

looked pale and oddly incomplete; also older and more vulnerable. It shocked him. He was not used to seeing her like this. The news of Christa's death seemed to have drained her of all colour and vitality.

'Tell me what happened,' she said in a low voice.

Alex began haltingly, finding it difficult to put into words the sequence of events which had led up to his discovery of Christa's body. It was difficult also to meet Ruth's eyes which regarded him steadily throughout his account and he had to keep glancing away or down at his hands. It was only when he had finished that he was able to look directly at her.

'I didn't kill her, Ruth,' he said, repeating the same words he had used to her over the phone.

'I know that, Alex,' she told him.

'But will the police believe me?'

'You haven't phoned them?'

'Not yet. I didn't know what the hell to say to them. And when you said not to . . .' He broke off, ashamed to admit that he had let her make the decision for him. Half rising from his chair, he added, 'I'd better ring them now. I'll use your phone –'

'No, wait, Alex!' she broke in. She had swung her feet to the floor and was leaning forward with sudden urgency. 'After you called, I had time to think. You're right. They're not going to believe you. You were there; you found Christa. And it'll look even worse if you phone them now. They're going to wonder why you waited. That's my fault. I'm sorry; I shouldn't have said anything to you. I realise that now.'

'Then what the hell am I going to do?'

'You could say nothing.'

'You mean pretend I wasn't there?'

The idea shocked him.

'Did anyone see you going into the house?'

'I don't know. No, I don't think so.' He broke off, remembering the elderly man with the dog. 'Yes, there was someone. A man. I passed him on the way to Christa's. He must have seen me. But even if he couldn't identify me, it's not going to work, Ruth. I must have touched things, left my fingerprints behind . . .'

'Where?'

'For God's sake, I can't remember!' he said, his voice rising. 'I didn't know Christa was dead until later. I just let myself in, like I told you. I wasn't paying any attention to what I was touching. The french windows perhaps? The door into the hall? Christ knows. I'm

15

sorry,' he added more quietly. 'I didn't mean to get angry. But I can't go through with it. I was never much good as a liar. I couldn't keep up the pretence. And I can't bear the thought of Christa lying there, perhaps for days, and no one knowing she's dead.'

'Yes, I understand that. I couldn't bear to think of it either. But it won't happen,' Ruth assured him. 'Today's Wednesday. Christa's cleaning woman comes on a Thursday morning. She'll call the police.'

'And then?' Alex asked.

'She'll phone me. She has my home number as well as the office. I gave them to her last winter when Christa was down with flu. I told Mrs Hunter then to ring me if ever Christa was ill again.'

'I don't follow you,' Alex said abruptly. 'If she phones the police, it won't make any difference to the evidence. I was there in the house. They'll find my fingerprints. They'll talk to the man who saw me. And what about the letters I wrote to Christa? If they get hold of those . . .'

'Knowing Christa, she probably burnt them. She hardly ever kept any mementoes, except one or two things of her father's.'

It was a small comfort to know this. He had dreaded the thought of the police reading the letters, knowing what they contained. But even so, this hardly altered the fact of Christa's murder and his discovery of her body.

He said, 'I still think I ought to –'

'Wait a minute. Let me think,' Ruth interrupted him. She had got up from the sofa and had begun to pace restlessly up and down the room, her arms tightly wrapped about herself as if to find consolation in this physical contact.

Alex watched her in silence, not liking to break her concentration. There was a tension about her which was almost palpable. He could feel it crackling in the air like a current of unseen energy.

Suddenly she halted and swung round to face him.

'All right, Alex. This is what you do. Yes, you admit you were at Christa's house this evening. But when you left, Christa was still alive.'

'I can't prove that,' he pointed out. He felt bitterly disappointed that, for all Ruth's intelligence, she hadn't managed to come out with anything more inspired than this.

'No, but I can,' she told him.

Alex looked at her in bewilderment.

'How?'

'Because I shall tell the police that I spoke to her after you'd seen

16

her. You don't have to lie about anything else that happened this evening except that one fact – Christa was alive when you left. You tell the rest exactly as it happened. Christa phoned and asked to see you. You can make up a reason –'

'But I've told you, I don't know why she rang, except she sounded angry about something.'

'For God's sake, you mustn't tell them that!' Ruth said quickly. 'Just say she was sorry about breaking off your relationship. Tell them she wanted to apologise and explain. So you went round to her house and discussed it with her. If you like, you can bring me into it. You can say you'd already spoken to me about it, which is true. Remember the time we met outside Sainsbury's and afterwards you came here and we talked about Christa? I'll back you up on that. I'll also tell them I'd mentioned to Christa that I thought she'd treated you badly, which is also true. I did talk to her about it. And that's why she wanted to see you. Christa still liked you but she didn't want to commit herself and she felt you were getting too serious about her. We discussed all this that evening, remember? All you have to do is make Christa say it instead of me.

'Then, after you and Christa had talked this evening, you left the house. You were naturally upset that Christa wasn't prepared to continue the relationship but you felt better because you'd had a chance to discuss it with her. You'd parted friends and you wanted me to know this. You'd better not say you phoned me. It might seem a bit suspicious, as if I knew beforehand you were going to see Christa. Just say you decided to call on me on your way home, which you did, and we talked about what Christa had said –'

'Is all this necessary?' Alex interrupted.

'Yes, because the nearer you keep to the truth, the more convincing it will sound when you make a statement to the police.'

Alex said abruptly, getting to his feet, 'I'm sorry, Ruth. It's all too complicated and I still don't think it'll work. I'm going to phone the police now and tell them what really happened.'

He was half-way to the door before she caught up with him, clutching him by the arm and forcing him to turn and face her. He was taken aback by the fierceness of her expression, the way her eyes looked directly into his willing him to hear her out.

'Don't be a fool, Alex,' she told him. 'You'll have to make a statement anyway. You found her. And you'll have to explain why you didn't phone them straight away. That's going to look even worse. In heaven's name, listen to me! I'm trying to help you.'

17

'I'm sorry,' he said.

'You'll wait then?'

'All right,' he conceded, returning reluctantly to his chair. Ruth remained standing in front of the fireplace. Hanging on the wall behind her, he could see the portrait of the child's head, one of Christa's charcoal drawings. The two pairs of eyes, Ruth's and the young girl's, were fixed on him, seeming to mesmerise him with their steady gaze.

'I'll make this as brief as I can,' Ruth was saying. 'You called here on the way home. All right? We'll have to work out what each of us said but we can do that later, after we've agreed on the rest of it. Then you left and went back to your flat. What's the time now? I haven't got my watch on.'

'About five to ten,' Alex said, looking at his own watch.

'Then we'll say you arrived here about twenty-five past nine and left soon after ten, say at five past. It's better if we keep roughly to the right times. Someone may see you leave. After you left, I went round to Christa's house and spoke to her. I'll make the excuse I had to go over to the office to pick up some papers I needed. On the way back, I decided to call on her to tell her you'd been to see me. It'll take about twenty minutes to make the round trip. That'll give you enough time to get back to the flat, won't it?'

The full realisation of what she was saying suddenly struck him.

'You mean you're actually going to go over there?'

'Of course, Alex. What else can I do? I can't say I phoned her. The police could check up on the call.'

'But supposing someone sees you?'

'It won't matter. In fact, it'll be better if I am seen. It'll back up my story.'

He said, 'I can't let you go through with it, Ruth. Christa's lying dead in there, for God's sake!'

He saw the muscles in her face flinch as if he had hit her across the mouth and when she spoke her voice had a high-pitched, almost hysterical ring to it.

'I won't go in, Alex! I couldn't bear to do that, even for you! I'll say I spoke to her briefly on the doorstep. She wouldn't ask me in; she said she was busy. I could tell the police she seemed on edge, as if she had someone with her. It'll make them think whoever it was must have killed her. Don't you see, it puts you in the clear?'

'Yes, I realise that,' Alex said, trying to sound grateful. 'I still think it's expecting a hell of a lot from you.'

18

'What's the alternative?' Ruth asked. 'You're innocent. I can't stand by and see you accused of something you didn't do.'

After that brief outburst, she was back in control of herself, her voice again normal. It was only her eyes which showed the tension she was still feeling. The pupils were contracted, the lids taut and stretched. She looked exhausted and he felt guilty for putting her under so much stress.

She was saying, 'When you get back to the flat, make sure some-one knows you're home. That way, the police won't think you went back to Christa's house after you left here. You see the point of that, don't you?'

'Yes,' he agreed bleakly.

There was nothing else he could do except go along with what she suggested. It was too late now to turn back. He was in too deep. It was like walking into a marsh, he thought. With each step, he seemed to be sinking deeper into the morass. And yet there was an awful inevitability about it which he acknowledged. As Ruth had said, he had no other choice.

'You think you can arrange that?' Ruth was asking.

He looked up and met her eyes.

'I'll think of something,' he told her.

Although God alone knew what. He knew the couple in the downstairs flat but not intimately, only to exchange greetings with if they met in the hall or on the front doorstep.

Ruth was saying, 'I'll also tell the police that I tried ringing Christa after I got home, only there was no reply. That way, they'll assume she must have died after the time I spoke to her at the house and before I made the phone call. It'll give you an alibi.'

'Won't the police be able to tell what time she died?' he asked.

'I don't think so; not exactly. She won't be found until tomorrow, remember.' Seeing his expression, she added, 'You've got to go through with this, Alex. Christa's dead. There's nothing either of us can do to bring her back. And it won't help her if you're arrested for her murder. Do you want me to go on?'

When he nodded, she continued, speaking more rapidly.

'Tomorrow, after Mrs Hunter, Christa's char, phones me, I'll ring you at work to tell you Christa's body has been found. As soon as that happens, we'll both get in touch with the police ourselves, as if we've only just heard about it. But we've got to make sure we both make roughly the same statements. So we have to decide now what we're going to say. You remember that evening when we talked about Christa? I told you then about that disastrous affair she'd had when she was in London and how it'd made her very wary about committing herself to any relationship. Well, that's what we talked about tonight. Agreed?'

'Yes, all right,' he conceded. He felt he was entirely in her hands as he had been on that occasion when he had relied on her to help him come to terms with Christa's rejection of him.

Ruth's reference to that earlier affair reminded him of Murray, Christa's latest lover, and of his suspicions that Murray might have killed her. In the shock of finding her body, he hadn't, until now, given any thought to the logical sequence of events which must have taken place before his own arrival at the house.

He said, 'When I make my statement, I'll tell them about Murray. He must have called on Christa this evening soon after she rang me. God, Ruth, I could have met the bloody man coming away from the house! He'd've had about fifteen minutes before I turned up, long enough, I suppose.'

He was taken aback by the vehemence of Ruth's reaction.

'For God's sake, Alex, don't say anything about Murray! It'll only make it worse for you. If you admit you knew Christa had thrown you over for another man, the police are going to think you killed her out of jealousy. Don't you see it gives you a motive? And then the rest of it is bound to come out – how you followed her and found out where he lives. That's going to make them even more suspicious. No; whatever you do you mustn't mention Murray. As far as the police are concerned, you and Christa parted quite amicably. So you had no reason to kill her. Keep Murray out of it.'

'But what if he killed her?'

'Leave that to the police. If he had anything to do with Christa's murder, they'll find it out for themselves. His name and phone number are probably in her address book. But that's not your problem. Your only concern is to make sure the police don't suspect you.'

'Yes, I see that,' he agreed but something in his tone of voice must have roused her suspicions because she said, 'You're still not convinced, are you?'

He said, 'Supposing they don't find out about Murray?'

'I tell you they will. They're bound to.'

'But if they don't?' he persisted.

'Then I'll tell them myself.'

'How? Won't it seem strange if you suddenly come out with Murray's name?'

'Let me worry about that,' Ruth told him. 'I'll think of an excuse when the time comes. If it comes. But I'm sure it won't. I've told you, they'll find Murray's name in Christa's address book. As far as you're concerned, you've never heard of him. You don't even know the man exists. Agreed?'

'Yes, all right.'

He still hesitated and Ruth asked, 'There's something else, isn't there? What is it?'

He said, 'It's Christa's cleaning woman . . .'

'Mrs Hunter? What about her?'

'She'll find Christa's body. Ruth, I don't like the idea of her . . .'

They had begun to walk towards the door and Ruth paused to put a hand on his arm.

'I know, Alex,' she said. 'I understand. But there's no other way out, is there? If you admit you found Christa dead when you went to the house, the police'll think you killed her. They're not going to concern themselves with Murray. Is that what you want? To be arrested? And supposing you're right and Murray's guilty?'

'Christ!' Alex said softly. Until that moment, it hadn't crossed his mind that he might be charged with Christa's murder in Murray's place. The situation took on a new, nightmarish proportion, bizarre and terrifying in its implications. But it was possible. It had happened before. He thought of miscarriages of justice he had heard about – Timothy Evans hanged for the murder of his wife when all the time Christie had been guilty. Or the Birmingham Six, sentenced to life imprisonment. Fifteen bloody years! And Murray left to go free. It was unthinkable.

'Don't worry. I'll make sure Mrs Hunter's all right,' Ruth was saying although he hardly heard her. 'She's a sensible woman and she's got a very supportive son. She'll survive, I'm sure of it. You'd better go now, Alex. I've got to leave the house soon myself.'

They had reached the front door and Ruth stretched up to kiss him on the cheek again but this time the gesture meant nothing to him at all. When he got into the car and drove away, he wasn't really thinking about Ruth and what she was prepared to do for him nor, to his shame, Mrs Hunter. Not even Christa. It was Murray who dominated his thoughts.

Murray had to be guilty. There was no question about that. And with Murray guilty, his first consideration had to be his own survival. That was paramount. For the time being, everything and everybody else seemed to have dwindled into insignificance.

Part of that survival meant setting up an alibi, as Ruth had suggested, and that, in turn, meant he had to make sure the couple in the downstairs flat knew what time he had got home. Although he had assured Ruth he'd think of something, he had, in fact, still no idea how he could arrange it. Call on them? But with what excuse? Or give the front door an extra loud slam as he shut it? It tended to stick anyway and had to be pulled hard to close it properly. That seemed the best option although he was concerned it might not be enough to establish the exact time he had got back to the flat.

He'd have to work it out somehow, he told himself. Even at that very moment as he was driving home, Ruth would be starting out to establish her part of his alibi. Absurd though it seemed, he felt he would be letting her down if he failed in his own attempt.

In the event, the Milners were out. He was aware of that as soon as he turned on to the cramped asphalted forecourt which had once been the front garden of the house. The downstairs window to the room the Milners used as their sitting-room was in darkness and, although Mrs Milner's Fiat was parked in the space immediately in front of the window, her husband's Volvo was not there. They had obviously gone out for the evening.

He drew in beside the Fiat and sat for a few minutes starting at the unlit window. What the hell was he going to do now? Drive over to Nick's place? It was a possibility although it was now too late for him to use the excuse of inviting him out for a drink. And besides, he couldn't face the thought of meeting Nick and having to act as if nothing had happened, Christa wasn't dead, he hadn't found her body, seen her lying there . . .

Thrusting away the memory, he turned to release his seat-belt. It was then that he caught the glare of headlights in his rear mirror and saw over his shoulder Milner's Volvo swing on to the forecourt behind him, stop and then slowly reverse into the gateway before moving forward again into the parking space on the far side.

He found himself trembling with relief as he got out of the car although somehow he managed to control his voice.

'Do you want me to move?' he called out.

Milner's face appeared at the open driver's window.

'No, it's okay,' he said grudgingly. 'Except you won't be able to get your car out until after I've left tomorrow morning. I'm blocking the entry.'

'That's all right. You usually leave before me anyway,' Alex replied.

He locked his own car and, taking out his key, let himself into the house before Milner had time to engage him in any further discussion. Parking was something of a sore point and, given the opportunity, Milner would go on about it at length.

Upstairs, Alex turned on the lights and drew the sitting-room curtains. As he did so, he heard the front door slam shut as the Milners entered and then subdued sounds from the television as the set was switched on. These faint background noises, reminders of other people's lives going on below him, seemed to make the flat appear unbearably empty and silent. Flinging off his jacket, he went through to the bedroom. But although physically and emotionally exhausted, he knew he wouldn't sleep. His mind was too active, his thoughts scurrying this way and that, like some frantic creature trying to escape from a cage.

Christa. Christa. His mind kept turning back to her. Not even Murray had any importance for him now.

As he entered the room, the sight of the bed brought him to a sudden halt just inside the doorway, jolting him back to the pain of the present reality. It was on this bed they had first made love. Christa had lain here, her hair spread out on this pillow as, in a kind of wonderment, he had traced round her mouth and eyes with one finger.

Shutting the door quickly behind him, he went into the kitchen to make coffee for himself. With the mug in his hand, he stood at the window looking down into the darkened garden.

Tomorrow he would have to make a statement to the police but, before he did so, he had to get quite clear in his own mind all that had happened between himself and Christa. It was also, he realised, the only way he knew of exorcising the memories which still haunted him. Only then might her unquiet spirit release him and allow him finally to come to terms with the past.

3

He had met her, he remembered, one Friday evening four months before in March, a few weeks before the end of the spring term, and, extraordinary as it seemed now, he hadn't liked her at that first meeting or even thought her particularly attractive, although he supposed a lot of men would consider her beautiful. She was one of those pale, fine-skinned blondes, the type of colouring that didn't normally appeal to him. It was too neutral, too lacking in warmth and vitality. The way she had worn her hair, pinned up on top of her head with a big tortoiseshell clip, had given her a severe, almost spinsterish appearance.

He was put off, too, by her aloofness, a quality of *noli me tangere*. She had seemed to create a space about her which no one was allowed to enter and from the centre of which she had observed those around her with a cool, watchful detachment.

Of the two women, he had preferred her friend, Ruth Page, who had more energy and animation. There was an air about her of quick intelligence which had also attracted him. Even as Nick Duffield had introduced her, it had occurred to him that she would make an amusing companion. He remembered thinking then that he would like to know her better.

It was Nick who had phoned him up that evening to ask him out for a drink. Both of them were at a loose end at the time, Nick in the middle of his divorce from Jean, his own affair with Barbara Lynford ended at his instigation. It had been an unsatisfactory relationship. She had wanted marriage; he had been unwilling to commit himself. Even so, he missed her or, rather, he had felt the absence of female company in his life. He liked women, even those for whom he felt no sexual desire, such as Joyce Stanley, the head of the English department. With men, he knew where he was. With women, there was always the excitement of discovery. It was probably why, at the age of twenty-eight, he was still single. There were too many attractive women around whom he hadn't yet met and who, like uncharted islands, offered the pleasure of unknown possibilities.

As usual, he picked Nick up from the flat he had moved into after the break-up of his marriage. Nick liked to drink, more so since he and Jean had separated, and he couldn't risk losing his licence by being caught over the limit. As chief reporter on one of the local papers, the *Essex Gazette*, he needed his car for work. As for himself, he found it no problem to keep to a couple of halves when he knew he was driving.

It was Nick who suggested that, for a change, they went to the White Swan at Elmsfield that evening, largely, Alex suspected, because the drive there gave him the opportunity to talk at length about his divorce. In those days, it was his main topic of conversation.

He had known Nick for about three years, having partnered him one evening in a game of squash at the leisure centre he had joined soon after moving to Chelmsford to take up the post of deputy head of the English and Drama department at Ashwood school, a large comprehensive in the Melbourne district of the town. Unlikely though it seemed, he had struck up a friendship with Nick, one of those easygoing, male relationships which demanded little from either of them except a liking for beer and, until the break-up of Nick's marriage, jokey, anecdotal conversations. It was difficult not to like him. A large, untidy, energetic man, he was totally lacking in self-consciousness, a quality which amused Alex although at times he found his exuberance exasperating.

It was a mild evening for March, a harbinger of the hot summer to come, and they had carried their drinks out into the pub garden where Nick had gone on and on about Jean and her treatment of him. Although it was six weeks since she'd filed for divorce and ordered him out of the house, Nick was still complaining bitterly about it. Alex had listened and made sympathetic noises, at the same time thanking the Lord that he had never married or felt the need to commit himself to any one relationship. Knowing also that Nick had had extra-marital affairs with at least two women in the time he'd known him, he had wondered, too, God help him, what Nick was making all the fuss about.

When it grew dark, they had moved inside the pub, where the lights and the noise and the crowds of other drinkers had cheered Nick up, to Alex's relief. It was while they were standing at the bar, ordering another round of drinks, that Nick drew his attention to two women who were seated at a table on the far side of the room.

'That's Ruth Page over there,' he announced, sounding pleased to see a familiar face. 'I interviewed her four years ago when she first opened that employment agency, Personelle, in Moulsham Street. You know, the one that specialises in finding jobs for graduate women. The article made quite a nice little feature. Come over and meet her.'

Holding his beer glass above his head, he began to shoulder his way towards them and, given no option, Alex followed, wondering which of the two women was Ruth Page, the thin, vivacious dark one, her hair cut into a fashionable short bob, who seemed to be doing most of the talking, or her quieter, fair-haired companion. Apparently, it was the dark one for, as they approached their table, it was to her that Nick spoke, grinning broadly as if sure of a welcome.

'Ruth Page. Remember me, Nick Duffield from the *Gazette*? I did a piece on you. Fancy running into you like this. Mind if we join you?'

Not giving Ruth Page time to signal her permission, Nick dragged out a couple of stools and sat down, waving a hand to Alex to join him and using the same gesture to act as a form of introduction.

'Alex Bennet, a friend of mine; teaches English at Ashwood comprehensive. I was telling him about Personelle.'

'Hello,' Ruth Page said, smiling at Alex across the table but, before she could say anything else, Nick had gone barging ahead.

'And who's your friend?' he was asking, turning his attention and his smile towards Ruth Page's companion.

She answered before Ruth Page had a chance to introduce her.

'Christa Wyatt,' she said.

There was a cool note in her voice which should have warned Nick but he seemed oblivious of it.

'Christa? Unusual name, that.'

'It's short for Christabel,' she said dismissively, effectively putting an end to that topic of conversation.

Not at all daunted by Christa Wyatt's coldness, Nick hitched his stool nearer to the table and leaned towards her, one eyebrow quizzically raised in what he himself referred to as the 'old come-on treatment'.

'So what do you do for a living, Christa?'

Alex was amused to see her back away from this too intimate invasion of her private space which Nick, for all his interviewing expertise, still seemed unaware of.

'I'm a freelance illustrator, mainly of children's fiction,' she replied shortly. The tone was designed to forestall any further questions, but Nick, scenting a story, was determined to press on.

'Fascinating!' he said. 'Tell me more.'

'There's nothing more to tell. I'm an illustrator. Of books,' she added, as if Nick was too dense to grasp this particular fact. 'And, as a freelance, I work from home.'

She looked pointedly at her wrist-watch and then, picking up a light jacket which lay beside her on the seat, she said to Ruth Page, 'Isn't it time we left?'

Ruth got up with her and the two men were obliged to stand also to allow them to squeeze past the end of the table, Christa Wyatt first, who neither looked at them nor spoke, and then Ruth Page who smiled her thanks. It was an oblique smile that was at the same time apologetic and a little wry, as if she, too, found the situation amusing.

'Bitch!' Nick remarked almost before the two women were out of

26

earshot. Alex assumed he was referring to Christa Wyatt and was inclined to agree with him. 'God, I hate women like that! They think they're so frigging superior when what they really need is a bloody good screw.'

Since Jean had chucked him out, Nick seemed to have lost several layers of skin. Normally, he would have grinned and shrugged off the situation with some remark about not being able to win them all. Alex wondered if the problem between him and Jean wasn't sexual after all, despite Nick's insistence that it was all down to his job and his irregular hours.

They themselves left shortly afterwards. The encounter with the two women had taken all the pleasure out of the evening. Nick had turned morose, hardly speaking, not even about his divorce, and when Alex suggested it was time they, too, pushed off, he had agreed without any of his usual protests about losing good drinking time or having a final jar.

But he cheered up when they emerged from the bar to find Christa Wyatt and Ruth Page still in the car-park, standing disconsolately under one of the lamp standards examining a dark grey Peugeot, its left-hand wing badly damaged and the headlight broken.

'Look at that!' Nick said exultantly. 'Makes you believe there might be someone up there after all.' Strolling across to them, he remarked with a jaunty air, 'Damsels in distress, I see. Is there anything a mere male can do to help?'

It was Ruth Page who answered.

'Some fool's backed into me. Look, you can see where they've smashed their own rear light.' She indicated the shards of orange glass lying on the ground among the debris of her own headlamp.

'Any idea who did it?' Alex asked.

'No, worse luck. It was like this when we found it. Not another car in sight, of course, and no note on the windscreen.'

'Some people!' Nick exclaimed in mock outrage. 'No consideration for others. They ought to be hung up by their thumbs.'

It was obvious he was hugely enjoying the situation and Alex saw Christa Wyatt turn away with a quick movement of distaste. To divert her attention as well as Nick's, he squatted down by the car to look more closely at the damage.

'I'm afraid you won't be able to drive it,' he announced, sliding his hand in under the crumpled bodywork. 'The wing's been pushed in on to the wheel. It must have taken a hell of a bashing. Sorry about that.'

He stood up, wiping his hand on his handkerchief.

'Who's your garage?' he asked Ruth Page.

'Morton's in Chelmer Street.'

'I don't know them. Do they run a twenty-four hour service?'

'No, I'm afraid not.'

'Then I suggest you either leave the car here overnight and get them out tomorrow to tow it away or phone one of the garages which runs an all-night service. Either way, I could take both of you home; save you hanging about here for a taxi. You could leave the car keys with the pub landlord. I'm sure he wouldn't mind.'

'Yes, thanks,' Ruth Page said, acknowledging the advice but not apparently accepting the offer of a lift for she turned to Christa. 'What do you think? It seems sensible, doesn't it, to let Nick Duffield's friend run us home?'

It was then that Alex felt the first stirring of interest in Christa Wyatt. As he and Ruth Page waited for her reply, he realised she had a stronger personality than he had at first imagined. Not only had she successfully put Nick in his place, but it was obvious that even Ruth Page, whom he had thought the more positive of the two women, deferred on occasions to her wishes. At the same time, he also recognised, like hearing a small warning bell sounding in his head, that this woman could be challenging; perhaps even dangerous in some obscure way; certainly different from all the other women he had ever met.

It was a strange sensation. He still felt no real physical desire for her. The attraction was more complex than that and yet at the same time oddly predictable. It was like a magnetic force, the irresistible drawing of iron towards the lodestone, simple, inevitable and yet difficult to explain.

Christa Wyatt was saying with a shrug, 'All right. I suppose it is more sensible than waiting for a taxi.'

It was a grudging agreement as if she were accepting the lesser of two evils.

'I'll phone Morton's tomorrow morning and get them to pick the car up,' Ruth Page said, addressing Alex. 'If you don't mind waiting a few minutes, I'll hand the keys over to someone in the pub.'

Christa walked off with her, leaving the two men alone.

'Shame about the car though,' Nick said. The remark was made as a form of apology, intended more for the women than for Alex although he took it as a general peace-offering. Even so, Nick couldn't resist the urge to kick at the wheel as if to express some lingering aggression and to add with gloomy satisfaction, 'It's going to cost a bloody packet to get that lot fixed.'

'You don't mind me giving them a lift?' Alex asked, making his own contribution to the truce which Nick seemed to have called.

'No. Why the hell should I?' Nick demanded, still a little truculent as if Alex were deliberately misinterpreting his motives.

It was for this reason that, when the two women returned, Alex put them into the back of his car, letting Nick get in beside him.

There was very little conversation between them on the drive back to Chelmsford and almost all of it was between Ruth Page and himself, Ruth thanking him again for his help and Alex protesting that it was nothing; anybody would have done the same under the circumstances. They also discussed the merits and demerits of their respective garages. It was a stilted conversation, both of them merely filling the silence of the other two occupants of the car.

During these exchanges, Alex glanced occasionally into his rear mirror, not so much to keep eye contact with Ruth Page as to observe Christa Wyatt. He caught only fleeting glimpses of her in the dipped headlamps of other cars, mostly in profile as she gazed out of the window at the darkened landscape they were passing. Caught in these brief flashes of light, her face looked very pale and clear-cut, reminding him of a cameo brooch which his grand-mother had worn years ago when he was a child, a memory he thought he had forgotten. Christa Wyatt's head had the same remote, classic beauty and clarity of outline as if it, too, had been cut from some glassy, translucent stone. The light also caught her hair, making it gleam like gold filaments and, at the sight of it, he felt the first jolt of physical desire; not just sexual although that was certainly part of it. It was more a longing to possess her, as a collector might yearn to own some fragile, exquisite object which seemed unattainable. It was only later he realised that, from this moment, he was obsessed by her.

They had reached the outskirts of Chelmsford and he fell silent, working out a route which would allow him to drop Nick off first, then Ruth Page without it appearing too obvious that he had de-liberately arranged it so that he could have Christa alone with him in the car.

Nick was easy. It was simply a matter of driving along Parkway, which took him past the turning to Nick's flat. Ruth Page was more difficult. In order to reach the Springfield Road area where she lived, it meant doubling back on to the ring-road. Had either of them questioned his choice of route, he would have given the excuse that it avoided the town centre.

But neither of them seemed to notice. Now that Nick had gone,

29

the two women had begun talking to one another. Although Alex strained to hear, their voices were too low for him to make out much of their conversation, apart from the tail end of it. Christa seemed to be suggesting she picked Ruth Page up the following morning and drove her to work, an offer which Ruth Page refused.

'I'll cycle,' she said. 'I need the exercise. And since I bought it, I've hardly used that bike.'

When he reached Ruth Page's turning, Alex had his first piece of luck. It was a cul-de-sac which meant he had to make a three-point turn once he had dropped Ruth off at her house. Christa got out with her and the two women stood together at the gateway. At first he thought she intended going into the house with Ruth Page, leaving him to drive home alone. But to his relief, when he had backed and turned the car, Christa came walking towards it. It was therefore perfectly natural for him to lean across and open the front passenger door so that she had to get in beside him.

As she bent towards him to fasten her seat-belt, he caught a breath of her scent. It was light and subtle and seemed to come from her hair, as if the hair itself was exuding its own fragrance.

They spoke little on the drive to Clifford Street, the address she had given him. He made some comment about the damage to Ruth's car which sounded forced even to his ears and to which she replied with some conventional remark about the cost of repairs. Despite her proximity to him in the darkened interior of the car, she might have been miles away and he felt at a loss as to how to reach closer to her across the void she seemed to create between them without appearing too brash. It was an uncertainty he hadn't experienced since he was thirteen and had fallen madly in love with a girl two classes ahead of him at school. A similar sense of remoteness and inaccessibility had affected him then, leaving him tongue-tied. He remembered also that, although he couldn't now recall the girl's name, she, too, had been fair-haired with a similar clear-cut profile, and he wondered if, for some reason he couldn't properly rationalise, he was programmed to fall in love with that type of woman.

He tried again, mentioning the White Swan at Elmsfield. It was an attractive pub, he said, one of his favourites. Did she go there often?

But he had mistimed the remark. Before she could reply, he had turned off London Road and had reached the corner of Clifford Street.

'You can drop me off here,' she told him, adding briefly as he drew up by the kerb and she opened the passenger's door, 'Thanks for the lift.'

30

With that, she walked quickly away down the road, the light streaming down from one of the street lamps giving that same glassy sheen to her hair as she passed under it.

Alex didn't like to wait to see which house she went into; it might seem too obvious. But, as soon as he got back to the flat, he looked her up in the telephone directory. There was no one listed under her name so he asumed she was ex-directory. Nor was there an entry for Ruth Page although he found her business number and address in Moulsham Street under 'Personelle'.

It was an indirect contact but better than nothing although he wondered how the hell he could find a plausible excuse for calling Ruth Page and finding out from her Christa's address or phone number.

He mulled over the problem during the next few days, finding himself thinking about it even in the middle of giving a lesson. Although he wasn't exactly haunted by her, he kept remembering Christa's face, in particular that profile, glimpsed so tantalisingly in the rear mirror of his car. It left him abstracted to the extent that Joyce Stanley, his head of department, asked him on one occasion if he were all right. He managed to shrug the question off with some remark about it being near the end of term and feeling a bit tired.

It was something Joyce Stanley said the following Friday at one of the regular after-school departmental meetings which gave him the idea of how to approach Christa through Ruth Page. As a department, the teaching was shared out as fairly as possible between the eight members of staff, no one monopolising the more able groups and each of them allocated at least one of the bottom stream classes. That year, his was a seventh-year form. It was also departmental policy wherever possible to invite outside speakers to address the senior pupils at least once a term. At the meeting, Joyce Stanley announced that she had managed to book a group of professional actors, the Strolling Players, to come at the beginning of the summer term to perform some scenes from *Hamlet*, one of the GCSE set texts for the upper school examination classes.

The idea then struck him that here was a way in which he could plausibly contact Christa through Ruth Page. As soon as the meeting was over, he approached Joyce Stanley to put the proposal to her.

Was there any reason, he asked, why this policy of inviting outside speakers should apply only to the upper school? Last term, he'd got his seventh-year group to write a project on children's literature. If this idea could be extended to all the seventh-year classes, it would encourage reading and the use of the library. They could perhaps invite an author of children's fiction to speak on the subject and also judge the pupils' own stories.

'As a matter of fact,' he added casually, 'I met someone the other day who illustrates children's books. She might agree to come along and give a talk.'

To his relief, Joyce Stanley welcomed the idea, suggesting he raised it at the next meeting. She would personally give it her support and would also suggest that he was put in charge of organising the project.

Professionally, of course, it did him no harm at all. He was already aware that Joyce was grooming him, as her deputy, to take over as departmental head on her retirement in two years' time. But it wasn't this aspect of the project which excited him as much as the opportunity it gave him to get in touch with Christa Wyatt.

4

The proposal for the seventh-year project was passed at the following Friday's departmental meeting. Although the scheme had begun merely as a means by which he could contact Christa, Alex had become interested in it for its own sake and, in the intervening week since he had first suggested the idea to Joyce Stanley, he had given it considerable thought, drawing up a report in which were included such additional proposals as a book exhibition in the school library, individual projects on children's authors and the involvement of the art department in illustrating the pupils' own stories. It was also decided that he should be in charge of organising the scheme which would take effect in the following autumn term with the new intake of seventh-year pupils.

After the meeting, Joyce Stanley had congratulated him on the way he had presented the project and professionally it was, of course, a feather in his cap and a useful addition to his CV. At the same time, he was eager, now that the proposal had been accepted, to get in touch with Ruth Page and, through her, Christa.

It was for this reason that, on the way home from school that Friday afternoon, he decided to call on Ruth Page at her office in Moulsham Street, instead of phoning her as he had at first intended. He also felt that a direct approach might be better. It would be less easy for her to put him off if he met her face to face.

Personelle was on the ground floor of a modest three-storeyed office building, given over to other commercial firms which included an accountant's and a solicitor's.

There was little to see from the outside, apart from the name 'Personelle' in elegant, flowing black letters on the window which was protected from the casual view of passers-by with a white venetian blind. The interior, as he discovered when he pushed open the door, had the same air of discreet, understated style which also managed to look expensive. Black leather and chrome chairs, several exotic indoor plants in white china tubs, and water-colours, probably originals, hanging on the walls gave it the appearance of a room in an exclusive club or the foyer of a modern, international hotel.

A young, attractive-looking woman was sitting behind an ebonised desk; not Ruth Page but almost certainly her secretary. She looked up as he entered and obviously mistook him for a potential client for when he asked to speak to Miss Page, she began, to his embarrassment, to explain that the agency handled only female clients.

'It's a private matter,' he said hurriedly.

He had then to give his name and wait while the young woman spoke to Ruth Page on the internal phone. As he stood there, he half regretted his decision to come in person. Contacting Christa had become more complicated than he had imagined. He felt exposed and oddly vulnerable, too, in this all-female world.

And then the door behind the desk opened and Ruth Page came out to meet him, smiling and holding out her hand.

'Alex Bennet! How very pleasant to see you again. Do come in.'

As she ushered him into the inner office, he had time to recover from his surprise at the change in her appearance. When he had first met her at the White Swan at Elmsfield, she, like Christa, had been casually dressed, in her case, in grey woollen slacks and a white cable-knit sweater. Now she was wearing a well-fitting black skirt and jacket and a cherry-coloured silk blouse, the female equivalent, he supposed, of a businessman's suit. Its formality, however, was softened by jet earings and several fine gold chains worn round her neck. Her face looked different, too; more sophisticated, and, as he took the chair facing her desk, he saw that it was skilfully made up, her lips reddened and her eyes emphasised with mascara and a silvery eye-shadow. But her expression hadn't changed. It still had that look of quick intelligence which had attracted him at their first meeting.

He was impressed, too, by the physical trappings of Ruth Page's world. If, as Nick Duffield had said, she had started up the agency only four years before, it appeared she had made a success of it. There were certainly signs that it was well organised. Apart from the sleek metal filing cabinets against the far wall, he noticed a photocopier on its own steel trolley and an IBM computer standing on the desk beside two telephones and the answering and fax machines.

Like Ruth Page herself, this impression of businesslike efficiency was softened by other touches. There were more potted plants and water-colours but these were additions, he felt, not essentials, which had been introduced to create a relaxed and comfortable setting.

Ruth Page herself was experienced at making people feel at ease. 'So what can I do to help you, Alex?' she was asking pleasantly. 'You don't mind me calling you Alex? And do please call me Ruth.'

'Thank you, Ruth,' he said, grateful for this friendly informality which made his task so much easier as he began his little prepared speech about the seventh-year project and how much he hoped that her friend, Christa Wyatt, might be persuaded to take part in it.

'Only I don't know how to get in touch with her,' he concluded. 'She's not in the phone book.'

As he spoke, he had the impression he was being interviewed, as if the occasion served as some kind of test which he had to pass in order to gain access to Christa. It was subtly done. When he had finished speaking, Ruth Page, who had listened with what seemed to him genuine interest, began to question him about details of the project such as who else had he considered contacting.

'Certainly a writer,' he replied. 'A publisher, too, if I can find one who'd supply publicity material, posters and so on. We're planning to organise a display of children's fiction in the school library which would be run in tandem with an exhibition of the pupils' own stories. We're hoping that either a publisher or an author might be willing to judge the runners-up and present a prize for the best.'

'And you have the backing of your department, you said?'

'Yes, of course. My head of English is very keen to get the project off the ground. If it works, it could become a regular feature, like the outside speakers for the upper school I mentioned.'

He hadn't objected to her questions. As Christa's friend, she was entitled to find out a little more about him before she handed over Christa's private address and phone number. He would have done the same in her place. At the same time, he felt that, as a business woman, she was testing out his commitment to his idea much as a bank manager might have questioned him about a commercial proposal, and he found this challenging.

Apparently, he passed whatever test Ruth Page had set him. She was saying, 'It sounds a very interesting project, Alex. Of course, I can't promise Christa will want to take part in it. That's up to her. But I'm sure she wouldn't mind if you contacted her about it. I'll give you her phone number as well as her address in case you want to ring her.'

She wrote them down on a page in a notebook which she tore out and passed to him across the desk.

Alex took it with pretended casualness, not even glancing down at it as he folded it in half and slipped it into his inside pocket.

'And good luck with the scheme,' Ruth Page added, as she showed him to the door. 'Perhaps we'll meet again some time. I hope so.'

'So do I,' he assured her. He meant it. If all went well with Christa, he might indeed meet Ruth Page again, he thought as he walked back to his car.

He tried phoning Christa as soon as he got back to the flat. But even then she proved elusive. All he reached was an answer machine and her recorded voice, cool and distant, giving her number and a brief message merely stating that she was unavailable and asking the caller to speak after the tone. It lasted a few seconds only and, he noticed, she hadn't included the usual apology for not being there in person. He left his own name and message, making it, like hers, brief and to the point, and asking her to phone him back when it was convenient. After giving his own number, he rang off.

He half expected that she would ring him later that evening or at least over the weekend but no call came and on the Sunday afternoon, he tried phoning her for the second time only to be answered again by her recorded voice. This time, he hung up without leaving a message. It wasn't until the Tuesday evening, five days later, when he had given up hope of ever hearing from her, that she finally rang him.

It was half-past seven in the evening, he remembered. She had sounded aloof and also a little impatient when he tried to explain in more detail about the project.

'There's no point,' she told him. 'I never give talks.'

It was said with the same coolly dismissive tone of voice that she had used with Nick Duffield and there was no apology either to soften the refusal any more than there had been in her recorded message.

For a few seconds, he felt utterly rejected only to be buoyed up again when she added, 'But I could put you in touch with another illustrator who might be willing to come. Would you like to meet and discuss it?'

'I'd be delighted to,' he said, hardly daring to believe his luck. 'Would tomorrow evening suit you?'

'I can't make it until Friday; say, seven o'clock at the Hollybush in Markham?'

She gave no explanation why she had chosen this particular pub, five miles out of Chelmsford, but he accepted the arrangement without any query.

'Yes, of course,' he agreed.

She had then rung off without saying goodbye or giving him the opportunity to prolong the conversation with some conventional remark about how much he was looking forward to seeing her again.

At the time, he had been too exhilarated by the prospect of meeting her to consider any of this. It was only with hindsight he realised that the pattern of their relationship was already established with that first phone call. It was she who was to set the pace, who decided where they were to meet and when, even when they were to become lovers. He should have been warned, too, of her capacity to raise and lower his expectations in a roller-coaster of emotions which was to become a feature of their affair.

As soon as Christa had rung off, he phoned Nick to change their planned meeting on Friday evening to the Saturday, giving as an excuse some urgent school business which had suddenly cropped up and which he had to attend to.

By dropping Joyce Stanley's name into the conversation, he was able to lead him to believe it was she whom he was meeting. Although he told himself it was only a white lie, he consciously came to the decision to say nothing to Nick about Christa, knowing Nick's dislike of her. Had he known it at the time, he would have realised that this, too, was a portent of the future, the first in a series of untruths which, over the coming months, was to develop into a web of deceit in which he was to find himself entangled.

The meeting at the Hollybush went well, better than he had dared hope. The evening was warm and they had sat outside in the garden. It was strange how memory worked. He could recall exactly what she was wearing on that occasion – a long-skirted dress of red wool, drawn tightly in at the waist with a black patent-leather belt, and a black jacket with a high Chinese collar. Her pale honey-gold hair was plaited into a long, loose braid which had hung down her back. She had looked exotic and yet at the same time oddly innocent, a mixture of English schoolgirl combined with a suggestion of Far Eastern mystery and glamour. As he carried out their drinks from the bar into the garden, he noticed how people, even the women, had turned to look at her and he had felt proud that she was with him.

Disconcertingly, her behaviour belied both images her appearance seemed to suggest. She was brisk and businesslike, handing over to him a typed page of names and addresses which he might find useful. They included an author of children's fiction as well as an illustrator, both of whom lived in London and who she thought might be willing to give talks for a small fee or, if he handled it properly, for just their expenses, considering the project was educational.

If he handled it properly. He was conscious throughout that evening that he must do just that with her, letting her set the pace. She hadn't flirted. She hadn't even tried any of those feminine tricks which, in his experience, women tend to use on a first date with a man in order to rouse his interest and to make themselves more appealing. She had met his gaze quite directly, almost with a child's candour. Her eyes were blue, he noticed for the first time; the pupils very bright, the irises flecked with tiny specks of darker blue and gold which made them look iridescent like the plumage of a bird or quartz which glitters with opalescent colours as the light catches it.

They talked mainly about children's fiction, he remembered. The conversation was light, companionable and astonishingly easy and yet, looking back on it, he was aware that there had been a curious lack of intimacy about it. Although she spoke of her own delight as a child in those pictures in which objects are hidden in the foliage of a tree or the details of a landscape, he was left with no clear impression of her childhood. She had made no attempt either to link that experience with her own work as an artist. It was only later in the week when he went to the central library and found in the children's section some books which she had illustrated that he discovered she used this same technique herself. The pictures, mostly pen and ink drawings, were beautiful, fascinating in their fine detail and in the way in which tiny objects were hidden amongst the rich, intricate patterns she had created on the page: a cat almost concealed in the voluptuous folds of a woman's skirts, a child's face at a high window, peeping out through the intertwining branches of a climbing rose which covered the walls of a tower.

It hadn't occurred to him that these illustrations were a clue to her own personality, another warning which he should have taken more heed of.

While they talked, he was acutely aware that, before they parted, he would have to find the opportunity to suggest a further meeting but, for the first time for many years, was uncertain how to go about it. What if he made a hash of it? Supposing she turned him down?

In the event, it was much simpler than he had imagined. When she glanced at her watch and announced she ought to be going, he walked her to her car. It was getting dark by then which made it easier. As they halted by her Renault, he could see only the pale glimmer of her face and hair in the dusk.

He said awkwardly, 'Perhaps I could take you out to dinner one evening to thank you for your help over the project?'

He half expected her to refuse or, at best, to put him off with some vague promise she had no intention of keeping.

Instead, she said, 'Yes, I'd like that very much.'

She seemed to mean it.

'When?' he asked eagerly, feeling an instant lift of his spirits.

'I'll phone you in the week,' she replied and, getting into the car, drove away.

He remembered standing there dejectedly, watching her car turn into the road and thinking that she probably wouldn't phone and wondering if he dared ring her or would that be a crass move on his part? He decided it would.

It wasn't until the middle of the following week, when he had again given up hope, that she called him to suggest they met on Saturday evening. She had offered no apology or explanation for the delay and, taking his cue from her, he had not so much as hinted to her that he expected either. Instead, he had acted as if her behaviour had had no effect on him at all, although he had taken the initiative by suggesting he picked her up in his car at her address on the Saturday. He was both surprised and delighted when she agreed.

Before that evening, he drove a couple of times past her house in

Clifford Street, not realising then, of course, that this, too, was setting a pattern of behaviour which was to be repeated months later after their affair was over. At the time, he put it down to curiosity. He knew so little about her. It was only natural to want to see where she lived.

The house had intrigued him. It was so different from all the others in the road. Even on that first occasion, he was struck by its air of secrecy which seemed to reflect the same quality of remoteness he was aware of in her. Closed off from the pavement behind the tall iron gate and railings, it appeared to hold itself aloof. There was no sign of life inside it either. The sash windows were blank, giving nothing away and when, two days later, he deliberately drove past it again after dark, he saw nothing more than light streaming out through the shell-shaped fanlight over the front door and a yellow glow behind the drawn blind at the ground-floor front window. The rest of the house was in darkness.

He was disappointed when he picked her up as arranged on Saturday evening. He had expected she would invite him into the house. Instead, when she opened the door to him, he saw nothing more than a glimpse of the hall before she came out on to the porch and closed the door behind her.

Remembering that event now, it seemed to him particularly poignant that his first view of the place where Christa lived should be the same setting in which she had died – the long, narrow hall floored with bare polished boards, the round, white paper lantern hanging from the ceiling and, to the left, the little rosewood table with the telephone standing on it and, above it, the oval mirror in its tarnished gilt frame.

It also seemed a cruel twist of fate that he had booked a table at Hartfield House at Eppingham, the same hotel where later her new lover, Robert Murray, was also to take her, although he realised he was perhaps being paranoid by reading too much into it. It was, after all, an ideal choice of rendezvous for a married man who was carrying on an affair with another woman. He himself had first been taken there by Nick Duffield who had written a piece about it in the *Gazette* when it opened; the owner, pleased with the publicity, was good for a free drink whenever Nick felt inclined to drop in there which he did from time to time.

Once the mansion of a private estate, it was a large Georgian house set in a couple of acres of garden. Apart from landscaping the grounds and modernising the interior with central heating and bathrooms, the new owner had left it very much in its original condition and had furnished it in period as a family residence. It was comfortable, discreet and, of course, expensive, not that he had begrudged the money. He had intended to make it a special occasion, one which he hoped would impress Christa. The food was excellent, the service impeccable. He and Christa had dined that evening in the main dining-room although there were a couple of small supper rooms, the former study and morning-room, which could be hired at a price for more intimate occasions. He assumed Robert Murray, who was obviously wealthy, had made use of one of these when later he also entertained Christa at the hotel.

On that evening, he was, of course, aware of none of this. All of that was in the future. As he and Christa had sat down opposite each other at their table, he had felt only a great surge of happiness such as he had not felt for years, a feeling of exhilaration simply to be there with her and an overwhelming hunger to touch and possess her.

5

Possession came after their fourth meeting although he still wasn't sure who was the possessor, who the possessed.

On that evening, they had gone again to Hartfield House, for a drink only on that occasion. There had been, he recalled, a special quality about the light. Although dusk was falling, the sky was still luminous, streaked with gold and violet, the last of a magnificent sunset which they had watched through the windows of the bar. She had spoken about Turner's genius for conveying light and he had asked her if she ever painted landscapes.

'Occasionally water-colours,' she said in that cool voice she used whenever the conversation became too personal and he had dropped the subject.

And yet, when they had left the bar and had walked down the terrace steps into the garden, it was she who had initiated their first real physical contact. He had taken off his jacket which he was carrying slung across one shoulder and, as they reached the bottom step, she had put one hand on his arm as if to steady herself. She had left it there as they walked across the lawn towards a little copse of silver birches. It was the lightest of touches which, for all his experience, he hadn't known how to interpret. He remembered

40

feeling again that adolescent uncertainty which had tensed up the muscles in his chest and made it difficult to breathe normally.

Should he kiss her? Was she expecting him to? Or would she repulse him if he tried?

In the event and to his enormous relief, it happened quite naturally. As they reached the trees, he had turned towards her and suddenly she was in his arms. He had kissed her like a man slaking his thirst, drinking in her lips and skin and hair, until she had drawn her face away and had said, leaning back a little from him, 'We'll go back to your flat, shall we?'

Her expression was enigmatic, half smiling, half serious, but, before he had time to analyse it, she had begun to walk away from him towards the hotel car-park.

Later, he was to recognise a similar expression on the face of the bust of the Greek goddess in Christa's garden, the lips parted but the eyes curiously wary as if the figure was poised between staying and taking flight. Even then, after he had visited Christa's house and seen the statue, he was still no nearer solving the enigma, either the goddess's or Christa's. Both remained inexplicable.

But by then, it no longer seemed to matter. Like an alcoholic or a drug addict, he was already in too deep, utterly dependent on Christa, on her beauty and, above all, on her sexuality, that combination of outward coolness and untouchability with a frank sensuality which, once he had experienced it, became impossible to resist. She had no inhibitions about nakedness, even that first time they made love or on any of the other occasions, except she would not let him undress her. Instead, while he watched in an agony of desire, she calmly slipped out of her clothes with as much naturalness as if he were not there and she was alone.

And it was she who came to him, walking straight-backed with a dancer's balance, her hair falling loose over her shoulders like a glistening cape. Of the two of them, he was the more unsure, awed by her beauty, afraid even then of losing her. If, that is, he had ever possessed her. Even on that first occasion, he was aware that he hadn't really entered her except sexually. At the moment of orgasm, he caught sight of her face on the pillow, haloed in her hair. Her eyes were open, fixed on a point somewhere beyond his right shoulder. And then, as she, too, had reached a climax, they had suddenly closed, as if she had wanted to shut out the image of his face so close to hers.

After that, they made love whenever they met. By then the term was over and the Easter holidays had begun. He was free to meet

41

her during the day as well as in the evenings. Several times they drove out into the countryside and made love in the open air, once in a wood under the budding trees. He could still vividly recall how cool the grass had felt and how warm her skin, smooth like silk under his hands, and how, afterwards, she had knelt upright to shake back her hair, rising like a Venus from among the long grass stems, her breasts golden in the sunlight.

Sex served as an entry, or a partial entry, into her world although he felt he never knew it in its entirety. There were still areas which he was not invited to enter; actual spaces such as her studio upstairs. The door was fitted with a Yale lock and, whenever he was in the house, it remained closed even though he was given the freedom of the rest of the place, including her bedroom.

And yet, even though he grew familiar with the house and the garden over the weeks, he always felt something of an intruder there, never exactly at home. Such visits always came by invitation only and, during the whole of their affair, he was aware of a constraint, never actually put into words, against calling on her casually. In fact, all their meetings were pre-arranged, usually by phone. Occasionally she would agree to a date for their next meeting during the previous one but, as he learned from experience, these were often cancelled by her a few days later with no real explanation apart from a vague excuse that she wasn't free after all.

More disturbingly for him, he felt excluded from large areas of her life. She never spoke about her past, her work or even what she was doing when he wasn't seeing her. He felt all of this was private territory which he was not permitted to enter without possessing a secret password which he never quite managed to acquire. The little he knew about Christa he gleaned from Ruth Page whom he met on several occasions during his affair with Christa. Usually, Ruth was already at the house when he arrived, casually dressed as she had been when he had first met her at the White Swan in Elmsfield, having changed out of her business clothes and cycled over, leaving the bike in Christa's back garden. He gathered it was something she did fairly frequently, whenever she felt she needed the exercise after a day spent in the office. She had never stayed long and he had not resented her presence. Instead, he had enjoyed it. Relaxed and informal in shorts or pedal-pushers, she was good company as he had imagined she would be. He felt comfortable with her, largely because she had accepted him as Christa's lover with every right to be there. It had made him feel less of an interloper in Christa's world.

One occasion was more formal. It was Ruth Page's birthday and she had asked him as her guest together with Christa to dinner at an expensive restaurant at Merstead. All of them had dressed up for the occasion, he in a dinner jacket, Ruth in dark red with a sequinned jacket. As for Christa, he had never seen her look more beautiful. Her dress was black silk, very plain, with narrow straps over the shoulders and, against the dark fabric, her skin had an alabaster sheen. She had worn her hair up, as she had when he had first met her, fastened on top of her head with the big tortoiseshell clip, leaving her neck bare. He remembered thinking how fragile it had looked, like the stem of a flower, a memory which reminded him so poignantly of that other more recent image of her lying on the floor in the Clifford Street house that he flung out a hand as if physically to thrust the thought of it aside and forced himself to return to that evening at the restaurant although those memories brought with them their own pain and sense of loss. He recalled how, watching her across the table, he had ached with desire for her. It was like a deep hunger which he knew making love to her would only partly assuage.

After the meal, he had driven her and Ruth back to Christa's house for coffee and they had talked until the early hours of the morning.

It was during these conversations that he picked up those little scraps of information about Christa which he might never have learned from Christa herself – the fact that she and Ruth had first met when they were students, for example, or that occasionally the two women went to London together to an art exhibition; even that the bust of the Greek goddess which stood on a pedestal at the end of Christa's garden in a niche of closely clipped yew was a copy taken from a statue of Artemis which Ruth had found in a junk-yard and had given to Christa as a twenty-first birthday present.

Although none of these facts were important in themselves, he had welcomed them as rare glimpses into Christa's life which created a form of intimacy not only between himself and Christa but also with Ruth Page, Christa's oldest friend.

For, although he and Christa were lovers, they were not intimate apart from the bond of sex. They never spoke of love. There was not even an exchange of endearments between them nor any reference to a mutual commitment. Was he in love with her? He wasn't even sure of that. What he felt for her was not love in any conventional sense of the word. Certainly, he felt desire for her; passion, too. And yet, although he was held captive by her sensuality, he was never entirely satisfied. He was always longing for some indefinable gratification which seemed to elude him; a closeness which he himself couldn't properly rationalise.

It was this craving for a greater intimacy which had prompted him to persuade Christa to spend a night with him at Hartfield House. Now, with hindsight, he wondered if that hadn't been a mistake. At the time, she hadn't wanted to, preferring to have dinner there only, as they had done before, and then to return to his flat. But, for once, he had got his own way. It was the last Saturday of the Easter holiday, he told her. On Monday he'd be back at work and he wanted something special to mark the occasion.

'Please, Christa,' he had said. 'Just this once.'

He hadn't told her the real reason – that he had wanted to spend the whole night with her and wake up to find her beside him.

Like a married couple, he thought wryly. Yes, he was prepared to admit that now. Although marriage had not seriously crossed his mind, he had fantasised about the two of them living together in a more permanent relationship in which there would be some form of commitment.

Sentimentality had played a part, too; ridiculous though that seemed now. He had always avoided sentiment in the past, feeling ill at ease whenever the woman with whom he was having an affair at the time had talked about 'our song' or 'our restaurant'. And yet, he had felt that the hotel was special. It was where he had first taken Christa to dinner and where they had kissed before making love for the first time.

Why had she agreed? At the time he had not really thought about it. He had simply been delighted that he had managed to persuade her. He wondered now if it hadn't been some kind of test on her part of her feelings for him, so that she, too, could find out how far she had wanted their relationship to develop. But like everything else connected with Christa, he wasn't even certain about that.

They had booked into the hotel as Mr and Mrs Bennet, dined in one of the small supper rooms, made love in the double bed in a room overlooking the gardens. They had then taken a shower together, their naked bodies pressed close under the jets of warm water, flesh to flesh, Christa's wet hair clinging to his skin. Afterwards, he had rubbed her hair dry and brushed it out, lifting up the gleaming strands and then letting them drift downwards in the light of the bedside lamps. It was a moment of intimacy which he still couldn't remember without feeling a pang of loss, like a hollow emptiness inside him.

But in the morning, when he woke at six o'clock, she was not there beside him. Going to the window, he had seen her, a distant figure in a white dress, walking alone under the trees.

Thinking about it now, he realised that the image epitomised his relationship with her.

On the Monday, he returned to work at the beginning of the summer term, picking up the threads of his old life. Now that the project was approved, he began to work on it seriously, writing off to publishers and to the author and illustrator whose names and addresses Christa had given him as well as putting into operation his other ideas about arranging exhibitions. The work on it filled much of his spare time when he wasn't meeting Christa in the evenings.

He met Nick Duffield, too, from time to time for a drink although not as often as in the past. Nick had found himself a girlfriend, someone called Trudi, and no longer felt the need to talk about his divorce which he seemed to accept as inevitable. The house was up for sale. Jean was looking for a place of her own. Nick himself was thinking of buying a bigger, unfurnished flat. When he did, Trudi might move in with him. Or, then again, she might not. He hadn't yet made up his mind on that one. Alex had the impression that Nick was glad to be relieved of all commitments and was once more free to play the field.

Alex said nothing to him about Christa, giving Nick the impression that he, too, was uncommitted and grateful for it. There seemed small chance Nick would see him with Christa. They rarely met in the town, preferring to drive out into the country, sometimes in her car, sometimes in his. They would walk together, dine or have a drink in a local pub and either find somewhere quiet to make love or go back to his flat or her house before separating for the night. It came, therefore, as an unpleasant surprise when Nick phoned him one evening.

'You cunning old sod!' he announced, without any preamble.

'What on earth are you talking about?' Alex demanded.

'You and Christa Wyatt. What else?'

Nick had sounded jubilant at catching Alex out.

'I don't get you,' Alex said stiffly.

'Come off it! You can't play the innocent with me. I saw the pair of you having dinner the other evening at the Bull in Westbury. Trudi and I were in the bar.'

'Oh, that. Yes, I'd happened to run into her a few days before,' Alex said, improvising quickly. 'I've been asked to run a project at school on children's fiction. Christa gave me a few useful addresses to contact. I asked her out to dinner as a sort of thank-you, that's all.'

Nick wasn't impressed.

'It didn't look like that to me. I'd say you two were an item.'

'Then you've got it wrong.'

'So you're not having it off with her?'

'For God's sake!' Alex said. He was angered by Nick's crudeness although, in the past, he wasn't usually offended by it. That was men's talk, acceptable from someone like Nick whose attitude to women when in male company had always tended to be macho, part of a freewheeling image he liked to create for himself.

'So what's she like, the ice-maiden?'

'A lot nicer than you might think.'

'Get away!'

'No, I mean it,' Alex said quickly, feeling a sudden urge to protect her. 'You got on the wrong side of her that evening in the Swan.'

'Could be, I suppose,' Nick conceded although he didn't sound all that convinced. 'I must say, though, she's a hell of a good-looker. So are you going to see her again?'

'Possibly,' Alex said. Caution warned him to hedge his bets on this one. He might run into Nick on some other occasion when he was with Christa and he didn't want to appear an outright liar. But even this small concession to the truth led him into deeper water.

'Well, if you do, what about making up a foursome one evening, me and Trudi, you and Christa?' Nick suggested.

It was a ludicrous idea which he had blocked as best he could.

'I'll bear it in mind, Nick. I haven't any plans at the moment for seeing her again but yes, it might be fun for all of us to meet up for a drink.' Cutting the conversation short, he added, 'Look, I must go now. I've got a hell of a lot of marking to get through. See you around sometime.'

They hadn't, in fact, met again until after his affair with Christa was over although Nick rang him a couple of times, ostensibly to arrange a date for them to play squash but merely using it as an excuse to quiz him about Christa whom he always referred to as the ice-maiden. It became, on Nick's part, a standing joke.

'How's the ice-maiden?' he'd ask. 'Seen her again?'

It was easy enough, as Alex discovered, to field Nick's questions with some half-joking, non-committal remark such as, 'I'm still working on it,' and then to deflect Nick's attention by switching the conversation to Trudi about whom Nick was happy to talk at length. But to Alex's relief, they never actually agreed on a date to play squash so he was saved the embarrassment of meeting him face to face. Nick was heavily involved with Trudi, thank God, and for the few evenings he was free, Alex was able to find some excuse of his own for not meeting him.

He still went to the leisure centre but less frequently than in the past and only on those evenings when he knew Nick wouldn't be there. It was an added complication to his life which he could well have done without and, even then, he had been conscious of a net that was closing about him; or, more precisely, of the need to lead his life on two different levels. One was the day-to-day existence of school and teaching and going back to the flat to mark pupils' work, a humdrum, ordinary routine. The other was those evenings he spent with Christa which were quite separate, like going through a door into a secret world which no one, with the exception of Ruth Page, knew existed.

6

Her letter breaking off their relationship came as a complete shock to him. It arrived one Saturday morning in late May, only hours before he was due to take her out to dinner again at Hartfield House to celebrate the fact that it was the beginning of half-term and he'd have the following week free. Like her first telephone call to him, it was short and to the point.

'Dear Alex,' it read. 'As you are probably already aware, our relationship seems to have reached the end of the line. I think it better for both of us if we make a complete break. Please don't phone or write. Christa.'

His first reaction was of total disbelief, accompanied by a sensation not unlike panic when the adrenalin sets the blood racing and the heart seems to swoop upwards out of control. It was followed by a sudden surge of anger.

No, he hadn't bloody known their relationship was over. When he had last met her on Tuesday, only four days before, there had been no sign on her part that anything was wrong between them, not a look nor a word nor even a gesture which might have suggested she was thinking of ending their affair. They had made love as usual, on that evening at her house which had given the occasion, at least for him, a special significance.

47

Afterwards, still naked, she had gone downstairs to fetch two glasses and a bottle of Chablis from the fridge. He remembered her walking towards the bed with a mock-solemn expression and putting the bottle and glasses down on the bedside table with the exaggerated deference of a stage butler. They had both burst out laughing at the absurdity of the situation. Later, lying side by side drinking the wine, they had even talked about the possibility of going to France together in the summer, perhaps to the Dordogne. Although Christa hadn't made any definite promise, she hadn't seemed averse to the idea.

He had tried to phone her, of course, immediately after reading the letter but had reached only her answer-phone. All over that weekend, he rang her again and again, each time hearing her cool, disembodied voice announcing that she was unavailable and would the caller leave a message after the tone. At the sixth attempt, he had done just that, pleading with her to phone him back. He had to see her. He wanted to know what had gone wrong. Was it something he had said or done? If so, he was sorry. On the Sunday afternoon, he had left another message, adding at the end of it, despite the unspoken taboo between them, 'I love you, Christa.'

Although the words seemed to be torn out of him, he really meant them. He did love her. He always had. He'd been blind not to recognise it before and a fool not to admit it.

Throughout the weekend he had stayed in the flat, anxious that, if he went out, he might miss her call. But she hadn't phoned. Finally, on the Sunday evening, he had written to her, the first of a series of letters he was to send her. Leaving his own answer-phone switched on, he had driven to the nearest pillar box to post it, intending to return immediately to the flat in case, in his absence, she might have rung him.

Instead, he had decided to go to her house. It was a sudden urge although he had no idea what he would do when he got there. Bang on the door? Insist on speaking to her? He only knew he couldn't return to the flat and wait by the phone, knowing it almost certainly wouldn't ring. At the time, he had no idea either that, like the letters, this was to be the first of many such excursions he was to make over the next few weeks.

As often happened, he was unable to park near her house and had to walk back along Clifford Street. There was no sign of her Renault outside the gate and no lights on in the house, apart from the one in the hall shining out through the fanlight over the door. It was only then it occurred to him that she might have found a new lover. Part

48

of him rejected the idea as absurd. He felt he would have known on that last evening if she had met someone else whom she preferred. Something in her manner would have told him. And yet, as he acknowledged, he knew so little about her. As he walked back to his car, he realized that he couldn't leave it there. He had to know the truth, however painful it might be.

After that Sunday evening, the excursions to Clifford Street took on a different purpose. He went there to keep a watch on her house. Almost from the start, these surveillances took on their own pattern. To begin with, he would drive past the house and, if her car wasn't outside, he'd simply go back to the flat, knowing he was too late to find out where she might have gone. If the Renault was there, he'd park his own car as near as possible and facing in the same direction as hers so that, if she did drive off, it would be easier to follow. Having parked, he'd wait there until ten o'clock when he'd give up and drive home, assuming it was then too late for her to keep an assignation.

On at least one occasion, he was seen by someone living in the street. A woman, whose parking space he was occupying, had come out of her house and, bending down to look in at the window, had asked him to move. He had immediately apologised and driven away. But he had no doubt she would be able to identify him to the police. For his part, he could remember her quite clearly. She was middle-aged with dark hair turning grey and thin features tense with indignation. For all he knew, she might well have taken the number of his car.

Looking back, he could see it was a form of madness, that obsession to find out who Christa was meeting, if indeed she was. Even at the time, he had tried to rationalize his behaviour, telling himself that, once he had found out the truth, he'd give up, forget all about her, try to find someone else although he knew that any other woman would only be second-best.

Once half-term was over and he had to return to work, he managed to keep up a semblance of normality even though it wasn't easy at times. The weather helped. Every day the temperature was up in the eighties and it took its toll on everyone, pupils and teachers alike. No one seemed to notice he was withdrawn, less sociable than usual. The heat had sapped everyone's energy. Even so, he avoided contact as far as he could with his colleagues by keeping clear of the staff-room during break-times and lunch hours, using as his excuse the lower school project which he worked on alone in his form-room.

There was a feeling, too, of the school year winding down. It was examination time and most of the upper school pupils were either sitting GCSE or A-level papers or were absent on home-study leave. Other groups were away on field trips or work experience. The amount of marking and preparation he had to do was therefore reduced and he could fit it in during the day, leaving the evenings free to keep watch on Christa's house.

She had no visitors apart from Ruth Page who called twice, once by car, the other occasion by bike, and she left the house only rarely. In fact, over the next few weeks, he followed her only four times and on three of these outings she drove to Ruth Page's house in Bishop's Close, off Springfield Road. As soon as he saw her car turn into the cul-de-sac, he had gone straight on, comforted by the thought that perhaps he was wrong after all and there wasn't a lover. But the fourth time, he was lucky enough to catch her driving off in a different direction, if luck had anything to do with it. As on the other three evenings, he had followed her along Parkway and, assuming she was making as usual for Ruth Page's, had kept his distance. But at the roundabout where she would have turned left if she was going to Bishop's Close, she had gone straight on. It was a Wednesday, earlier in the evening than the other occasions when he had followed her, and there were more cars about. A queue was waiting to filter into the roundabout and he was forced to sit there watching her Renault disappear ahead of him into the traffic. It was then a new thought had struck him, adding further fuel to his obsession.

Supposing she had seen him parked in Clifford Street and had realised he was watching her? She would recognise his car quite easily. She had been a passenger in it enough times. The realisation that Christa might be deliberately eluding him only confirmed his suspicions that she was meeting a new lover and made him more determined to find out who he was. The problem was how?

He considered employing a private inquiry agent to follow her on his behalf and even went as far as to look up the name of one in the Yellow Pages but, in the middle of dialling the number, he had second thoughts and replaced the receiver. There was something shameful, he felt, about paying someone to spy on Christa. It would also mean having to confide in the man and a sense of distaste at revealing his private life to a stranger dissuaded him.

Instead, he rang Nick Duffield and arranged to meet him on the Friday evening at the Crown for a drink, the only time Nick was free, hanging up before Nick had time to ask about Christa.

50

But, as he had expected, Nick put the inevitable question as soon as they met in the bar.

'How's the ice-maiden?'

It was no use trying evasive tactics and, sounding as indifferent as he could, he said, 'Oh, that's all over. I haven't seen her for several weeks.'

'So you were having it off with her?'

'Not really. I met her a few times. It wasn't serious,' Alex replied, thinking, Christ, if only Nick knew the truth!

Nick said, 'I can't say I'm surprised, you chucking her over. I always thought she was a toffee-nosed bitch.'

Alex said nothing to disabuse him, finding it a small comfort that Nick believed it was he who'd put an end to the affair. And anyway, he wasn't given the opportunity. Nick had launched into an account about some woman who worked in the front office at the *Gazette* and whom he, Nick, had once asked out for a drink, only she'd given him this look, cold enough to freeze your bloody balls off.

'Anyone'd think I'd tried touching her up. Lovely pair of knockers, though,' he'd concluded reminiscently. Then, cheering up, he'd added, 'What about another swift half?'

It was when they were finishing their second drinks that Alex slipped the proposition in casually, as if it were of no great importance.

'By the way,' he said, 'I suppose you wouldn't mind swapping cars for a week? You've got third party insurance, haven't you?'

As he had guessed, Nick, with his reporter's nose for sniffing out a story, wasn't willing to leave it there.

'What for?' he asked.

Knowing Nick, Alex had prepared himself for the question. He said, 'I've met someone else only it's getting a bit tricky.'

'Husband trouble?'

Alex shrugged, a gesture he hoped Nick would interpret as reluctant agreement to the suggestion but implying that it was a situation which he didn't want to explain in detail.

Even so, Nick wouldn't give up.

'He's not having you followed, is he?' he asked and then, without waiting for Alex's reply, had added, 'You want to watch out or you'll find yourself on the sticky end of a divorce. Take my tip, never mess with a married woman.'

Which was rich coming from him, Alex thought wryly. Only last year, Nick had been heavily involved with a married woman and had been worried sick in case Jean had found out about her.

He said ironically, 'Thanks for the advice, Nick. I'll bear it in mind next time. What about the car, though? Can I borrow yours?'

'Of course, old son. What are friends for? And the best of British luck to you.'

They had swapped cars in the pub car-park and Alex had driven off in Nick's Vauxhall which had an overflowing ashtray and smelt of cigarette smoke overlaid with the musky odour of a woman's scent – Trudi's, he assumed. He drove back to the flat with all the windows wide open.

It was the Wednesday of the following week before anything happened. Every evening he kept up the surveillance but Christa hadn't left the house and he had begun to think he had been wrong in assuming she was meeting someone else. Sitting in Nick's car, he had felt reassured and yet oddly cheated. To know the worst seemed infinitely preferable to being kept in suspense.

And then, when he had given up hope of anything happening that evening, he saw her in the distance coming out of the gate and getting into the Renault, a hold-all slung over one shoulder. He started his own car and, when hers turned into London Road, he had followed, keeping at a discreet distance.

It was eight o'clock, still sunny, and the conditions were perfect, the traffic light enough to make it easy to keep her in sight but with enough cars on the road for it not to be too obvious he was tailing her. Not that she would have recognised Nick's car. At one point, he was so close behind her that he could see the back of her head through her rear window. She was wearing her hair in the loose braid down her back, a style which gave her the air of a schoolgirl, innocent and yet tantalisingly poised on the edge of sexual awareness.

At the Army and Navy roundabout, her Renault turned left on to the A12 where it picked up speed. Alex kept his own speed down, letting other cars overtake him but making sure he kept hers in sight. After about six miles, he saw her signalling to turn left again to take the slip-road which led to Buckleigh Green, one of those villages which, because of its picturesqueness and its proximity to Witham station, had developed into a commuter area. He knew it fairly well. He and Nick had driven out there a couple of times in the past to drink at the George and Dragon, an old coaching inn which stood in the centre of the village where some of the original plaster and thatch houses, tarted up with window-boxes and neo-Georgian, double-glazed conservatories, were known to change hands for a couple of hundred thousand pounds.

Alex kept his distance as they drove through the new estate of executive-style houses on the edge of Buckleigh Green. Once off the main road, there was little traffic about and he was anxious in case Christa might notice that the same dark blue Vauxhall was still on her tail. For that reason, he slowed down to allow a pick-up van, coming out of a side turning, to get between them. It was a mistake, as he soon realised.

The three of them drove in convoy through the village centre and then out on to a road which was unfamilar to him. It was narrow and twisting, little wider than a lane, with a wood on the left and houses on the right, hidden behind more trees and high hedges. The effect was like driving down a leafy tunnel. The subdued light and the frequent S bends meant he had to keep his eyes on the road as well as on the van immediately in front of him which kept braking sharply at every bend, forcing him at times to drop down into second gear.

Alex swore at the driver under his breath, urging him to get a bloody move on. What the hell did he think he was playing at?

He had lost sight of Christa's Renault which he assumed was still ahead of him. There were no turnings off the road which she could have taken. Even so, he nearly missed her. He had just come out of another sharp bend and was almost nose to tail with the van which had slowed down to fifteen miles an hour when he saw her car drawn up on the other side of the road near a pair of white-painted gateposts. He dared not stop; he dared not even take his eyes off the pick-up in case he ran into the back of it. It was only after he had driven past that he risked a quick glance into his rear mirror. The image was fleeting and yet so vivid that afterwards he was able to recall every detail of it.

The right-hand door of the Renault was open and the figure of a man was stooped down in the act of getting into the passenger seat. He was too far away for Alex to make out his features although he had a distinct impression of someone tall and dark-haired, wearing what looked at that distance like jeans and a denim jacket. Like Christa, he had some sort of luggage with him, either a briefcase or an overnight bag. The next moment, the road swung to the left and he lost sight of both the car and the man.

There was nothing he could do except drive on until he could find somewhere to park. As he turned the next bend, he saw an opening on the left which gave access to a bridle-path leading into the wood. Another quick glance in his rear mirror assured him the road behind was empty. Christa's car hadn't yet come into sight round the corner. Slowing down, he bumped the car up the verge and into the opening. He had barely time to snatch a map out of the glove compartment, spread it open across the steering-wheel and bend down over it before the Renault drove past. As soon as it had gone, he looked up but by then it was too far away for him to see anything except a pair of heads side by side in the front of the car before it disappeared round another twist in the road.

Flinging the map to one side, he set off in pursuit, still careful to keep his distance. He caught up with the Renault a little further on at a crossroads where it turned left. After that, tailing it became easier. The road was straighter and the countryside more open. The wood had dropped back and there were only fields, separated from the road by low hedges. Even though he kept well back, he had no trouble keeping the car in sight. Eventually, the road joined the A12 and Christa turned on to it, before signalling left again after about another three miles.

He knew at once where she was making for – Hartfield House. As he topped the brow of a hill, he could even see the hotel lying in a hollow, the sunlight glittering on its windows and the drive snaking away between the trees. When the Renault turned into the gateway, he didn't even slow down or turn his head to watch it disappear towards the little spinney of birch trees.

He had seen enough to convince him Christa had a new lover. That was why she had thrown him over. As he turned the car and drove back towards the A12, he had felt at first, he remembered, oddly relieved and vindicated. His suspicions had been confirmed and the guilt he had felt when he had kept watch on her seemed somehow mollified. He had been right, after all. But that sense of justification was almost immediately replaced by another more complex emotion.

It began with an acute awareness of loss. Christa had left him for another man whom she obviously preferred to him. For the first time, he realised properly that she was gone for good. There was no chance now that he would ever get her back. He wondered who the man was, what he looked like, what made him so bloody special. He was angry, too, at her defection and humiliated by it as well. His anger was directed at them both; at Christa for her deceit and rejection of him; at the man for taking her away from him. He thought of the two of them together in the hotel, dining in one of the small supper rooms, strolling across the lawn, perhaps making love in the same bed which he and Christa had shared. She would step out of her clothes, letting them slip to the floor, and then walk towards him, naked, holding out her arms as she had once come to him.

It was this jealousy and anger which he felt the most keenly. The humiliation was too painful to think about. And with the anger came a new obsession. He had to find out who the man was, put a name and a face to him. That glimpse of him in the rear mirror wasn't enough.

The decision he made on the drive back that evening to discover more about the man who had replaced him came as a kind of consolation. It gave fresh impetus and purpose to his life, a positive objective which needed careful planning.

The next evening, he set about it systematically. As soon as he got back from school, he rang Nick at the newspaper office to arrange to swap back their cars later that evening. Then, having changed into more casual clothes, he left the flat to make the return journey to Buckleigh Green in Nick's car, following the same route he had taken the previous evening.

Once through the village centre, he drove slowly, looking for the place where Christa had picked up her new lover. He had no difficulty in finding it. It was just beyond a particularly sharp S bend. He remembered the warning arrows on the side of the road. About twenty yards further on, he saw the white gateposts on his right. It was too dangerous to park immediately opposite them. It was too near to the S bend; too near, also, to the house. So he drove on to the bridle-path where he had left the car the evening before. Getting out, he walked back along the road.

There was no one about, thank God, and no cars passed him. The place seemed deserted. It was, he realised, as he retraced the route on foot, part of a much older residential development than the new estate on the other side of the village. Here the houses were spaced out in large, mature gardens, set well back from the road; Victorian or Edwardian, judging by the two he passed before he reached the pair of gateposts and a white-painted five-barred gate which was set open. A plate, with the name 'Roselands' on it in black gothic letters, was screwed to the top bar.

Beyond it, he could see a drive leading past a shrubbery to a circular sweep of gravel with a rose bed in the centre. The house which faced it was solid, built of red brick and slate, with large, square bay windows and a porch of fretted wood, painted white like the gate and the rest of the woodwork. It was handsome and had that well-tended look which suggested money. The lawn was immaculate, the paintwork pristine. In contrast, his own flat seemed small and shabby, although he thought the two ornate urns, full of pink geraniums, which stood on either side of the porch steps were pretentious, like the name 'Roselands'. He wondered if these were a clue to the man's personality – a need to display his wealth. He had already assumed that he was married. The house suggested a family; it was too large for a single man, whether a bachelor or divorced, to occupy alone. It was probably why Christa had picked him up at the gate rather than going up to the house. He imagined the man had made some excuse to his wife about a business meeting with a colleague which meant staying away from home overnight.

Anxious in case he was seen, he took only a quick look at the place before going on as far as the S bend where he turned and walked back to the car. He was bothered, too, at not knowing the name of the road in which the house was situated. If, as he intended, he looked the man up in the electoral register, he'd need a precise address.

The problem was easily solved. On the way back through the village, he stopped at the George and Dragon for a drink and simply asked the barmaid. He'd already got an excuse prepared in case he needed it. He was calling on an old friend who lived in the road leading towards Witham but wasn't sure of its name.

In the event, the excuse wasn't necessary. Without showing the least curiosity, the barmaid had said, 'Oh, you must mean the Old Rectory Road; the one with the posh houses in it.'

Nick was less easy to deal with. When later, as arranged, Alex met him at the Crown, he was already in the bar and eager for news.

'So how did it go?'

'All right,' Alex said with a shrug, trying to play it down.

'No hassle with her old man?'

'No, like I said, it went all right.' He pushed Nick's car keys across the table. 'Thanks for the loan of the car. I'll do the same for you any time you want.'

'Not necessary, old son. I'm off married women for good. The game's not worth the candle, take my word for it.'

'You could be right,' Alex said, as he pocketed his own car keys. 'How's the divorce going?'

As he had intended, the conversation shifted to this much more interesting topic, to Nick at least, than Alex's supposed affair with a married woman. It seemed Jean had a lover; in fact, had been having an affair for the past year which was why she wanted a divorce. Nick was outraged at her deception even though he'd had several affairs himself during their marriage, a fact he appeared to have forgotten.

He was able to put a name to Christa's lover the following day by going to the central library and asking to look at the electoral register. And there it was in black and white. Robert Edward Murray, Roselands, Old Rectory Road, Buckleigh Green. He was married, too, as Alex had suspected, to Helen Patricia Murray.

Robert and Helen. The rhythm of the combined names made them sound like an ideal couple.

'I, Robert Edward, take thee, Helen Patricia, to be my lawfully wedded wife . . .'

But, as he closed the register, it occurred to him that the other pair of names chimed together with equal harmony.

Robert and Christa. Christa and Robert.

Better, perhaps, than Christa and Alex? Better suited as lovers?

He consoled himself with the thought that at least he had a name for the man. All he needed now was a face to put with it. But that, he realised, was not going to be so easy.

7

Knowing he would have only the one opportunity to confront Murray, he spent the next few days thinking about the best way to set about it. It would have to be a weekend, he decided. He didn't know Murray's daily routine and he couldn't risk keeping a watch on the house as he had on Christa's. The area was isolated. A car parked regularly at the side of the road would be too conspicuous. Neighbours, perhaps even Murray himself, might notice it and become suspicious. Someone might even phone the police.

A Sunday seemed the best option. On Saturdays, people were often out shopping. He might arrive at the house and find no one there. The lunch hour was probably also a good time to catch Murray at home.

As for his excuse for calling on Murray, he gave this careful consideration as well. It had to be simple. He himself tended to be suspicious of over-elaborate explanations which pupils sometimes made for forgetting their homework or being absent from school. And it had to sound plausible so that Murray would accept it without question.

By the following Sunday, he had his excuse ready and also the prop to go with it – an old briefcase of his own which he had filled with papers before locking it. He then drove over to Buckleigh Green, this time parking the car, as Christa had done, on the right-hand verge, close to the gateway to Roselands and well off the road. For a few moments, he remained seated in the car, going over in his mind again what he would say and telling himself that, when he came face to face with Murray, he must remain calm. He must say and do nothing to arouse the man's suspicions. Then, after taking a few deep breaths to relax himself, he set off up the drive towards the house with the briefcase in his hand.

His choice of day and time seemed right. A silver-grey BMW, which he assumed was Murray's, was parked on the gravelled forecourt, together with a Peugeot, almost certainly his wife's. So they were both at home. As he walked up the four steps of the porch, past the urns of pink geraniums, he wondered who would answer the front door. Murray, he hoped. It would be a hell of a waste of time and effort if the only person he saw was Murray's wife.

At first he thought he was out of luck. A woman opened the door. Behind her, he could see a long hall, floored with black and white tiles, leading to a glass door at the end which was set open, giving a distant view of a garden. But the hall was empty. There was no sign of Murray.

'Yes?' Mrs Murray was saying.

There was nothing else he could do except launch into his pre-pared story.

'I'm sorry to trouble you,' he began. 'I'm trying to trace someone . . .'

He stopped there. A man had emerged from a room at the back of the house and was walking towards them along the hall. It was several seconds before the light from the open front door fell on his features and Alex was able to see him clearly. All he could make out was that the man was tall, dark-haired, and was dressed casually in denim slacks and a white polo-necked cotton sweater, details which exactly matched the figure Alex had seen bending down as he got into Christa's car. There was no doubt in his mind. He was about to come face to face with Christa's lover, the man for whom she had left him.

He felt a sudden uprush of emotion – anger, jealousy, bitterness – he wasn't sure quite what except it was a primitive reaction, the force of which frightened him by its intensity. In those few seconds, he understood the passion which could lead to murder, that blind impulse to strike out with fists, with feet, with anything to appease the savage desire for blood.

And yet something held him back. Shame, perhaps? An innate self-control? As he stood there on Murray's doorstep, he remembered shifting the briefcase to his other hand, a small trivial-seeming action but one which served, thank God, to steady him. His vision cleared and, in the time it took Murray to reach the front door, he was enough in control of himself to concentrate on other aspects of his appearance, absorbing them quickly as if he were making notes on the man.

Age: in his forties. Older than Alex had expected but still in good shape. There was an athletic quality about him which suggested he played some sport such as golf or tennis or worked out regularly in a gym. He gave off an impression of energy, controlled but simmering just below the surface; a sexual energy, he thought, although this was only an impression.

Face: interesting rather than conventionally good-looking. Strong, positive features; perhaps a little heavy. A well-used face with laughter lines round the eyes and a deep V of concentration between the brows. Intelligent. Self-assured. And shrewd, too. As Alex went through his story, he was aware that Murray was listening, taking it all in but not prepared to accept it at face value.

He'd given a man a lift home yesterday evening from Witham station, Alex explained. His car had broken down. He'd dropped him off somewhere along this road; he thought opposite this house only he couldn't be sure. It was dark. It was only that morning he'd found the man had left his briefcase in the back of the car.

'Isn't there anything in the briefcase to identify him?' Murray asked, taking charge of the situation. His voice had a confident ring to it with a touch of impatience in the tone as if he wouldn't suffer fools gladly.

'It's locked,' Alex said. 'And I can't remember the man's surname so I can't look him up in the phone book. It's Harry something or other.'

'Sorry, I can't help you.' Murray sounded dismissive. It wasn't his problem. But he seemed to accept the story. At least, there was nothing in his expression to suggest he doubted it. It was Murray's wife who showed more interest.

'Did you say his name was Harry?'

Alex turned his attention to her. She was an attractive woman, younger than her husband, probably in her early thirties, with

59

auburn hair which might have been rinsed that colour. It had a dark, rich sheen to it like the patina on polished wood.

'Yes, that's right. Harry,' Alex replied.

'I don't know anyone of that name living in the road,' she was saying. 'But we don't have a lot of contact with neighbours. Perhaps you could ask at one of the other houses.'

'I'm afraid I'm rather pushed for time this morning,' Alex said. 'Oh, well. I'll have to get a locksmith to open the briefcase on Monday. I'll probably find his name and address inside. It's a nuisance and I hate prying into other people's business but it seems the only answer. Anyway, thanks for your help and I'm sorry to have troubled you.'

He walked away down the drive, turning to glance back only when he reached the gate. Murray had gone inside the house but his wife was still there, removing dead heads from one of the urns of geraniums. She wasn't looking in his direction and seemed absorbed in the task.

So he had got away with it, Alex thought as he unlocked the car and slung the briefcase on to the back seat. But the sense of triumph at having pulled it off was short-lived.

He had seen Murray, as he had planned, and without rousing the man's suspicions. But what, after all, had he achieved? Nothing really, except he now knew what Murray looked like which in the final analysis had done nothing except satisfy his curiosity. In every other respect, he was worse off than before. By giving the man a face, he had brought him into sharper focus so that, whenever he thought of Christa and her new lover together, he would imagine her with Murray – see his face, hear his voice. It only confirmed Christa's defection and sharpened his own sense of loss. There seemed no hope now of ever getting her back.

True, Murray was married but that only made it worse. Christa must have fallen in love with the man. He could think of no other explanation. She was too fastidious, too cool and aloof, to welcome the kind of deceit which such a relationship would inevitably involve. Or was she? When he thought about it, he realised how little, in fact, he knew about her. She might, after all, enjoy the excitement of a clandestine affair. He remembered her unwillingness to talk about herself, the locked door to her studio. Didn't that suggest a desire for secrecy?

And what the hell was he to do now? Over the past few weeks, his need to find out the truth about Christa had kept him going. The hours he had spent watching her house, though painful, had at least given him a sense of purpose, a *raison d'être* which had occupied his time and thoughts. With Murray's identification, that quest was over. He had no wish ever to return to Clifford Street, no desire even to see Christa again. All that was left was an empty void inside him, like a great hunger, which nothing would ever fill.

He got through the next few days somehow, carrying out his duties at school but shutting himself away from all contact with the other teachers, even at morning assembly which members of staff were expected to attend. He was aware, however, that Joyce Stanley suspected something was wrong. Several times he caught her looking at him with obvious concern but his air of preoccupation dissuaded her from questioning him. His abrupt, aloof manner also helped in the classroom. The pupils, even the less well-behaved ones, watched him warily and, seeming to sense that something was wrong, got on quietly with their work.

The days seemed endless and he longed for the end of term, which was less than a fortnight away, and for the chance to escape, although where to, he had no idea. Although nothing had been arranged, he and Christa had talked about a trip to France, touring the Dordogne. That, of course, was out of the question now but he might take off somewhere by himself if only to get away from the bloody place, the flat, the whole town and the surrounding countryside which reminded him too painfully of Christa. He began avoiding certain roads, simply because it meant passing a pub where he and Christa had once met for a drink, or even going anywhere near the area where she lived, in case he saw her driving away in the Renault or, worse still, Murray's BMW parked near her house.

It was the Friday afternoon of the following week that he met Ruth Page outside Sainsbury's in the town centre. Although it was a late-night shopping day, he usually called in there earlier on his way back from school to stock up for the weekend. But the weather was so hot, he had stopped off at the flat first to shower and change. On his way out of the supermarket, he met Ruth coming in.

He had not seen her for weeks, not since Christa had written to him breaking off their affair, and he felt awkward meeting her in public, not knowing if Ruth was aware that he and Christa were no longer lovers. He assumed she must have guessed even if Christa hadn't told her in so many words. She couldn't have failed to notice that she hadn't seen him at Christa's house for nearly two months.

Even so, that apparently hadn't altered her feelings towards him, judging by the warmth of her greeting.

'Alex!' she said. 'How lovely to see you again. It's been ages.'

'Yes, it has,' he agreed. He felt embarrassed, as if he were masquerading under false pretences, and he added abruptly, 'I suppose you know Christa and I have broken up?'

Her face changed, her pleasant, rather plain features taking on a concerned expression.

'Yes, Christa told me. I was so sorry. You two seemed so –'

At that point, they were jostled by a woman pushing a loaded trolley past them and Ruth said, 'We can't talk here. Come round to my place later this evening. Say at eight o'clock? In case you don't know my address, it's 5 Bishop's Close. I'll see you later.'

She had gone before he had time to reply or even consider whether or not he wanted to talk to her about Christa. Part of him wanted to refuse. He had discussed Christa with no one and the thought of expressing his feelings out loud to anyone filled him with revulsion. On the other hand, Ruth was Christa's friend and she might be able to explain why Christa had rejected him in so cold and sudden a manner.

On balance, though, he decided as he drove home that it was probably better not to talk to Ruth that evening. He shied away from exposing his pain. It would be like one of those bloody awful women he sometimes overheard in pubs talking about childbirth or their operations. Or Third World beggars exposing their scars, looking for pity. He would phone Ruth and cancel their meeting.

It was only after he got back to the flat that he realised he had no choice in the matter. He had no idea of Ruth Page's home telephone number which was ex-directory and it was too late to phone her at the office. When he'd met her at Sainsbury's she was obviously on her way home from work. So he'd have to go after all although he made up his mind to say as little as possible.

He arrived quarter of an hour late on purpose in order not to appear too eager and with an excuse prepared for leaving early. He had a set of essays to mark before the morning.

As he drew off Bishop's Close on to the paved forecourt, he saw the house properly for the first time, having only glimpsed it in the headlights that evening when he had dropped Ruth off after giving her and Christa a lift back from Elmsfield. It was a newish, detached house with a low-pitched roof, rather like a Swiss chalet, and cedar cladding on the upper storey. The rest of the house, including an integral garage, was built of reddish-brown brick. There was a small, flat-roofed porch extension where a tub of pink and white petunias was standing, reminiscent of Murray's urns of geraniums. At the sight of it, he nearly turned and walked away without ringing the bell. But Ruth must have heard his car or seen his shadow through the reeded glass panel because, before he could retreat, she had opened the front door. He had no option but to follow her through the hall to a large sitting-room at the back of the house, overlooking the garden.

The room reminded him of her office in Moulsham Street. The furniture was similar, a leather-covered sofa and armchairs, only olive green this time, not black. There were potted plants standing about, too, and water-colour landscapes hanging on the walls. The only difference was the absence of office equipment and a large portrait hanging above the fireplace.

The general effect was stylish, comfortable and expensive although, like the office, it was oddly impersonal. He thought of Christa's sitting-room with its idiosyncratic second-hand furniture and the shabby carpet laid over the bare polished boards.

Ruth was saying, 'What would you like, Alex? A glass of wine? Coffee?'

'Coffee, please.'

He would have preferred wine if only to relax him a little but was anxious it might loosen him up and he'd say too much.

Ruth left the room and, in her absence, he walked across to look more closely at the portrait above the fireplace. It was a charcoal drawing of a young girl's head, quickly executed in a few simple strokes and yet oddly tender and evocative. The sitter's face was turned to look out of the frame as if her attention had suddenly been caught by the viewer's unexpected presence, in this case his own. There was an expression of startled appeal in the eyes, as if she were pleading with him, but why he couldn't decide.

He was still looking at it when Ruth re-entered the room, carrying a tray of coffee things which she put down on a low table by the window.

'That's one of Christa's,' she said.

'Is it?' Alex asked, surprised. 'It's not like any of her other work I've seen.'

'You mean the book illustrations? Oh, they're just her bread and butter. She ought to be a portrait painter. That's what she was trained for.'

'Why isn't she then?'

'Not enough commissions. And she wasn't prepared to flatter her clients. When she painted them, it was as they really were, warts and all.'

'Yes,' Alex agreed. He could understand that. There was an un-compromising quality about Christa which he had found both challenging and at times intimidating.

Ruth had poured the coffee and was holding out his cup to him. He joined her, sitting down in the leather armchair opposite hers. As he took the cup from her, she looked him directly in the eyes and said simply, 'You mustn't mind too much about Christa. It wasn't anything to do with you.'

'She told you that?'

'Not in so many words. But I know her. She finds it hard to commit herself to any relationship. You see, she had a bad experi-ence two or three years ago. Someone she was very much in love with let her down. It was why she left London and came here. I'd already set up Personelle and she needed to be near someone she knew. Her father had died about the same time and had left her enough money to buy the house in Clifford Street. He brought her up after her mother died of cancer when Christa was eleven so she was very close to him. His death and the disastrous love affair had a devastating effect on her. She had some sort of a breakdown. She couldn't work; couldn't concentrate on anything. It was then she gave up portrait painting. Once she'd left London, it wasn't easy to get commissions anyway and she'd become very wary of people she didn't know, even her sitters. It was why she took up book illustrating. It meant she could work on her own at home and not have to meet people if she didn't want to.'

All of which, as he acknowledged to himself, was no doubt true but it failed to explain Christa's abrupt rejection of him or her haste to get involved with another man. He said as much to Ruth.

'I expected more from her than just a couple of lines out of the blue telling me it was all over. I thought I meant more to her than that.'

'Is that how it happened?' Ruth asked. 'She didn't try to explain?'

'No; she simply wrote she didn't want to see me again. There was no reason, no explanation. I've tried calling her but all I got was her bloody answer-phone. She hasn't even bothered to answer the letters I sent her.'

He stopped there, afraid to continue in case he said too much. He could already feel the anger and frustration beginning to build up, tensing the muscles in his throat.

Ruth said, 'I'm so sorry, Alex. That was unkind of her. I'm sure she doesn't realise how much she's hurt you. She may have thought it was better to make a clean break. That affair I was telling you

64

about has made her – well, not exactly hard but very cautious about any commitments. She finds it difficult to deal with emotions, hers and other people's.'

'That didn't stop her from taking up with Robert Murray,' Alex said, letting his bitterness show.

'How did you find out about him?' Ruth asked quickly.

He knew he had gone too far but it was too late to withdraw the statement. Ruth was intelligent enough to know that, if the break with Christa was as sudden and as complete as he had described it, then he couldn't have learned about Murray from her but must have found out by some other means. He would have to give Ruth some sort of explanation although he could not bring himself to tell her the whole truth.

'I happened to see her driving through the town one evening,' he said, 'so I followed her. She picked him up outside his house in Buckleigh Green and then they drove to an hotel about five miles away. If she's that wary of relationships, why the hell has she got mixed up with Murray? She must know he's married.'

'Perhaps that's why. With him, there's no real commitment,' Ruth said.

It was an aspect of Christa's relationship with Murray which hadn't occurred to him although, now that Ruth had expressed it, he could see it might be true. It was small comfort to think that Christa might not, as he had assumed, be in love with Murray after all even if it hardly helped him come to terms with her rejection of himself.

'So it's just another affair to her, like the one she had with me?' he said bitterly. 'I didn't think Christa was like that.'

Ruth looked away from him and made no reply although an expression of sadness on her face seemed to suggest that he had come uncomfortably close to the truth.

Unable to contain the rising anger and frustration which he had struggled for weeks to control and which now threatened to over-whelm him, he got abruptly to his feet. The anger was directed not so much at Christa as at himself. Yes, he could see now that Christa had used him but it was his fault for letting it happen. He'd been a fool not to realise from the beginning that she had never really cared for him. Perhaps, as Ruth had suggested, she was incapable of love, so damaged emotionally by that early disastrous affair that she found it impossible to feel anything more than physical desire.

It also struck him as ironic that he, who had always in the past avoided any form of commitment, had been caught in the same snare. It was like a retribution, he thought wryly; a nemesis which he richly deserved.

Ruth, too, had got up from her chair and had gone over to a bureau on the other side of the room where she was writing something down on a slip of paper. As he came towards her, she turned and gave it to him.

'It's my home phone number,' she told him. 'If at any time, Alex, you want to talk, please give me a ring. I only hope what I've told you about Christa has helped. What has happened between you is not your fault, believe me. It's just the way Christa is and she's not to blame for that either.'

'Thanks,' he said, pocketing the piece of paper although at the time he had no intention of phoning her.

'I'm truly sorry, Alex,' she added. Her face held an expression of genuine distress. He understood her feelings. She was Christa's friend. His friend, too; or so he liked to believe. He could see how difficult the situation was for her. But he was glad he had come to see her. She had talked a lot of sense and given him a better understanding both of himself and of Christa. He was grateful for that. Although he could still feel the pain of Christa's loss, he could now dimly imagine a time when he might eventually come to terms with it, even though a scar would always remain which would never entirely disappear.

'I'm sorry, too,' he replied.

There was nothing more to be said.

He had left the house, he remembered, believing that it was all over. He would never see Christa again. Nor Ruth either, come to that.

That was ten days ago. How bloody wrong he had been.

Turning away from the window, Alex began to walk restlessly up and down the kitchen. That sense of loss he had felt at Christa's defection was nothing compared to the present pain of her death; the ultimate and irrevocable loss.

No, he would never see her again.

Now that the initial shock of finding her body had passed, he knew that, if he gave way, he would drown in despair. He would not remember, he told himself fiercely, the fixed blue stare, the chin strained upwards, the one bare foot exposed below the hem of her gown.

He would concentrate instead on Murray and on Murray's guilt. It was like a rock to which he would cling. But it wasn't as simple as that. Murray's guilt was inextricably bound up with his

66

own innocence. Once that was proved, the other was beyond doubt.

Ruth had been right in insisting he said nothing himself about Murray. He could see that now. If he brought Murray into the picture, he would only be giving himself a motive for Christa's murder. He had to leave Murray to the police.

And tomorrow, with these memories of the past fresh in his mind, he would have to go to the police and give them a suitably censored statement which would have to sound convincing. He wasn't at all sure that, in his present state, he was capable of such a sustained and deliberate deception.

8

The alarm clock rang at a quarter past seven the following morning and Alex woke suddenly, jerked into consciousness from a troubled sleep which had been like a delirium, full of confused snatches of vivid dreams which he couldn't now recall. The confusion spilled over into wakefulness. For a moment, he was uncertain where he was; something seemed wrong with his surroundings, and then he remembered that, in the early hours, he had made up a makeshift couch for himself on the sofa, unable to face going to sleep on the bed where he and Christa used to make love.

Stumbling to his feet, he carried the bedding and the alarm clock back to the bedroom where he dumped them before going into the bathroom to shower and dress. The water revived him a little but, as he shaved, he was aware that he was avoiding his own eyes in the mirror above the basin as if ashamed of meeting their glance.

Given the choice, he would have rung the school to plead illness. But he had no option. It was vital that he behaved as if today were no different from any other, as if he were unaware that Christa was dead, that at some time during the morning Ruth would phone him and he would have to present himself to the police to make a statement. The only way he knew of coping was to distance himself from it all, to cut off all memory and emotion as if he had switched to a sort of automatic pilot which acted for him.

At twenty past eight as usual, he gathered up the books and notes he'd need for the day's classes and went downstairs to the car. Milner's Volvo had gone and, turning into Maynard's Avenue, he set off along familiar streets, keeping his speed down and concentrating on the act of driving.

On his arrival at school, he avoided the staff-room and went straight to his own classroom to take registration, going across to the hall for assembly only at the last minute, where he slipped into a vacant chair at the end of the back row behind the headmaster. Joyce Stanley, seated in the front, turned and, catching his glance, smiled at him. He smiled back, pretending normality. But as he went through the familiar routine, rising to his feet for the hymn, sitting down again while the headmaster gave out the notices about the end-of-term arrangements, he felt as if he were watching it from underwater. Sounds seemed muffled and the rows of faces turned up towards the platform were oddly distanced, anonymous pale ovals above the regulation blue and white checked dresses or white shirts and striped ties.

It was another hot day and the sunlight fell in great oblongs through the tall windows, glittering on the parquet flooring and on the silver sports trophies in their glass case on the far wall.

When assembly was over, he left the platform as soon as he decently could before Joyce Stanley had time to catch up with him.

His first two lessons that morning were, thank God, in the upper school block, separate from the main building. He went straight there from the hall to wait for the class he still thought of as the lower sixth, twelfth-year pupils due to sit their A-level examinations the following year, to straggle in and take their places at the semi-circle of chairs and tables facing his desk. The set play was *Hamlet* and, the previous Monday, he had given them an assignment to prepare notes on Hamlet's remark to the Queen: 'Seems, madam! Nay, it is; I know not "seems" ', asking them to consider the quotation with regard to all the relationships in the play. Under normal circumstances, he would have discussed the subject with them in an informal seminar, encouraging them to make their own comments. Now, watching them settle down and turn their faces expectantly towards him, Alex suddenly lost his nerve.

How the hell could he stand there as if nothing had happened and calmly discuss a play which involved murder, madness and the betrayal of love? He remembered the description of Ophelia's death – how, as she had drowned, her clothes had floated wide in the stream. It was a vivid image which recalled in a sudden flash his own mental image of Christa's long gown spread out across the polished boards which had gleamed like water under the hall light.

Even the word 'seems' had its own special significance. Nothing was as it seemed, certainly not Christa's feelings for him. And at some point during the morning, Ruth would phone and he would have to steel himself to make his statement to the police. Another lie. Another form of seeming.

Taking some file paper from the desk and handing round the sheets, he said abruptly, 'Monday evening's assignment. I assume you've all made the notes. I'd like you to expand them under headings – Hamlet's relationship with his mother; Ophelia's with Hamlet and so on.'

Turning to the board, he wrote up a list of the headings, hearing as he did so a low muttering break out behind him in protest at having to do written work the day before the end of term. He swung back to face them.

'Just settle down and get on with it. I'll take the work in at the end of the lesson.'

Once their heads were bent over the task, he sat down at the desk, glancing at his watch as he did so to check the time. It was a quarter to ten. In fifteen minutes, Mrs Hunter would put her key in the front door of Christa's house and would enter the hall.

Blanking out the image, he transferred his attention to the scene outside, watching but not really seeing a group of lower school girls in navy and white gym kit playing rounders on the top field. Their cries came drifting in through the open window.

So normal, he thought. So very ordinary.

And at some time during the next hour, Ruth will phone and then there will be no going back.

The summons came when he was collecting up the papers. Mrs Reynolds, one of the school secretaries, tapped on the door before opening it and putting her head inside the room.

'Urgent call for you, Mr Bennet,' she announced. 'I've switched it through to the telephone room.'

Although he had been expecting it, the shock of it still came like a physical blow although he managed to cover up his panic in the flurry of shoving the papers into his briefcase and dismissing the class. Minutes later, as he set off across the courtyard towards the main building, the bell rang for mid-morning break. By the time he reached the office, classes were already dispersing and the corridors were crowded with pupils scrambling for the doors which led out into the school grounds.

The telephone room, situated off the general office, was set aside for any teachers wanting to make or receive private calls. The small room was quiet, minimally furnished with a table, a shabby chair and a wall-mounted pay-phone.

Picking up the receiver, he heard Ruth's voice speaking softly and urgently.

'Alex? Is it all right to talk?'

He knew what she meant – was there any danger of their conversation being overheard?

He said, 'It's safe.'

'Then listen. I went round to Christa's house last night as we agreed –'

'Oh, God, Ruth!' he exclaimed. In his obsession with Christa, he had pushed the thought of Ruth's part in the deception to the back of his mind. Now, reminded of it, it suddenly came home to him what she, too, must have gone through.

'It was all right,' she assured him quickly. 'Christa had given me a set of keys that time she was ill with flu. I simply opened the front door a couple of inches.' He heard again that quick, harsh intake of breath as if she were struggling for air. 'I didn't go in. I didn't see anything. But I think someone saw me. A man. He walked past the house as I was standing there –'

'Ruth, we can't go on with this –' he began. She cut across him.

'We have to. It's too late now to go back. And it doesn't matter about the man, Alex. In fact, it's better that way. As I said to you yesterday, I'll have a witness to back up my statement. At that distance, he can't have seen anything much – just a woman on the doorstep apparently talking to someone inside the house. It'll work, believe me. It has to. It gives you an alibi.'

'I see that but –'

'Let me finish. There isn't much time. Mrs Hunter rang me this morning. You'd better know what she said in case there's any query. She said Christa's been strangled although that's not official yet. The police are at the house. I've already rung the local station and I've been asked to go to Divisional headquarters to make a statement. Evidently the inquiry's being organised from there. I suggest you do the same – ring the police, I mean. And listen, Alex, there's something else I have to know before I make my statement. The police may ask me about it. What was Christa wearing last night?'

Alex closed his eyes and leaned against the wall, still holding the receiver to his ear. Since yesterday, he had struggled to blank out all recollection of the dead Christa, substituting instead memories of her when she was alive. Now, for a searing moment, that Ophelia-like image of her lying in the hall flashed again into his mind – her gown spread wide as if she were floating away on some dark stream.

The sound of Ruth's voice came to him, too close, too real.

'Alex, are you still there?'

'Yes,' he said.

'Did you hear? What was –?'

He answered quickly to prevent her from repeating the question. 'That cream-coloured kaftan.'

She was silent for a moment and then she said, her voice rising in distress, 'Oh, God, Alex! It's so awful! Like a nightmare. But we've got to go through with it. You're innocent. Whatever happens, we have to hang on to that.'

'Yes, I suppose so,' he replied.

'So you'll ring the police?'

'I'll phone them now,' he told her. Just before he hung up, he added with awkward abruptness, 'Thanks, Ruth, for all you're doing.'

There was a dog-eared telephone directory lying on the table and he picked it up, turning over the pages to find the entry for 'Police'. Ruth had said it was like a nightmare and, as if he were taking part in a dream, he watched his hands go through the motions of putting money in the slot and dialling the number of Divisional headquarters in New Street.

A woman answered him, impersonal, efficient.

He heard his own voice speaking.

'I'm phoning about the death of Christa Wyatt. I may have some information about it.'

Was it his imagination or was there a small, startled pause before the woman said, 'I'll put you through to Detective Sergeant Craddock, sir'.

Craddock came on the line almost immediately; a deep voice, pleasant and courteous but with the same non-committal tone.

'How can I help you, sir?'

Alex repeated the statement he'd already given, conscious of a rising sense of tension and frustration. He wanted to get the whole ghastly business over now, as quickly as possible, make his statement, tell the lies which had to be told. He plunged on, 'I saw her yesterday evening. At her house. She's a friend of mine. Was, I mean.'

'Just a minute, sir.' Craddock's voice cut in, registering nothing more than polite professionalism. 'If I could have your name and address first.' When Alex gave them, he continued, 'May I ask, Mr Bennet, how you heard about Miss Wyatt?'

'A mutual friend's just rung me. Ruth Page. She heard about it from Christa's cleaning lady, Mrs Hunter.'

If the names meant anything to Craddock, he gave no sign.

'Thank you, Mr Bennet. Well, sir, if you care to call in here at Divisional headquarters as soon as you can, I'd be grateful. Ask for me at reception.'

And that was it. Craddock had replaced his receiver and, after a moment of disbelief, Alex, too, rang off.

Reaction set in almost immediately, surprising him by its force. As if some inner control had suddenly burst apart, he began trembling violently and a sensation, like physical nausea, came swooping up from his stomach to fill his chest and throat. Fumbling for the chair, he sat down and put his head between his knees.

It was delayed shock, he realised. Until that moment, he had not properly registered anything, not even Christa's death. In some way which he still couldn't understand, he had protected himself against the full reality of it, repressing his emotions in his attempt to behave normally. It would have been far better if he had told the truth from the beginning, protested his innocence and admitted everything he knew about Murray. But it was too late now. He was stuck with the lies, like some monstrous burden he was forced to pick up once more and carry on his shoulders.

He got to his feet and went through the main office into the corridor just as the bell rang for the end of mid-morning break. He was free for the next two lessons and it had been his intention to shut himself away in one of the upper school classrooms which would be empty now that the GCSE exams were over and most of the pupils had either left or were on home-study leave. But, as he made for the door leading out of the main building, Joyce Stanley came out of the staff-room and hurried after him.

'I'm glad I've caught you. You're free for period four, aren't you? I wondered if we could get together to discuss next year's class allocations . . .' she began and then stopped as she saw his face. 'Alex, what's happened?' she asked, her own face full of concern. 'You look dreadful.'

'I've just heard a friend of mine's been killed,' he said. He couldn't bring himself to use the word 'murdered'. He had meant to leave it there but some compulsion to tell her at least part of the truth prompted him to add, 'I've got to go to the police sometime today to make a statement.'

'Come in here,' she told him, turning back to the staff-room and almost pushing him ahead of her into the marking-room beyond where a solitary young geography teacher was frantically writing comments on a set of end-of-term reports which should have been finished on Monday.

'Do me a favour, Bob,' she said to him. 'Keep an eye on 8C, room 17, for me, will you? I'll take over as soon as I can.'

As the door closed behind him, she turned to Alex.

'Go home,' she said. 'No I mean it, Alex. You're in no fit state to carry on here. I'll arrange cover for your lessons. And take tomorrow off as well. I'll clear it with the head.'

He nodded, grateful for her briskness which was like a shower of cold water; grateful, too, that she asked no questions.

At the door, she added, 'You're all right to drive?'

'Yes,' he said.

She regarded him with a long appraising look but said no more except, 'Take care.'

He had intended taking Joyce Stanley's advice by going back to the flat first to change and prepare himself for the interview with Craddock but, on the drive there, he changed his mind. All he wanted to do now was get it over and done with. He was afraid, too, that if he waited, the control which he had so carefully built up might break down again and he would lose his nerve completely.

At the next junction, he signalled right and drove to New Street. Getting out of the car, he went through all the right motions, locking it up before walking across to the white modern block of Divisional headquarters. The heat, striking back from the tarmac, made every step a physical effort, like wading through deep water.

It was cooler inside the building. As instructed, he gave his name and Craddock's at the reception desk and was directed towards one of the chairs against the wall where he sat down, deliberately registering nothing. Instead, he picked up a Sunday colour supplement magazine from a nearby table and turned over the pages, concentrating on the printed images. Advertisements for cars, for fitted kitchens, a page of horoscopes, a crossword puzzle partly completed in blue biro.

'Mr Bennet?'

The voice was familiar; polite, pleasant, non-committal.

Looking up, Alex saw a tall man in his thirties; clean-shaven, dressed in a grey suit, white shirt and dark red tie. The face above the tie had the same pleasant, non-committal expression as the voice.

73

'I'm Detective Sergeant Craddock. Thank you for coming in, Mr Bennet. If you'll come this way.'

Alex followed him along a corridor and up a flight of stairs. The interior was like any other modern block, functional, impersonal, artificially lit. Occasionally, an open door gave a glimpse into an office, a glowing computer screen, a potted plant on a window-sill. The building was strangely quiet although Alex was aware of activity going on around him. A phone rang behind a closed door. A WPC passed them on the stairs carrying a pile of folders.

Craddock was saying something over his shoulder which Alex only half registered – some apology about there being no empty office and having to use an interview room. He paused to push open a door before ushering Alex into a small room, furnished with a plastic-topped table and a couple of chairs. A shelf on the wall held recording equipment.

'Of course,' Craddock was saying, nodding towards the shelf, 'that's used for suspects' statements, Mr Bennet. As you're only a witness, yours won't be recorded.'

Only a witness!

It was absurd to feel so much relief at such an ordinary remark. But just to hear Craddock say it seemed to lift some of the tension.

And, in the event, giving his statement wasn't the ordeal Alex had feared. Craddock wrote it down in longhand, only occasionally stopping to ask about some minor matter, to verify a time or a date, but never once questioning the basic truth of what Alex was saying.

When he had finished, Alex read through the statement and signed each page at Craddock's request. It read better than he had dared hope. Except for that one big lie, that Christa was alive when he left the house, the rest was close enough to what had happened and seemed plausible even to him.

Although the necessity to have his fingerprints taken came as a shock, one he hadn't expected, Craddock's explanation that it was merely a routine matter, sir, for purposes of elimination, softened its effects. After that, he was free to leave.

He came out of the building into the bright sunlight feeling an enormous sense of relief. The worst was over.

The phone rang soon after he returned to the flat. He picked up the receiver, assuming it was Joyce Stanley calling to find out how he was. But it was Nick Duffield, ringing from the *Gazette* office, judging by the background noises. His voice, speaking too close to the mouthpiece, sounded eager and anxious.

'Alex? Thank God I've got hold of you. I tried ringing you at work but someone said you'd gone home. You're not ill, are you?'

'No,' Alex said.

'That's all right then.' Nick sounded relieved. 'I thought perhaps . . .' He broke off and began again, his voice taking on a concerned note which wasn't altogether convincing. 'Look, Alex, I'm afraid I've got some bad news for you. It's about Christa. I realise you two split up some time ago –'

'I already know,' Alex said. It didn't occur to him to ask how Nick had found out. He assumed that, as a reporter, Nick would have been routinely informed.

Nick was saying, 'Who the hell told you?'

Alex could hear the surprise in Nick's voice at not being the first with the news.

'Ruth Page.'

'And how did she find out?'

'It's a long story,' Alex said. He would have preferred Nick to have left it there but he wasn't going to be done out of his scoop.

'So you know Christa was murdered?'

'That's been confirmed?' Alex asked sharply, suddenly alert. 'Where did you hear that?'

'Oh, I have my contacts,' Nick replied. It was said in an airily throw-away manner which managed at the same time to sound conspiratorial.

With the police, Alex assumed. The implications of Nick's remark suddenly struck him. If Nick had access to inside information, what else might he turn up which could find its way into the *Essex Gazette*? It was an aspect of the situation which hadn't occurred to him before and he thought what a bloody fool he'd been not to have taken this into account. And if Nick had a line to the police, it meant the police in turn had a line to Nick. Wasn't that the way such contacts worked? Scratch my back and I'll scratch yours? Although he didn't for a moment believe Nick would speak out of turn, he knew Nick's ability to loosen up when he'd had a few drinks. God knows what he might say. 'Alex Bennet? Yes, I know him. Is he involved? Why the hell didn't he tell me?'

It might look suspicious if he said nothing to Nick. With the thought came the realisation of circumstances closing in on him again, of more lies that would have to be told, of more deceits to be maintained.

And the car! God, he had forgotten about that! Supposing Nick mentioned he'd borrowed his car?

He said quickly, 'Can we meet? I'd like to talk to you.'

'Yes, of course. When?'

'As soon as possible. Can you make it this afternoon?'

'Okay by me. Where'd you suggest? The Crown?'

'Let's make it somewhere out of town.'

Better that way. They were less likely to run into someone they both knew.

'All right. The Swan at Elmsfield?'

'No, not there.' That was where he had met Christa. 'The Bell at Ramstead in three-quarters of an hour?'

'Right, you're on.' His voice full of curiosity, Nick added, 'What's this about, Alex? Is it something to do with Christa?'

So he had guessed but that couldn't be helped.

'I'll explain when I see you,' he said and rang off.

He showered quickly and changed before driving over to Ramstead. Nick was late as usual and, while he waited, Alex sat in the garden behind the pub, choosing a table well away from the others although there were few customers. It was a weekday and the Bell was too far out of town to attract many lunchtime drinkers.

It was pleasant under the trees. On the far side, the lawn sloped down to a small stream edged with willows. In the other direction, he could see the rear wall of the pub hung with the heavy mauve tassels of wistaria. Dragonflies, their glassy wings iridescent in the sunlight, flashed backwards and forwards across the water. He caught himself thinking Christa would have liked it here and then deliberately switched off the thought, emptying his mind of everything except the feel of the sun on his face and the sound of some distant tractor working in an unseen field.

He was startled out of his reverie by someone calling his name and, turning his head, he saw Nick emerging from the rear door of the bar, carrying a tray containing two glasses of beer and a plate of sandwiches.

'Get some of this down you, old son,' he said, putting the tray down on the table. 'I bet you haven't eaten.'

It was one of those spontaneous acts of kindness which Nick made from time to time and which Alex appreciated as a mark of genuine friendship. He knew what the signals meant. Look, Nick was saying. I'm here as your friend. You can trust me.

And Nick seemed to mean it when he said, 'I'm sorry about Christa. It must have come as a hell of a shock.' But he was still a journalist under the skin as Alex realised when he continued, 'So how did Ruth Page find out about her?'

There was a look of bright-eyed curiosity about him of the reporter on the prowl.

'Through Christa's cleaning woman.'

'You mean she found Christa?'

'According to Ruth, yes,' Alex replied. He decided it was time he took control of the conversation. 'Listen, Nick,' he said. 'I know whatever I tell you won't go any further.'

'Of course not. You know me.'

Only too well, Alex thought wryly.

'The fact is, I've had to make a statement to the police. I saw Christa last night.'

Nick made no attempt to hide his astonishment.

'But I thought you'd finished with her weeks ago.'

'For God's sake, let me finish!' Alex broke in.

Nick lifted both hands, palms open, in a gesture of conciliation.

'Okay, okay! Sorry. Go on; I'm listening.'

'Yes, it was all over between us. I hadn't seen her for weeks. Then she phoned me yesterday and asked me over. She wanted to talk to me. I don't want to go into details right now. It's a personal matter and I've explained all that to the police. I just didn't want you to think I was holding anything back from you, in case my name gets mentioned. I suppose there'll be something in the *Gazette*?'

'There's bound to be. There'll be a police press release sooner or later.'

'But not yet?'

'Not officially, no. Probably later today or tomorrow.'

'And unofficially?'

'Oh, that.' Nick grinned deprecatingly as he put down his glass. 'Shall we just say I know someone on the inside who does me a favour from time to time? Civilian bloke on the office staff but he gets to hear things. He gave me a bell when the news broke this morning. That's strictly between us, though. Right?'

'Yes, of course. Will you cover the case?'

'Almost certainly as soon as there's anything to report. But it's okay, Alex. I get your drift. I may be thick-skinned but I'm not thick-headed. There's not going to be a banner headline in the *Gazette*, "Local Teacher Had Affair With Murder Victim", if that's what's bothering you. Your name won't come into it, not unless you get yourself arrested. And then even I couldn't keep that under wraps.'

'Thanks,' Alex said sardonically. 'You're a real friend.'

Nick immediately looked contrite.

'Sorry, Alex. I was way out of order. I mean it must be hell for you, seeing Christa not long before she was murdered. You've no idea, I suppose, who might have done it? No mention of a new boyfriend? No sign she was having an affair with someone else?'

'No,' Alex said. 'Nothing. And talking of affairs, about the car . . .'

'What car?'

'Yours. You remember I borrowed it?'

'Oh, yes, I'd forgotten. What about it?'

'I'd rather you didn't mention it to anyone.'

'Why should I?' Nick looked surprised. 'You were having it off with a married woman, weren't you?'

Alex regretted saying anything but it was too late to withdraw. He said, 'Exactly. I wouldn't want her name brought into it.'

'I get your drift. It could be awkward if her old man found out. How's it going anyway; that affair, I mean?'

'It's over,' Alex said curtly, hoping to dissuade Nick from pursuing the subject any further. He was so deep in lies, he wanted to be finished at least with this one.

He got to his feet.

'I ought to be going,' he said.

Nick gulped down the last of his beer and also stood up.

'I'll come with you. I suppose I ought to be pushing back to the office. I told them I was meeting an informer.'

He gave Alex a sideways grin and then added, 'Who'd you see when you gave your statement?'

'Detective Sergeant Craddock.'

'I know him. Nice bloke. Any problems?'

'No, it was all straightforward,' Alex replied.

They had reached his car and he stopped to find his keys.

It was then that Nick made his parting remark, probably for no other reason than to impress Alex with his inside knowledge.

'Craddock's experienced but he won't have much to do with the investigation. Detective Chief Superintendent Davies'll be in overall charge of that; he's mainly a desk-wallah, though. The chap who'll be doing the leg-work is Detective Chief Inspector Jack Finch, or so my dicky-bird tells me. A sharp operator, Finch. Looks like a farmer but he's damned good at his job. Not much gets past him. Anyway, old son, I'd better get going. Sorry again about Christa. Bloody awful business. I'll see you around.'

And with a cheerful wave, he went loping off across the car-park towards his own car, leaving Alex still standing there with the keys in his hand.

At about the same time as Alex Bennet was driving to Divisional headquarters, a car containing Detective Chief Inspector Jack Finch, with Detective Sergeant Boyce at the wheel, drew up outside number 47 Clifford Street. Getting out, Finch stood for a few moments on the pavement with his hands in his pockets, surveying the front of the house as if he were estimating its value.

The blind was still drawn over the front downstairs window, he noticed, and a light was burning in the hall. It was also an end property which meant it had only the one neighbour who might have seen someone entering or leaving the house. Not a good start for a case although his face, which had the guileless, open look of a countryman, remained bland, giving nothing away.

Jerking his head at Boyce, he set off up the path towards the porch where Parsons, a uniformed PC, was on duty logging the names of everyone who came and went from the scene of the crime.

'Who lives next door?' Finch asked after Parsons had added his name and Boyce's to his list.

'It's an architect's office, sir,' Parsons replied. 'The woman who found the body phoned from there earlier this morning.'

So it would be closed in out-of-business hours. No hope of finding witnesses there, Finch thought gloomily, if, as he already suspected from the drawn blind and the lights left burning, the murder had been committed after dark the previous evening.

'I've been asked by the SOCOs to direct everyone round to the side entrance,' Parsons added with an apologetic air although the decision wasn't down to him. 'The body's lying in the hall, sir, and they want to avoid contamination of the scene. There's not much room either to get in and out.'

Finch merely nodded before setting off in the direction Parsons had indicated, a stocky figure followed by the taller, broad-shouldered sergeant.

As he turned the corner into Henrietta Street, which ran at right angles to Clifford Street, the chief inspector's gloom deepened. The entrance was a wooden door set in a high brick wall and was overlooked by the side elevation only of the houses across the road, blank except for a couple of small first-floor windows of frosted glass, almost certainly those of a bathroom and lavatory. Small chance there either of finding any witnesses who'd seen anything useful.

The garden which lay behind the wall was as secluded as the approach to it. The door leading into it was open and Maguire, one of the SOCO team, wearing gloves and coveralls, was dusting over the white-painted surface for fingerprints. Finch nodded to him as he edged past, followed by Boyce. It was a long garden, with a lawn at the far end and a paved area immediately inside the gate which extended along the back of the house. But it wasn't the flower beds, nor the rose trellises, nor the artistic touches in the form of wrought-iron garden furniture and a marble bust standing on a pedestal in its own little niche of dark, close-clipped yew which caught the chief inspector's attention. It was the high wall which surrounded the whole garden and the trees in full leaf which effectively shielded the place from its neighbours. As far as the inquiry was concerned, the house might have been set miles from anywhere in the country. Even the hope of finding any footprints was a non-starter. Although it had rained heavily the evening before, the flagstones had long since dried.

Viewing the back of the house, he noticed that the blind was pulled down over the downstairs window by the back door and that the curtains were also drawn over a pair of french windows which were set open and which led out on to the paved area.

So far, he knew little about the case apart from a few details included in the preliminary report sent in by the two officers in an Instant Response Vehicle which had arrived first on the scene. The victim, who had apparently been strangled, was a young woman; name, Christabel Wyatt; single; living alone; in her late-twenties. The body had been discovered at approximately 10 a.m. by her cleaning lady, a Mrs Hunter, who had telephoned the police – according to Parsons, from the architect's office next door. The two men in the IRV had taken a preliminary statement from her and she had since been allowed to go home. Parsons had her address. Finch had subsequently been informed that the SOCO team had been called out and were already on the premises together with Pardoe, the pathologist. The police surgeon had left after certifying death.

Finch was already building up his own mental dossier on the case from what he had so far seen. If he were right and the murder had been committed the previous evening, then it had probably taken place after 8 p.m. when, because of the threatened storm, it was already beginning to get dark. Finch remembered turning on his own lights at home at about that time.

It was also possible that the murderer could have entered, as he had done, through the back garden although that would need checking out. Turning, he walked back the few yards to where Maguire was still brushing over the paintwork on the door with aluminium powder.

'Was this open when you got here?' he asked.

'Closed but not bolted, sir,' Maguire replied. 'Have a look for yourself.'

The door was fitted on the inside with two black-painted bolts, top and bottom. In addition, there was a box-lock, also painted black, and above it an old-fashioned catch, of the type used on cottage doors, which could be lifted on the outside by a thumb-latch.

So, he thought, if neither the bolts nor the lock were secure, anyone could have entered through the back garden, almost certainly unseen, as his own observations tended to suggest.

Jamming his hands even deeper in his pockets, Finch tramped back towards the french windows. He was already getting bad vibes about the case, a gut feeling that the odds were stacking up against it being one of those straightforward inquiries where the evidence was handed to you on a plate.

He and Boyce were met at the french windows by Barney, in charge of the SOCO team, who handed out protective clothing including overshoes which they put on standing one-legged on the patio before Finch pushed aside the curtains and they entered the room.

It was large, a combined dining- and sitting-room, and was full of people, Barney and Rogers fingerprinting, and two civilian photographers, one taking still shots, the other video-recording the scene. Finch, too, took his own mental shots with a few rapid glances as he stood just inside the room, storing up these first few vital impressions which he'd later use to supplement the recorded images.

Furniture basic and unconventional, the sort you'd pick up cheap second-hand. Two lamps burning on low tables on either side of the fireplace, the alcoves of which were filled with floor-to-ceiling bookcases.

No sign of any disturbance. If there had been an intruder, he'd been remarkably neat. There was none of the confusion of strewn possessions the average burglar leaves behind.

But there were signs of occupation. The cushions on the rocking chair and sofa were flattened, suggesting two people might have sat there.

Two doors led off the room. The one in the dining-room end was partly open and through it he caught a glimpse of a kitchen, an oblique view of a sink unit, the window above it fitted with a blind which was lowered.

The other, also open, which Barney was indicating with his thumb, apparently led into the hall.

'The body's through there, sir.'

With Boyce at his heels, Finch crossed the room, taking care to keep to the protective plastic squares which were laid out across the floor and which, like stepping-stones, led to this second door.

As Parsons had said, there wasn't much room to get in and out. The body took up most of the space. It was lying on its back although that was almost certainly not the position in which it had been found. He'd have to check with the still photographs and the video-recording to establish that. Barney would have moved it when he bagged up the head, hands and feet and it would have been further disturbed when Pardoe had made his preliminary examination.

Finch had seen many bodies during his career as a policeman, not only murder victims but those resulting from suicide and accidents of every kind: fires, car crashes, once a stockman gored by a bull, and yet he had never learned to look on the faces of the dead with equanimity. It always seemed to him an act of voyeurism, a form of violation which he found difficult to come to terms with even now as he stood there looking down at this latest victim.

She was young and was, or rather had been, attractive; that is if you looked past the puffy flesh, the effects of strangulation, mercifully softened by the transparent plastic bag, to the features which lay beneath. There was a classic curve to the forehead where the fine, shining strands of blonde hair were swept back. The hands and the one bare foot had the same delicate bone structure. Rigor mortis had already set in, giving the body the appearance of a statue cut from marble.

It was such a bloody waste of a young life.

At the same time, Finch, the professional policeman, was making mental notes. The long, cream-coloured gown suggested she was almost ready for bed when she had been murdered and this in turn supported his earlier assumption that the crime had taken place during the evening. The robe could also suggest that, if the murder wasn't the work of an intruder, it could have been committed by someone she knew whom she'd invited into the house and with whom she felt intimate enough to dress informally.

A lover, perhaps?

The position of the body, close to the table on which the phone was standing, could also be significant. Was she trying to ring someone when she was strangled? To call for help?

Squatting down, he looked more closely at the ligature round the neck. It was a length of fabric, broader than, say, a belt, and was made of a blue and white checked material of a type which seemed vaguely familiar. He bent lower to get a closer look.

As he did so, Pardoe, the small, sardonic pathologist, who was standing nearby observing Finch observing the body with the critical and slightly impatient air of a teacher waiting for a pupil to come up with some useful comment about a specimen in a school lab, suddenly barked out, 'Can you make out what it is, Jack?'

'It looks like a tea-towel.'

'Spot on!' Pardoe replied, sounding pleased. 'A common or garden tea-towel. Not your usual ligature, I admit, although I've seen odder ones in my time.'

And not the sort of object anybody might carry about in a pocket, Finch added silently. Which could suggest the murder was unpremeditated, the killer grabbing up whatever came to hand.

He looked down the hall towards the kitchen. Pardoe, following his glance, grinned ironically. Finding the origin of the ligature wasn't part of his job. That was up to Finch and his band of merry men.

He said, 'If you've seen enough, I'll get the body moved. Time of death? I bet you're dying to know. Well, I'm not sticking my neck out on that one.' He gave a little yelp of laughter at his own black humour before adding, 'Judging by the degree of rigor mortis and the body temperature, she's been dead for about sixteen hours. No obvious signs of any other injuries to the body although I'll need to have it on the slab before I can confirm that. And no flesh or skin that I can see under the fingernails. But, again, I'll need to take scrapings before that's established.'

'Thanks, Reg,' Finch said.

'All part of the service,' Pardoe said with another grin. 'I'd do the same for you any time. Right, then!' he added briskly, turning to PC Yeats, the Coroner's officer, who was standing with his back to the front door. 'If you'll whistle up the mortuary van, we'll get this show on the road.'

As Yeats let himself out, Finch gestured to Boyce who, because of the lack of room, had remained just inside the sitting-room doorway.

'Check the kitchen,' he told him. 'See if there's a tea-towel in there. I'm going upstairs for a little recce.'

Stepping carefully over the body, he began to mount the stairs.

He needed to be alone, partly to escape from Pardoe's mordant comments which had left a sour taste in his mouth even though he understood the pathologist's need to indulge in them. How the hell else could he cope day after day with his job unless he turned it into a macabre joke? It probably kept him sane.

He also needed time to consider the implications of Pardoe's last comments which suggested the murder had taken place at roughly 8 p.m. the previous evening, an estimation which confirmed his own suspicions. Pardoe's other remarks about the apparent lack of further injuries and absence of skin and flesh under the fingernails would also indicate that the victim hadn't put up a fight for her life. Because her attacker was someone she knew and trusted?

He reached the landing where he paused to look about him. There were three doors, two of them ajar, the other closed. The SOCOs hadn't yet examined this part of the house and he was careful to touch nothing, merely nudging more widely open those doors which were already ajar with his elbow.

The first led into a bathroom, probably converted from a boxroom or a small bedroom. It was neat, almost spartan, and contained nothing of particular interest that he could see.

The second door opened into what he took to be the main bedroom which overlooked the front of the house. He lingered there for several moments, standing just inside the doorway and listening to the sounds downstairs in the hall as the body was bagged up and was carried, decently covered, out of the front door to the waiting mortuary van.

Pardoe called up the stairs, 'I'm off then, Jack! See you later at the PM,' before the door slammed shut behind him and the Coroner's officer.

In the silence, Finch looked about him, taking in the details of the room which seemed to him to hold more of the essence of the dead woman than those on the ground floor where the SOCOs had taken charge. It was a large room, containing a minimum of furniture as if she preferred a simple, uncluttered life-style – just a pine chest of drawers and a small dressing-table which held nothing more than a mirror, a brush and comb, and a couple of cosmetic jars.

The floor, which was of the same stripped pine, was bare apart from two rugs of rough white wool on either side of a double bed which was fitted with a Victorian headboard of black enamelled iron. The bed had not been slept in, Finch noticed, and the white cotton quilt was still smooth. A telephone and an alarm clock stood on one of the bedside tables.

Unlike the rooms downstairs, the blinds were not lowered over the two sash windows and the sunlight came pouring in, shining on the polished floorboards and giving the white rugs and bed-cover a dazzling brightness. The impression was of virginal fresh-ness which was at the same time oddly bleak and uncompromising, like a nun's cell.

Here, Finch thought, was the one room in the house which should have reflected something of the dead woman and yet there were no personal mementoes, nothing in the way of ornaments; not much concession even to physical comfort.

He wondered if she conducted her private life along the same lines, discarding all emotional clutter and reducing everything to the bare, simple essentials.

His doubts concerning the case returned more strongly. If he were right, the inquiry into her death wasn't going to be easy.

The third door, which led into a room at the back of the house, wasn't only closed, it was fitted with a Yale lock which failed to yield when he leaned his shoulder against it. Whatever room lay behind it would have to be examined later, after the SOCOs had got the door open.

Retreating along the landing, he went down the stairs into the now empty hall, the body gone and nothing to indicate where it had been. The only record was contained in the video and still photographs which he'd have to study later.

Finch stood looking down at the space where the dead woman had been lying and then glanced across at the little table where the telephone and answer machine stood, wondering again if she had been making or receiving a call when she had been strangled. At the same time, he briefly registered the pile of telephone directories to the right of the receiver and a notebook and pencil which lay beside them. He had a vague feeling that something was wrong but, before he could decide what it was, Boyce had stuck his head out of the doorway at the end of the passage.

'In here, sir,' he announced. 'By the way, the tea-towel's missing but there's something else I think you'll find interesting.'

The door led into the kitchen which he had already glimpsed

from the dining-room. As he entered, Finch was struck again by the neatness and simplicity of the setting. There was the same use of pine in the floorboards and the fitted cupboards which were topped with black slate; the same absence of clutter. Cookery books occupied one shelf while kitchen equipment was either hung on hooks or stowed away in open shelves. The only objects left out were a half-empty bottle of white wine standing on one of the work-tops, open but lacking its cork, and two up-ended wine-glasses on the draining-board.

They had not yet been tested for fingerprints and Finch made no attempt to touch them.

'Looks like she had someone round for a drink,' Boyce commented.

Finch grunted in agreement.

'I want those dusted and bagged up,' he said. 'Get Barney on to it. And why the hell is the cork missing?'

'Perhaps it was chucked away,' Boyce suggested.

'Could be, I suppose,' Finch said.

Walking over to the bin beside the sink and pressing his foot on the pedal, he lifted the lid. The bin contained little apart from some crumpled white tissue paper which might have been wrapped round the bottle when it was bought.

'We'll have this lot bagged up as well.' Looking round the kitchen, he added, 'I see what you mean about the tea-towel. There's the hook for it beside the sink but it's empty.'

Boyce opened his mouth but before he could reply, Finch had turned suddenly on his heel and had set off down the hall towards the telephone table where he stood contemplating the pile of directories. Boyce hurried after him.

'What've you found?' he asked.

'Nothing,' Finch replied. 'And that's the point. Take a look at this lot, Tom. Local phone book, copies of Yellow Pages and Thomson's directory, note-pad and pencil. What's not there?'

Boyce shrugged, not getting the point.

'I don't follow,' he began.

'A private address book, listing friends' phone numbers. There isn't one. But shouldn't there be? Most people have one and keep it by the phone. I know I do. Like the cork and the tea-towel, it's gone walkabout, although we know where the tea-towel finished up – round Miss Wyatt's throat –'

He was interrupted by his call sign on the personal radio he was carrying in his breast pocket, a tinny voice going on to announce that two witnesses, a Miss Page and a Mr Bennet, had visited Divisional headquarters that morning to give statements.

'That settles it!' Finch said, turning to Boyce as the message ended. 'We'll get back to headquarters. When you've dropped me off, Tom, I want you to go on to Mrs Hunter's, the cleaning lady who found the body. Get her address from Parsons. All I need from her at this stage is the answer to a few questions: did Miss Wyatt have a personal address book; if so, where was it kept? And what did she own in the way of valuables, jewellery and so on, and where are those likely to be found? We'll do a full interview with her later.'

Before they left, he had a quick consultation with Barney, asking him to have the contents of the kitchen bin bagged up and a search made for an address book, including the upstairs room which was locked.

'Will do,' Barney agreed.

After Boyce had dropped him at headquarters, Finch went up-stairs to the canteen for a cheese sandwich which he carried down to his office and ate while he waited for a WPC to bring the two witness statements to him.

Once they had been delivered, he glanced through them quickly, briefly establishing a general outline of their contents before reading through them again with greater care, making notes as he went. By piecing the two statements together, it was possible to work out a fairly detailed account of some at least of the events which had taken place during the previous evening as well as a rough time-table of when they had occurred.

According to Alex Bennet's statement, the victim, whom he referred to as Christa Wyatt, had phoned him at approximately 8.15 p.m. and had asked him to call at her house which he had done, arriving there at roughly 8.35 p.m. They had talked for about half an hour and he had then left. At that time, Christa Wyatt was still alive. From Clifford Street, he had driven to Miss Page's house in Bishop's Close, arriving at about twenty-five past nine, and had stayed until roughly five past ten before returning to his flat in Maynard's Avenue, off Broomfield Road. The time had then been about twenty-five past ten.

Ruth Page's statement corroborated part of Bennet's. According to her, Bennet had arrived at her house at about 9.25 p.m. and had left at 10.05, which agreed with Bennet's own estimation of the time.

So far, so good. It all seemed to hang together satisfactorily.

It was what happened afterwards which, from the point of view of the timing of the murder, interested Finch the most. Some twenty-five minutes after Bennet had left, that is at about half-past ten, Miss Page had called at Christa Wyatt's house and had spoken to her briefly. However, about half an hour later, when Ruth Page had tried to phone her, there had been no reply.

There could, of course, be some quite innocent explanation for Christa Wyatt's failure to answer the phone. She could have been in the bath. But one fact was certain; she hadn't gone to bed. The bed hadn't been slept in. And even if she were getting ready for bed, that shouldn't have prevented her from taking the call. There was a telephone extension on the bedside table.

Which left Finch with what seemed like the most logical conclusion: that at eleven o'clock Christa Wyatt was already dead. And that would place the time of her murder between 10.30 p.m., when Ruth Page had spoken to her, and 11 p.m. when she had failed to reach her by phone.

Although it was too early to start making assumptions about the case, this theory tied in with his own observations at the scene of the crime: the lights still burning downstairs, the patio doors left open, the drawn blinds and curtains on the ground floor but not those in the bedroom as well as the unslept-in bed; all of which suggested the murder had not taken place during the night but at some earlier time in the evening.

The theory might also explain the position of the body. She could have gone into the hall to answer the phone call from Ruth Page but then been strangled before she could pick up the receiver. It was a possibility.

It didn't, however, agree with Pardoe's estimation of the time of death which he put at approximately 8 p.m. He'd have to check with Pardoe later in the day once the investigation was properly off the ground although, even as he made the decision, he was aware he was already making excuses to himself for not attending the PM or for turning up too late to witness the actual autopsy.

There were a couple of other points arising from the statements which he'd need to check out when he spoke to Ruth Page and Alex Bennet which he intended doing as soon as Boyce returned from seeing Mrs Hunter. Apart from finding out more about their relationships with the dead woman, particularly Alex Bennet's, there was something in Bennet's statement which struck him as a bit odd. Why, after calling on Christa Wyatt, had he gone to see Ruth Page? In his statement, Bennet had admitted he'd had an affair with the dead woman and was also a 'friend' of Ruth Page, one of those catch-all words which could cover a variety of relationships from lover to somebody one met occasionally for a drink. And on the face of it, it seemed a strange thing for Bennet to have done, to go from one woman to the other in so short a space of time.

The other aspect of Bennet's statement which interested the chief inspector was the question of timing. Bennet said he'd got home at about 10.25 p.m. Were there any witnesses to corroborate that? Or could he have driven back to Christa Wyatt's house and committed the murder after Ruth Page had spoken to her at half-past ten?

He was studying a large-scale map of Chelmsford which was pinned up on the wall behind his desk when Boyce came in.

'You were right about the address book,' he announced. 'There was one – a red-leather job – which was kept by the phone. And the only valuable item Mrs Hunter knows about is a box of jewellery; not much, just a couple of gold chains and a locket. It should be in the dressing-table drawer if it hasn't been nicked.'

'We'll check that later with the SOCOs,' Finch replied. 'As for the address book, that could be somewhere else in the house, I suppose. But first I want to interview these two who've already given statements.' He gave Boyce a brief résumé of their contents and then added, tapping on the street map with his finger, 'Bennet could have had enough time to make it from Maynard's Avenue back to Clifford Street between half-past ten and eleven o'clock.'

'So we go and talk to him?' Boyce asked.

'No, not yet, Tom. I'd rather see Ruth Page first and get her account before we speak to him. She'll probably be in her office. What's it called?' Crossing to the desk, he glanced quickly at her statement. 'Personelle in Moulsham Street. There's something else I want to ask her as well. Why did she call on Christa Wyatt at ten thirty yesterday evening? It seems a bit late to drop in on someone. And why try to ring her so soon afterwards?'

'Oh, women,' Boyce said disparagingly as he followed Finch to the door. 'They spend half their lives nattering on the bloody phone. Waste of time and money, if you ask me.'

10

However, Ruth Page hardly seemed to fit Boyce's description of either a time- or a money-waster when they were shown into her office behind the reception area of Personelle.

She was a smartly dressed, brisk woman, as Finch observed as he took one of the black leather-slung chairs facing her desk. Capable and efficient, too. She answered his preliminary questions directly and without hesitation. But behind that cool, businesslike façade, there was a sadder, more vulnerable woman, as Finch realised as soon as he turned to more personal aspects of the interview.

'How long had you known Miss Wyatt?' he asked, settling back in his chair and assuming his expression of the interested listener, leaving to Boyce the professional duty of taking notes. He noticed how quickly her face changed, as if the muscles had suddenly sagged, making her look tired and much older.

Even so, she still kept to the point, giving him a concise account of her relationship with Christa Wyatt.

They had first met when they were both students in London, she explained, Christa at the Royal College of Art, herself at the London School of Economics. In fact, they'd shared a flat during their first two years as students. Then Christa had moved into a studio and she had stayed on in the flat alone for several years while she was working for one of the large London employment agencies. She'd come to Chelmsford four years before to set up her own agency, Personelle, but had kept in touch with Christa and they'd met fairly frequently.

'So would I be right in thinking you and Miss Wyatt were close?' Finch asked.

'Yes, of course,' Ruth Page replied. Now that the interview had become more personal, both her voice and her expression showed signs of tension, he noticed, although she continued to regard him with the same directness. 'We were what I suppose you'd call best friends. As a matter of fact, it was because I was living in Chelmsford that Christa moved down here. Her father had died and left her enough money to buy the house in Clifford Street and she decided to work from there as a freelance illustrator, mostly of children's books. She'd just gone through a disastrous love affair as well and I think she needed to be near someone she knew. London can be a very lonely place sometimes. All of this may seem a little irrelevant, chief inspector, but it ties in with Alex and what happened last night.'

'Ah, Mr Bennet,' Finch said. 'Tell me about him.'

'Christa and I met him one evening about four months ago at the Swan in Elmsfield. Someone had backed into my car and he offered us a lift home. He and Christa went on seeing each other and eventually they became lovers.'

90

It was said with complete frankness and, as far as Finch could make out, no change of expression in either her face or her voice. It was simply a fact. In the same open manner, Ruth Page added, 'Christa broke off the relationship several weeks ago without apparently giving Alex any explanation and this upset him.'

'Badly?'

'I think so. I met him one evening outside Sainsbury's and he seemed pretty cut-up about it. I like Alex. I can't say I know him all that well but he's always struck me as being a very pleasant man. So I invited him round to my house that evening and we talked about Christa. He felt she had treated him unfairly and I agreed with him. I said as much to Christa the next time I saw her. I think she was more prepared to take it from me than from Alex because she rang him yesterday evening and asked him to go and see her. I gather from him that she apologised for the way she'd behaved and explained it wasn't his fault. Since that disastrous affair, she just didn't want to be tied down emotionally. And then he left.'

'And called on you. Why? Was it pre-arranged?'

Ruth Page regarded him with the same unwavering gaze.

'Oh, no, chief inspector. As far as I could make out, it was a sudden decision. He was still a bit churned up about Christa and I think he wanted to talk it out of his system.'

'Churned up?' Finch put in quickly. 'You mean angry?'

'No; more sad, I'd say. He seemed to have accepted the fact it was all over between them. I made some coffee and we talked about what Christa had said – about that old love affair of hers and how much she'd been hurt. Then he drove home.'

'This was at five past ten?'

'Roughly. He arrived at about twenty-five past nine and stayed for approximately half an hour.'

'You then went to see Miss Wyatt?'

'Not straight away. I'd been writing up CVs for some of my clients – it's one of the services Personelle offers as part of the package. I'd done most of them and had taken a break to have a shower just before Alex arrived. After he'd gone, I sat down to finish them when I found I'd left the notes on one of them at the office. It was a nuisance as I wanted to hand the CVs over to my secretary this morning to type up and run copies off on the word processor. So I decided to drive round to the office in Moulsham Street and pick the notes up.'

'What time was this?'

'Oh, only a few minutes after Alex left; say about ten past ten. I was on my way back from Moulsham Street when I thought I'd call in on Christa.'

'Why?'

'Why not?' she countered. 'It was only a few minutes out of my way. I'd intended phoning her anyway to let her know Alex had been to see me. It seemed just as easy to drop in and talk to her face to face over coffee or a drink.'

'Wasn't it a bit late for that?' Finch asked, voicing the objection he'd already put to Boyce.

'Late?' She gave a wry smile. 'I'm self-employed, chief inspector. I frequently work to one or two in the morning. So did Christa, for that matter. And anyway, it wasn't all that late. I didn't look at my watch but I suppose it was only about half-past ten.'

'I gather from your statement you didn't go inside the house?'

'No. When Christa opened the door, she wouldn't ask me in.'

'Did she give any reason?'

'She said she was busy but she'd phone me later to explain. She seemed . . .' Ruth Page paused for a second to consider and then continued, '. . . I'm not sure exactly – a bit tense, I thought; on edge. At the time, I didn't think that much about it. I simply assumed she might still have been upset about the meeting she'd had earlier in the evening with Alex. So I left it there. I just told her Alex had been to see me and we'd talk about it when she rang me. She said, 'All right,' and closed the door. But I've wondered since if she had someone with her who she didn't want me to meet. That's only an impression, though. I didn't see anyone.

'Anyway, after I got home, I started work on the remaining CVs but I couldn't settle. I was a bit on edge myself, waiting for Christa's call. It wasn't only Alex I wanted to talk to her about. I knew she had other things on her mind as well.'

'Such as?'

'Is this relevant?' For the first time during the interview, Ruth Page showed signs of impatience. Finch had already realised that he was dealing with a highly intelligent woman with a strong personality who was used to running her own business. The question might indeed be irrelevant to the murder inquiry but that was up to him to decide, not her. So he smiled but said nothing as he waited for her reply. After a moment, she shrugged and said, 'Christa's agent had written to her offering her a commission she wasn't sure whether or not to accept. I wanted to find out if she'd made up her mind.'

It was a small point and Finch decided to drop it and move on.

'I gather from your statement you tried phoning Miss Wyatt at about eleven but there was no reply?'

'That's right. As she hadn't rung me as she'd said she would, I thought I'd call her instead.'

'Weren't you concerned when she didn't ring you or answer when you phoned her?'

'Not really. She'd seemed very tired when I spoke to her earlier and I just assumed she didn't feel up to talking after all and she'd simply gone to bed and ignored the phone. I was going to ring her this morning from the office but instead Mrs Hunter called me . . .' The sentence trailed off and there was a moment's silence before she continued more briskly, 'Is there anything else, chief inspector?'

It was clear she considered the interview over but Finch remained seated.

'A couple more points, Miss Page. When you spoke to Miss Wyatt last night, what was she wearing?'

'A long cream-coloured kaftan. She often wore it in the evenings as a sort of housecoat.'

'And I assume she owned a personal address book? Where was it usually kept?'

'On the hall table, next to the phone. Why?'

Finch ignored the question and continued in the same easy, bland manner.

'You said you thought Miss Wyatt might have had someone with her last night –'

'That was only an impression . . .' Ruth Page put in quickly.

'Was she seeing another man after she broke off with Mr Bennet?'

'Not to my knowledge.'

'You would have known?'

'Almost certainly.'

'Miss Wyatt would have confided in you?'

'Yes, I would have expected her to.'

'But she didn't?'

'I've already said so, chief inspector. As far as I know, Christa wasn't meeting another man.' It was a sharp little exchange and Ruth Page herself seemed aware of it for she made a quick gesture with one hand which was meant to be conciliatory. 'I'm sorry,' she continued. 'You seemed to be suggesting Christa was promiscuous. She wasn't. And because she was such an intensely private person, I find it difficult to discuss her personal life with someone who didn't know her. I realise you need to find out who she might have

93

been meeting but I can only repeat what I've already said – if she was having an affair, she'd said nothing to me about it.'

'Which doesn't mean she hadn't found herself a new boyfriend,' Boyce pointed out when, a few minutes later, having taken their leave, he and Finch got into the car. 'He could have been with her last night when the Page woman called on her. Like she said, she had the impression she wasn't alone. It could be why Christa Wyatt didn't ask her into the house.'

Finch merely grunted in reply.

Boyce could be right, of course, in suggesting Christa Wyatt had a new lover. But if she hadn't told Ruth Page, her closest friend, about him, as she had apparently failed to do, had Ruth Page suspected as much? Or, more to the point, had Alex Bennet? If such a lover existed, it would give Bennet a strong motive for murder. But, until his existence was proved, if ever, then none of it added up to anything more than speculation.

'Where to now?' Boyce was asking. 'Bennet's place?'

'No,' Finch said, coming to a sudden decision. 'I want another look at the murder scene.'

Although he wanted to check on the call Ruth Page had said she'd made the previous evening to Christa Wyatt's number, he was more interested in the missing address book. It was an odd thing for someone to take, if that's what had happened to it. It might, though, tie in with the theory of another boyfriend. Bennet had no reason to remove it. He'd quite openly admitted his affair with the dead woman. But a new lover might well want to keep his name and address secret.

They went in by the front door this time, and, once inside, Finch immediately sought out Barney who, with most of the SOCO team, had moved upstairs, leaving only one colleague to search the cupboards and drawers in the downstairs rooms. They conferred briefly on the landing.

Yes, Barney reported, the contents of the waste-bin had been bagged up but the address book hadn't yet been found. They'd go on looking for it. And yes, he'd ring 1471 and find out what was the phone number of the last person to call Christa Wyatt.

'And while I'm here,' Finch added, 'could you also check the dressing-table drawer? There should be a box of jewellery in it. I'd like to know if it's still there.'

'I'll get Stevens on to it as soon as the table's been printed,' Barney told him. 'But if you're thinking of an intruder, it's unlikely in my opinion. You can usually tell when a place's been turned over.'

Which agreed with Finch's own gut feeling.

Barney nodded towards the door with the Yale lock at the far end of the landing.

'By the way, we've got that room opened up. I found the key to it downstairs. If you want to have a dekko, go ahead. It's been printed.'

He followed Finch down the landing, adding unnecessarily as the chief inspector pushed open the door, 'It's a studio, by the look of it.'

Indeed it was. Like the other rooms in the house, the blind was drawn and the light was on. And like those, too, it was plainly furnished, the floor bare boards. A large wooden table, similar to the one in the dining-room, was standing under the window. Next to it, a smaller table with a typewriter on it and a swivel chair drawn up to it, served as a desk. An easel and a metal filing cabinet stood nearby.

The rest of the room was fitted with open-fronted units which ran along two sides, the shelves below filled with artist's folders and racks of paper, the tops with jars of brushes, paint-pots and bottles of coloured inks. A small sink had been let into one of the units. The walls above them were lined with cork boards on which were pinned a collection of illustrations – postcard reproductions, photographs torn from colour supplements and samples of what he took to be Christa Wyatt's own work.

Apparently in no hurry, Finch strolled up and down the room, examining this display. It was an eclectic collection. Among the reproductions, he recognised paintings by Turner, Van Gogh and Renoir as well as several he thought were by Blake. Those he assumed were Christa Wyatt's included sketches in pencil or char-coal, rough outlines of a hand, or a tree, or a woman's profile which still managed, in a few, quick strokes, to capture the spirit of the object they were depicting. Others, such as two or three water-colours of landscapes or seascapes, were complete.

But the majority were pen and ink drawings of what seemed to be illustrations for children's books of dragons and castles, winged horses and witches and long-haired princesses wearing crowns. They were meticulously detailed and at the same time oddly old-fashioned, reminding him, with a sudden jolt of nostalgia, of a book of fairy stories he had owned when he was a child.

Pinned up amongst these pictures were three photographs, one a snapshot of a middle-aged man sitting in a garden – Christa Wyatt's father perhaps. The other two were of Ruth Page. In one, she was leaning over the gate of what looked like a cottage. In the other, she was standing by a signpost against a background of a high bank overhung with trees.

'I'd like this lot bagged up,' he told Barney, who had followed him into the room and who raised an eyebrow at Boyce behind the chief inspector's back. 'And this lot as well.'

He had moved across to the filing cabinet where, easing open the top drawer, he was examining the rows of neat manila folders, each one labelled according to its contents in clear black letters: 'Contracts', 'Correspondence', 'Finances'.

'Anything else?' Barney asked with a touch of irony which was lost on Finch who was taking a final look about him, confirming his impressions.

A workmanlike room, he was thinking. Plain, austere and, like the bedroom, almost nun-like in its simplicity. And at the same time oddly secretive. Why else was the door fitted with a Yale lock except to keep people out? Yet, despite its bareness, it seemed to suggest more of the personality of its owner than any other room in the house. It was here that Christa Wyatt had chosen to keep her correspondence and her few personal mementoes.

Ignoring the rest of the upstairs rooms which he had briefly looked at earlier in the morning, he went downstairs to the sitting-room where he again strolled about with no apparent purpose that Boyce could see, reading the titles of some of the books on the alcove shelves, looking at the cushions on the sofa and the rocking chair. The lights were now switched off and the curtains drawn back to reveal a leafy view of the back garden through the french windows.

Finch looked at that, too, standing at the doors for several moments and gazing out at that other secret, hidden place.

'Ready to go?' Boyce hinted. He hated this inactivity, this hanging about which seemed to achieve nothing.

Finch nodded and together they went into the hall where the chief inspector called up the stairs to Barney who came out on to the landing.

'Found the jewellery box?' he asked.

'It's still in the drawer,' Barney announced.

'Right!'

Finch seemed to be galvanised into action by this piece of information for he walked briskly out of the house and down the path to the car.

'Bennet's place?' Boyce asked, getting in beside him.

But evidently Finch wasn't yet ready to interview the victim's former lover.

'No,' he said. 'We'll talk to Mrs Hunter first.'

Even when they arrived at Mrs Hunter's small terrace house, Finch still seemed in no hurry. At Mrs Hunter's invitation, they sat together in the garden on a tiny lawn, drinking tea and eating slices of her home-made Victoria sponge. She was in her sixties, a short, shrewd-eyed woman who, although still a little shaky and tearful from shock, seemed glad of their company. Finch noticed that she perked up during the interview, pleased with the attention she was getting.

In Boyce's opinion, it wasn't a proper interview. Finch let the woman chat on in her own way which made the task of note-taking far from easy. And what she had to say didn't seem to Boyce to add up to very much in the long run.

She confirmed the time she had found the body and the fact that, after she had gone home, she had phoned Miss Page, Miss Wyatt's friend, to let her know what had happened.

'And what was Miss Wyatt like?' Finch had then asked conversationally as he drank his tea, and she was off like a bloody rabbit across a field with Boyce's pencil scurrying to keep up with her.

Miss Wyatt was nice enough, according to Mrs Hunter. A good employer, always regular with her payments, and the place didn't need much cleaning, not like some she worked for. Mess! You wouldn't believe it and one a doctor's wife who she wouldn't name but whose house was a tip, washing-up all over the kitchen and you should see the state of her saucepans.

You could say this for Miss Wyatt, everything was kept very neat; odd that, her being an artist. Mind you, she couldn't vouch for the state of her studio as she'd never been in it. Miss Wyatt always saw to that herself.

No, she didn't really know much about Miss Wyatt's private life. She wasn't the sort to chat about herself. When Mrs Hunter was there on a Thursday morning doing the cleaning, Miss Wyatt usually stayed upstairs in that studio of hers. She was a bit – well, not exactly stuck up but kept herself to herself.

Phone calls? Yes, a few although Miss Wyatt always left the answer-phone on, at least when she was there so she'd never heard her answering any calls, or making any, come to that. As for friends, she couldn't really say. There was Miss Page, of course. She'd met her a couple of times at the house last winter when Miss Wyatt was down with flu; a very pleasant lady, Miss Page, very friendly. In fact, Miss Page had written down her phone number on a bit of paper so she could ring her if ever Miss Wyatt was taken ill again, Miss Wyatt being alone in the house.

As for letters, she'd never seen any. The postman had always been by the time she arrived and Miss Wyatt never left any lying around, not that she'd dream of reading them, of course, if she had.

And she couldn't say if Miss Wyatt ever entertained anyone in the evenings. If she did, any glasses or plates were always washed up and put away by the time she got there on a Thursday morning.

'And what about overnight guests?' Finch asked guilelessly.

For once, Mrs Hunter paused to regard him with a long, shrewd look.

'Do you mean men?' she asked.

'If she had any to stay.'

'Not that I know of,' Mrs Hunter said slowly as if reluctant to admit to this particular lack of information. 'They usually leave something lying about, don't they? You can generally tell where they've been.' She spoke as if referring to some kind of spoor. 'Mind you, that's not to say she didn't have any – men friends, I mean. She was a nice-looking young woman with that long fair hair of hers, though a bit stand-offish, in my opinion. A lot of men would've been put off.'

'Thank you, Mrs Hunter,' Finch said, getting to his feet and holding out his hand. 'You've been most helpful.'

'Was she?' Boyce asked as they left the house. 'I can't see she told us anything worth knowing.'

'It was what she didn't know that was interesting,' Finch replied.

'Like what?'

'For a start, about Alex Bennet having an affair with Christa Wyatt which had apparently been going on for several weeks.'

'Oh, that.' Boyce didn't sound all that impressed.

'Think about it, Tom. Mrs Hunter's the sort who likes to find out all she can about the people she works for. It's meat and drink to her. And yet she knows nothing about Christa Wyatt's private life and that tells us something very revealing about Christa Wyatt.'

'Secretive,' Boyce suggested succinctly.

'Exactly.' Finch fastened his seat-belt. He seemed pleased Boyce had confirmed his own impression. 'And that means trouble for us when we start doing our own nosing about.' In a sudden little burst of exasperation, he added, 'God, I hate cases like this! You're not only dealing with witnesses who could be lying through their teeth but even the victim does sod-all to help. Let's hope Bennet has something useful to tell us.'

'You mean you want to talk to Bennet now?' It came as something of a surprise to the sergeant that Finch had at long last decided to interview Bennet who, after all, was one of the last persons to see the victim alive, apart from Ruth Page and, of course, her murderer.

'Why not?' Finch, in turn, sounded surprised that Boyce should question his decision.

'Right!' Boyce said with relief as well as a touch of impatience as he pulled smartly away from the kerb.

11

There was a message on his answer-phone from Ruth Page when Alex returned to his flat after meeting Nick Duffield at the Bell in Ramstead. Her recorded voice sounded brisk and matter-of-fact although he could detect a note of tension in it as well.

'Alex, it's Ruth. I can't say much; I'm phoning from the office. The police have been here. In fact, they've only just left. Ring me as soon as you get back, will you?'

He phoned her at once and judging by the alacrity with which she picked up the receiver, he guessed she had been waiting for his call.

'Just a moment,' she told him. 'I'll get Janet to take the letters to the post.' He heard muffled voices in the background and then she came back on the line. 'That's better. We can talk more freely. She knows about Christa. I had to tell her when the police arrived so naturally she's agog. They haven't been to see you?'

'No, not yet. How did it go?'

'All right, I think. Fairly straighforward to begin with. It was mostly about the statement I made this morning. But listen, Alex, don't be fooled by Finch. He's the detective chief inspector who's in charge of the case. He seems a very ordinary man; pleasant to talk to but he's a damned sight shrewder than he makes out.'

This last comment so closely echoed Nick's warning about Finch that Alex felt an empty sensation in his chest as if the air had suddenly been knocked out of him.

Ruth was saying, 'Just keep to what we agreed, all right? And try not to add too much detail. He's got this trick of waiting for you to say something more. I think he may ask you about Christa's phone call, asking you to go round to her house. He questioned me pretty closely about the visit I said I'd made to her. Wasn't it a bit late to call on her? And why did I try phoning her after I'd got back to the house? And talking of phone calls, remember you didn't ring me yesterday. You just dropped by at my place on your way home. I said I thought it was a spur-of-the-moment decision.'

'Yes, yes,' Alex said. He felt impatient at her efficiency and envious, too, of her ability to remain so calm; guilty as well at his own reactions. For God's sake, she was only trying to help him.

'You managed to find someone who'll verify the time you got home last night?' she was asking.

'Yes, I did.'

'Thank the Lord for that!' She sounded relieved for his sake. Then in a gentler, warmer tone, she added, 'Don't worry, Alex. It'll be all right if you keep it simple. Look, I must go now. Janet's just got back. Ring me this evening at home.'

She hung up and Alex replaced his own receiver.

Keep it simple! It was easier said than done although he could see Ruth's point. It was better to stick to what he knew than add extra details which Finch might later check on and find to be untrue.

He was longing now for the police to arrive so that the whole bloody business could be over and done with.

While he waited, he could settle to nothing and wandered aimlessly about the flat, looking for something to do which would occupy his mind. In the end, he sat down at his desk and read through his report on the seventh-year project although he knew he was merely going through the motions of studying it. The words meant nothing to him.

It was nearly five o'clock before they arrived. Because of the heat, the windows were thrown wide open and he heard their car draw up on to the asphalted parking space in front of the house.

Crossing to the window, he looked out. Two men were getting out of an unmarked Ford Mondeo, both in plain-clothes. The driver, a tall, broad-shouldered man, must be Finch, Alex assumed. The other, who was shorter, was wearing a pair of grey Terylene trousers and a beige lightweight jacket, the back of it badly creased where he had sat in the car.

He watched as they strolled over to where his Volkswagen was parked and the taller of the two wrote down its registration number in a notebook. As they turned to walk towards the front door, Alex ducked away out of sight.

The door bell rang seconds later and, taking a deep breath, Alex went downstairs to let them in.

'Mr Alex Bennet?'

It was the shorter of the two men who addressed him and it took Alex a couple of seconds to realise that he must be Detective Chief Inspector Finch and to direct his attention away from the bigger-built man to his companion. In this initial confusion, he registered only a fleeting impression of him. He had a pleasant, rather nondescript face. But there was something else about the chief inspector which he might not have noticed had it not been for Nick and Ruth's warnings. Behind the politely bland expression, there was an air of quiet watchfulness. As Ruth had said, he was a damned sight shrewder than he appeared.

'I'm Detective Chief Inspector Finch,' the man was saying, 'and this is my detective sergeant, Boyce. May we come in, Mr Bennet?'

'Yes, of course,' Alex replied hurriedly, glad of the excuse to turn away and lead the two of them up the stairs.

'Sit down,' he added as he showed them into the living-room. He saw Finch take a quick look about him as he settled himself in one of the armchairs, as if familiarising himself with his surroundings. He seemed immediately at his ease, as indeed he was. Like his own house, Bennet's flat had all the signs of a bachelor's apartment. A jacket was slung carelessly over the back of a chair and a used cup and saucer stood on the mantelpiece. One end of the dining-room table, which apparently served as an addition to his desk, was piled with exercise books and stacks of manila folders which Finch assumed was work he'd brought back from school.

'You're not married, Mr Bennet?' Finch asked.

'No,' Bennet replied.

He seemed on edge, Finch noticed; unable to settle. At first, he had gone to stand in front of the fireplace and then had abruptly moved away to perch himself awkwardly on one corner of the table.

'I thought we'd just run through the statement you made this morning,' Finch announced, taking a notebook out of his pocket and flapping over the pages. It was an old ploy of his to put witnesses at their ease. Start off with the simple stuff and then, if necessary, go for the jugular once they'd loosened up a little.

And it was surprisingly straightforward, Alex thought with relief. Finch hardly raised his eyes from the notebook as he checked

101

over the facts Alex had already given to Detective Sergeant Craddock earlier that morning only a few hours before.

'And you said you got back to the flat at about ten twenty-five
yesterday evening?' Finch concluded.

'Yes, that's right.'

'Can anyone verify that?' Finch asked.

'The couple downstairs,' Alex replied. 'They drew up not long
after I'd parked my car.'

'Their name, sir?'

It was the sergeant who asked the question. He had got out his
own notebook and was waiting with it open on the arm of his chair.

'Milner,' Alex said. 'I don't think they're back yet if you want to
check with them. They both go out to work and they're not usually
home until about six.'

'We'll have a word with them later then,' Finch said, cheerfully
offhand as if it was only a minor matter. 'To get back to your own
statement, Mr Bennet. You say you arrived at Miss Wyatt's house
at roughly 8.35 p.m. and she showed you into the sitting-room.
Were the french windows open?'

That, too, was easy although Alex had the uncomfortable feeling
that from now on the interview was going to get harder. There was
a subtle change in Finch's manner. He was more alert, his head
cocked at a slight angle as if he were not only waiting for the
answer but listening to the silence which preceded it.

'Yes, they were. It was very hot yesterday evening.'

'Were the curtains closed?'

'Yes.'

'What about the lights? Were they on?'

'Yes.'

Keep it simple, Ruth had said. Don't add any details.

'And where did you sit?'

The question threw him by its unexpectedness.

'Sit?'

'Yes; in the room.'

'I can't . . .' Alex began and then, with an effort, pulled himself
together. Think of another evening, he told himself, when Christa
was alive and we were still lovers. Suddenly he remembered the
occasion when, after the three of them had gone out to dinner to
celebrate Ruth's birthday, they had returned to Christa's for coffee
and had talked until the early hours of the morning, although God
knows why he should recall that particular evening out of all the
others.

He said, 'I sat on the sofa.' Running a hand over his face, he added, 'I'm sorry. I still can't believe Christa's dead.'

Finch gave a small nod as if in sympathy with his momentary confusion.

'And Miss Wyatt? Where did she sit?'

'On the rocking chair.'

'Did she offer you anything while you were there? Coffee, for instance?'

'No.'

'Or wine?'

'No, nothing. We just talked.'

He was taken aback by these references to coffee and wine, wondering what had prompted Finch to make them, but quickly forgot about it when Finch moved on; not, thank God, to ask about the conversation he was supposed to have had with Christa, a subject he was dreading, but to a more mundane inquiry.

'In your statement, you said you left soon after nine, Mr Bennet. Which way did you go? Through the front door?'

That question, too, was straightforward. As Ruth had advised him, it was better to keep to the truth as far as possible.

'No; through the garden.'

'You mean the side entrance into Henrietta Street?'

'Yes; that's right.'

'Was the garden door bolted?'

'No.'

'And did Miss Wyatt go with you to the door?'

For a moment, Alex was tempted to say, 'No, she couldn't, because she was dead,' and so have done with the lies. It would have been so simple.

Instead, he replied, 'No; she didn't.'

'So you wouldn't know if she bolted the door behind you?'

'I'm sorry, I've no idea.'

'Where were you parked, Mr Bennet?'

It was the sergeant who asked the question and Alex turned to him with relief, grateful for a moment's respite from Finch's inquiries, so innocent-seeming but which followed so relentlessly one after the other.

'At the far end of Clifford Street. It was the only space I could find.'

'So when you left Miss Wyatt's house you walked back to your car?'

'Not straight away,' Alex replied. He had given this part of his account some thought and, like the question of which door he had left by, he had decided to keep to the facts. 'I walked round the block for a while. I was a bit – upset.'

His mouth twisted painfully as he spoke. A bit upset! Christ, what an understatement!

'Then it began to rain so I went back to the car,' he went on. 'I was going to drive home but I decided instead to call on Ruth Page, Christa's friend. I wanted to talk to someone.'

'Yes, of course.' Finch resumed charge of the interview, as bland and as apparently sympathetic as ever. 'But to get back to Miss Wyatt. How was she dressed when you saw her?'

'In a cream-coloured kaftan, a sort of long robe.'

The image of Christa lying in the hall flashed momentarily into his mind and then he blanked it off, deliberately keeping his attention fixed on Finch, with his guileless face and interested, listening expression.

'Did Miss Wyatt happen to mention if she was expecting any other visitors later that evening?'

'No.'

There was a small silence in which Finch shifted his position slightly in his chair and Alex had the impression that the interview, too, had changed. It was moving into a higher gear and he held himself tense, waiting for the next more searching phase in the interview. But when the question came, it was not entirely unexpected.

'Tell me about your relationship with Miss Wyatt.'

'We were lovers,' Alex said. There was an angry abruptness in his voice which he regretted but couldn't control. 'We met in March and the affair lasted until the end of May. Then she wrote to me, breaking off the relationship.'

'Do you still have the letter?'

His first instinct was to say no. It would have been easy enough to say he had got rid of it but, small though the deceit would have been, he suddenly rebelled against telling another lie. Crossing to his desk, he took the letter from the top drawer and handed it silently to the chief inspector.

Alex had read the letter so many times that he knew its contents by heart but it was impossible to tell what Finch made of those few curt sentences. His face had suddenly gone blank as if a shutter had been pulled down, and his voice sounded deliberately flat and unemotional when he asked, 'May I keep this for the time being, Mr Bennet?'

Alex nodded and walked back to the table although this time he

104

jerked out one of the upright chairs and, turning it so that it faced the two policemen, he sat down. He felt exhausted, not just physically but mentally as well.

For God's sake, how much longer would the interview go on? He longed for sleep; for oblivion; for some escape, if only for a short time, from the whole bloody awful mess.

A need to bring the interview to an end and a desire also to take charge of the interview, however temporarily, prompted him to speak out before Finch could ask any more questions and dig it out of him. He meant it, too, as a form of confession, a small concession to the truth to counterbalance all the lies although he knew he dared not tell the whole truth.

'I was very distressed when I got that letter,' he said. 'And angry and confused as well. I couldn't understand why Christa had thrown me over. There'd been no quarrel; not even a disagreement. I felt I had to have some explanation. So I rang her but she'd left the answer-phone on and she didn't return my calls or the letters I sent her. And a couple of times, I drove round to Clifford Street in the hope of seeing her . . .'

He broke off suddenly, knowing the rest of it would have to remain unsaid. At the same time, he wondered if Finch had found his letters to Christa and had already read them. It was impossible to tell from the man's expression whether he had or not. But if he had, it was too late now. He would know their contents, all the outpourings of his grief and despair.

Finch, who had listened in silence, his head cocked on one side, asked, 'Can you remember the dates when you went to Clifford Street?'

'No, I bloody can't!' Alex said angrily. 'As for the rest of it, that's all in my statement. I met Ruth Page one evening. She knew Christa had chucked me over and she said she'd try to talk to her about it; get her to phone me so that we could discuss it. Which she did. That was why Christa rang me yesterday evening and asked me to go round to the house. She explained she didn't want to be committed to any relationship, with me or anyone else.'

'An amicable discussion, was it, Mr Bennet?' Finch asked.

'We didn't quarrel, if that's what you mean,' Alex replied shortly. 'After I left, I walked about for a bit, like I told you. Then I decided to go to Ruth Page's.'

'Was she expecting you?'

'No. As a matter of fact, she'd just had a shower,' Alex said. 'I stayed there until just after ten.'

'Talking about Miss Wyatt?'

'Yes. Ruth explained that Christa had been badly let down by a man in the past. It made her very wary of any relationships.'

'You're a friend of Miss Page?'

'Yes, I suppose so; in a way. She's been very supportive. But she was more Christa's friend than mine.'

Finch nodded, as if satisfied, and seemed to prepare himself to get up. But, at the last moment, he subsided once more into his chair.

'Had Miss Wyatt taken up with a new boyfriend, by any chance?'

Although Alex had been preparing himself for such a question throughout the interview, Finch's offhand manner and the fact that he asked it almost as an afterthought caught him unprepared. It was so tempting, too, to mention Murray's name. But he knew he mustn't.

'No,' he said, hoping Finch hadn't noticed his hesitation. 'Not to my knowledge.'

And that, it seemed, was that. The interview was over, thank God. Finch had got to his feet and was thanking him and shaking him by the hand.

'We'll see ourselves out,' he added cheerfully as Alex showed them to the door.

Shortly afterwards, he heard their car drive away.

As soon as they had gone, he poured himself a brandy and carried it through to the kitchen where he stood with the glass in his hand, staring out through the window at the back garden.

How hot it was! There was not a breath of wind and the trees stood motionless, the leaves heavy with heat. The sunlight had a dull, brassy quality to it, presaging another thunderstorm like the one yesterday evening after he had found Christa's body. He could feel the pressure in the air, matching his own inward stress. At some point, he knew both would have to break. The problem was how long he could control his own tension before that, too, gave way.

For Finch would be back. Alex was sure of that. The interview was merely a preliminary skirmish, like the first faint rumble of thunder before the storm finally broke.

He drank the brandy and then went to lie on the sofa in the sitting-room, staring up at the ceiling. Although he had not intended to, he fell asleep. It was as if he had been sucked down into a black, spinning vortex of unconsciousness from which he fought to escape and from which he was woken about half an hour later by a banging sound. He jerked awake, feeling sick and dazed, wondering where he was and what had wakened him. Then he realised it had been the sound of the front door slamming shut. The Milners were home which meant it must be about six o'clock. Ruth would also be home by now and he had promised to phone her.

Going to the bathroom, he splashed cold water on his face and then returned to the sitting-room to ring her. However reluctant he felt, it would have to be done although the last thing he wanted was to go over the whole bloody business again.

'How did it go?' Ruth asked anxiously.

'All right, I think,' he replied.

'You kept to what we agreed?'

'Yes,' he said abruptly. He was suddenly tired of being cross-examined. He added, forestalling her next question, 'And no, I didn't say anything about Murray.'

'Don't worry. The police'll find out about him,' she assured him.

'I suppose so,' he replied. He felt too exhausted to go over that point yet again.

'Oh, they will, Alex.' Ruth's voice sounded so strong and confident that he himself was convinced by her certainty. She added, 'Keep in touch, won't you?' and rang off.

Replacing the receiver, he switched on the answer-phone and went back to the bathroom to take a shower. In the meantime, someone must have tried to phone him because when he came out, the little red light was flashing and the buzzer bleeping with an infuriating persistence.

It was Nick, he discovered when he ran the tape back; bloody Nick sounding curious and excited.

'Any news, Alex? Have the police been to see you? I haven't heard anything official yet but I'll give you a bell as soon as I do. We must meet up for a drink. What about tomorrow evening? Ring me back and let me know.'

Instead, Alex jerked the plug out of the connection box, poured himself another brandy which he drank straight down before going to lie down again on the sofa. Once more, he fell asleep almost immediately, oblivious of everything, even the storm which finally broke about half an hour later.

12

'So what did you make of that?' Boyce asked as he pulled off the forecourt of Bennet's house into Maynard's Avenue. But before

Finch could reply, the sergeant had answered his own question, a maddening habit of his. 'I thought Bennet's statement hung together all right. Basically, it was much the same as Miss Page's and she alibis him at least for the earlier part of the evening. I suppose we'll check on the Milners tomorrow?'

They were approaching the bottom of the road when Finch said abruptly, 'Turn round.'

'Turn round?' Boyce said. 'I thought you'd want to get off to the PM?'

'I'll do that later. It's almost six o'clock. The Milners should be home soon. We'll talk to them now. I want to check on what time Bennet got back to his flat last night.'

'Okay by me,' Boyce said as he made a neat three-point turn and headed back up Maynard's Avenue.

'Pull in here,' Finch added a few seconds later and Boyce drew the car into the kerb.

It was a good place to park for they had a clear view of Bennet's place a little further up the road on the opposite side. The man was evidently on the chief inspector's mind for he suddenly said, 'Bennet.'

'What about him?' Boyce asked encouragingly. God knows what Finch was thinking although, had he been able to read the chief inspector's mind, the sergeant would have been surprised to discover, knowing nothing of Finch's private life, that he was brooding over his own past which in many ways mirrored Alex Bennet's and Christa Wyatt's. It was a train of thought which had been prompted by the letter the dead woman had sent to Bennet and which had aroused old emotions from which he had imagined he had long since recovered. He, too, had been thrown over, in his case by two women whom he had once loved. As a consequence he had become, like Christa Wyatt, wary of committing himself to any emotional attachment. Even to Nina, he was thinking, whom he had met since those two disastrous affairs and whom he thought he loved but still wasn't sure he wanted to marry.

Boyce was saying, 'Personally, I can't see anything wrong with Bennet's statement.'

'No; there were one or two things not quite right about it.'

'Such as what?'

'Odd details he didn't seem too sure about, like what chair he was sitting in last night when he and Christa Wyatt were talking. You'd think he'd remember something as simple as that.'

'Shock?' Boyce suggested. 'Give the man his due, he'd only heard this morning she'd been murdered.'

'The cushions on the rocking chair and the sofa were flattened,' Finch said in apparent agreement.

'There you are then. That ties in with what Bennet said.'

'And I'm damn sure he knows, or suspected, Christa Wyatt had a new lover,' Finch went on, ignoring Boyce's comment. 'If he did, it'd give him a motive.'

'But I can't see he had the opportunity, if Christa Wyatt was alive at ten thirty when Ruth Page spoke to her at the house,' Boyce argued. 'He says he got back to the flat at ten twenty-five and the Milners saw him. I know we've got to check with them, but it's unlikely he'd lie about something like that. It seems to me it all fits together. Bennet calls on Christa Wyatt and leaves when he said at about five past nine. After he's gone, someone else drops in on her; probably the new boyfriend. She opens a bottle of wine and they talk –'

'Presumably quite amicably at first,' Finch put in. 'No one's going to bother to get the wine out in the middle of a row. But things must have got more tense later on. Ruth Page said when she called at the house at half-past ten, Christa Wyatt seemed on edge.'

'Right. After Ruth Page leaves, Christa Wyatt goes back into the house where the boyfriend's waiting. They quarrel. Perhaps she wants to chuck him over like she did Bennet . . .'

'Or he may have overheard Ruth Page mention Bennet's name when she talked to Christa Wyatt on the doorstep.'

'That makes sense,' Boyce agreed. 'The boyfriend jumps to the conclusion that Christa Wyatt's been seeing another man. So they start to argue. In the middle of it, Ruth Page rings her up. Christa Wyatt goes into the hall to answer the phone. He grabs up the tea-towel and strangles her. That's why her body was found where it was.'

Boyce seemed particularly pleased with this last point.

'So according to your theory, Christa Wyatt was murdered at eleven, the time Ruth Page tried to ring her?' Finch said musingly. 'I suppose it would tie in with the other evidence – the lights left on and the bed not slept in.'

But it didn't agree with Pardoe's estimated time of death, Finch added silently to himself. He'd have to check on that with the pathologist although fixing a precise time was notoriously difficult.

Boyce was saying, 'We can make a reasonable guess what happened next. We've got the evidence for that as well. After he's strangled Christa Wyatt, the boyfriend takes the wineglasses through to the kitchen and washes them up. His fingerprints would be on one of them but perhaps he can't remember which was which so he washes them both. He then takes the wine bottle into the kitchen as well.'

'Why?'

'How should I know?' Boyce protested. 'He'd just bloody strangled somebody! People do strange things when they're in a panic . . .'

Finch, who seemed to be following a trail of his own, put in, 'He carries the bottle by the cork so that he won't put his prints on it or smudge Christa Wyatt's. He then pockets the cork in case his prints are on that.'

'Right!' Boyce agreed. 'Of course, he wouldn't know we can't lift fingerprints off a cork.'

'And takes Christa Wyatt's phone book because his name, address and number are in it . . .'

He broke off at the sight of a Fiat turning into the parking space in front of Bennet's house, a woman at the wheel.

'Mrs Milner,' Finch announced. 'Let's go.'

By the time they had reached the house, the Fiat was already parked and there was no sign of Mrs Milner. Finch rang the bell for the downstairs flat and a young, ginger-haired woman wearing glasses opened the door to them.

Producing his ID, Finch introduced himself and Boyce in his best official voice, adding, 'We're making inquiries into a sudden death. I wondered if we could ask you a few questions relating to it.'

'I've only just got home,' Mrs Milner protested but she showed them into the front downstairs room which served as a sitting-room where she invited them to sit down.

'A sudden death?' she asked, showing curiosity for the first time. 'You don't mean murder, do you?'

'We're still investigating,' Finch said in his blandest manner. 'At the moment, we're trying to establish the time of death which is where you may be able to help us. You know Mr Bennet?'

'Alex, the man upstairs? Yes, of course I do.'

'I believe you and your husband spoke to him last night.'

'Yes; that's right. He was just parking his car when Phil and I got home. We'd been out for a drink at the Six Bells. As a matter of fact, Phil was a bit annoyed. Alex'd parked right next to my car and Phil had to leave his on the far side. There's not much room for three cars and I know it's a question of first come first served, but Phil's got this big Volvo and he needs quite a bit of space.'

'What time was this?' Finch asked. It was obvious the problem of parking was a long-standing grievance but it hardly seemed relevant to Christa Wyatt's murder.

'A few minutes before half-past ten.'

'You're sure of that?'

'Oh, yes.' Mrs Milner sounded quite certain. 'There was part three of that spy thriller on ITV at twenty to eleven after the news and Phil didn't want to miss it. We caught the end of the regional news and the weather forecast so it must have been about twenty-five past.'

'Do you know if Mr Bennet left again at any time after you'd got home?'

'No, he couldn't have done. Not in his car anyway.'

'You're certain about that as well?'

'Yes, I am.' She sounded faintly annoyed. Her face, already pink with the heat, had flushed a darker red but whether at Finch's implied doubt over her statement or the old resentment about the parking space was hard to tell; probably the latter, for she went on, 'Like I said, Phil had to park over the far side by the dustbins which meant the Volvo was blocking part of the gateway. Phil mentioned this to Alex Bennet but he said not to bother. Phil always leaves earlier than he does so he'd be able to get his car out in the morning when he went to work. And even if he didn't use the car again last night, we'd've heard him leave anyway. That front door sticks – Phil keeps saying he'll plane a bit off it – so you have to slam it hard to shut it.' She paused and regarded them both with her head on one side. 'What's all this got to do with Alex Bennet?'

'We're just checking,' Finch said easily. 'I suppose you wouldn't have noticed any visitors who called on Mr Bennet?'

'Girlfriends, you mean?'

Finch merely lifted his shoulders in a non-committal gesture but it was enough encouragement for Mrs Milner.

'There was one who used to come here fairly often; a blonde girl. Christa I think her name was. I heard her and Alex Bennet talking once when they were getting into his car. But I haven't seen her for weeks. There was another one before her; dark-haired. That was months ago, though. Hang on a minute!' Her eyes behind her glasses suddenly brightened. 'You said a sudden death. It's not her, the blonde one, who's been murdered, is it? Wait till I tell Phil!'

Finch prudently made no reply to this, either to confirm or deny

111

it. He merely thanked her for her time and trouble, adding a formal request that she and her husband should present themselves at Divisional headquarters at their earliest convenience to make official statements, to which she agreed with alacrity. It was obvious she was excited by the prospect of taking part, in however minor a role, in a police investigation.

To her, it was probably almost as good as appearing on the telly, Finch thought sourly.

Outside, he paused briefly to examine the forecourt. It had obviously once been the front garden which had been asphalted over. Alex Bennet's Volkswagen was parked on the right, next to a low, open-fronted wooden construction which housed two dustbins on which the letters A and B were painted in white, presumably referring to the two separate flats. Mrs Milner's small Fiat was drawn up under the ground-floor bay window well over to the left, leaving a large space beside it where no doubt her husband's Volvo would normally be parked.

What he saw made sense of Mrs Milner's statement. If a large car like a Volvo was parked by the dustbins, it would stick out far enough to block access through the opening in the low wall which separated the forecourt from the pavement.

As for her comment about the front door, Finch had already witnessed that for himself. On both occasions he and Boyce had called, first on Alex Bennet and now on Mrs Milner, the door had had to be pulled quite hard to make it shut properly.

He remarked as much to Boyce whose reply was lost in the first rumble of thunder. In the quarter of an hour they had spent with Mrs Milner, the storm had been gathering. The sky was dark, boiling with great masses of clouds which were rolling in above the roof-tops, back-lit by the lurid glare from the sun. Seconds later, the first raindrops fell, as hard and as direct as bullets.

They sprinted for the car, reaching it just before the storm finally broke and the rain came deluging down. Boyce turned on the windscreen wipers and they sat looking out at the rainswept street for a few moments in silence.

'Well, it seems Bennet is in the clear,' Boyce commented at last in a told-you-so voice. 'There's no way he could have committed the murder. He's alibied all down the line.' Taking the chief inspector's silence for agreement, he added, nodding towards Bennet's house where the upstairs window to his flat was set wide open, 'Mind you, if he doesn't soon shut that, he's going to find the rain's coming in.'

Finch said suddenly, 'It rained yesterday evening as well. What time did it start?'

'I don't know,' Boyce replied. He seemed thrown by the inconsequentiality of the remark. 'Quarter-past nine? Half-past?'

'I need a more precise timing than that. Drive back to Clifford Street, Tom. I want to have a word as well with Barney.'

It was still raining hard when they arrived at the scene of crime and they had to make a dash for it up the path to the front door. The hall was already full of plastic bags of evidence, tied up and labelled, waiting to be taken away for examination. Barney was in the act of carrying another one down the stairs as they entered.

'You're wet,' he told them with the satisfied air of a man who was indoors in the dry. 'By the way, we've checked on 1471 for you. The last recorded call was a local one. I've written it down for you.'

He handed Finch a piece of paper which he glanced at before putting it into his pocket. He'd have to look up Ruth Page's home telephone number in her statement but he had no doubt it would be the same.

'What about the address book?' he asked.

'No luck there,' Barney replied. 'We've gone through everything now, even looked in her car, but there's no sign of it anywhere.'

'That settles that then,' said Finch, not letting on if he were pleased or disappointed by the news. 'Another thing, Barney, when you examined the floor in the dining-room, did you find any footprints on the boards?'

'Nothing worth writing home about. There was only a thin layer of dust so we couldn't raise much, only a few faint marks. McCullum photographed them under oblique light but they won't be much use as evidence. Could have been a size eight or a nine. That's as far as I can go.'

'And there were no signs they'd been made with a wet shoe?'

'No; I wouldn't have said so. Wet shoes, even damp ones, would've left a clearer print.'

'What time did it start to rain yesterday evening?'

'God knows. Is it important?'

'It could be.'

'Colin!' Barney turned to shout up the stairs and a head appeared over the landing banisters. 'The Chief wants to know what time it started to rain last night. Any idea?'

'Just before quarter-past nine,' Colin replied.

'You're sure of that?' Finch called back.

Colin came down a couple of treads, ducking his head to address the chief inspector.

'As near as soddit, sir. I'd forgotten to lock up the garage and the wife reminded me to do it before it got too dark. It was just after ten past by the clock in the sitting-room when I went out and it'd begun raining by then; only just though. The path was hardly wet. It started coming down heavily soon after I got back indoors.'

'Thanks,' Finch said briefly and, nodding to Boyce to follow, retreated out of the front door into the rain.

'I know what you're thinking,' Boyce said when they had reached the car and slammed themselves shut inside its warm, dry interior. 'If none of the footprints were made by wet shoes, then whoever killed Christa Wyatt must have arrived before a quarter past nine when it started raining.'

'It looks that way,' Finch agreed. 'And if we're right, he must have turned up not long after Bennet left at five past. It's a wonder they didn't run into each other, unless he came in by the front door as Bennet was leaving by the back. Even so, it was cutting it pretty damned close. And he must have turned up unexpectedly. I can't see Christa Wyatt inviting him round if she'd already arranged to meet Bennet.'

As he spoke, he had an uneasy feeling that there was something not quite right about the theory. It was too coincidental, the new lover arriving so close on the heels of the old, as if the whole event had been stage-managed in some way. But coincidences did happen, as he'd experienced for himself in more than one investigation.

Boyce was saying, 'It hangs together. The Page woman said she thought Christa Wyatt might have had someone with her when she called at the house at half-past ten. And, as you pointed out, he could've overheard her mention Bennet's name which was what sparked off the quarrel.'

'But it's still only a theory,' Finch reminded him. 'And it doesn't bring us any nearer to identifying the man.'

He glanced quickly at his watch. It was now nearly ten to seven.

He said, 'Drop me off at home, Tom. I'll push off from there in my own car to the PM. I want a word with Pardoe.'

'A bit late, isn't it?' Boyce remarked. 'You'll've missed most of it.'

'Yes, I suppose I will,' Finch agreed in a slightly surprised voice as if the thought had only just occurred to him. 'But Pardoe'll still be there. I sometimes wonder if he ever goes home.'

13

The air inside the house, which had been shut up all day, was stifling. It met him like a blast from an oven as he opened the door. The silence was just as thick and as oppressive.

Stepping over a small pile of letters lying on the mat, mostly junk mail by the look of it, Finch went upstairs to change out of his damp clothes, rattling about in the bedroom as he found a clean shirt and trousers with unnecessary energy in an attempt to lay claim to these silent rooms and reassert his possession of them.

As he changed, he could see the back garden through the bedroom window with its overgrown flower beds and the drenched lawn which needed cutting although God alone knew when he'd find time to do it.

Downstairs, he picked up the letters and carried them through to the kitchen where he set about making himself tea before leaving for the PM although, as he shuffled through the envelopes as he waited for the kettle to boil, he realised he was putting off the moment when he'd have to get into the car and drive over to see Pardoe. Attending a PM was not a duty he relished and he always went reluctantly, more out of a need to show solidarity with Pardoe than from personal preference.

As he had suspected, the letters were mainly circulars, promotions from firms selling insurance, double-glazing and a pizza take-away. Further down, he came to a bank statement and an appeal from Oxfam, a charity he supported. And right at the bottom, a postcard from Nina, showing a view of a marina with an impossibly blue sky and sea with boats at anchor.

He turned it over eagerly, trying to decipher the message which she'd squeezed into the small space alongside the address. No superscription, he noticed. No 'My dear Jack' or even 'Dear Jack'; just a few staccato sentences in a sort of telegraphese written in an almost illegible scrawl. 'No trace yet of Danny. Have made inquiries at the hotel he was staying in but no luck. Not arrested, not so far anyway, thank God, and not in hospital either. Will return as planned next Fri. Nina.'

Along the side of the postcard she had added as an afterthought and perhaps also as a sop to the conventional picture postcard message, 'Weath. v. hot. Comf. hotel w. balc.', which he took to mean the weather was very hot, the hotel where she was staying comfortable and her bedroom had a balcony.

The kettle boiled and he poured the water over a tea-bag in a mug, dunking it a couple of times before fishing it out with a spoon and adding milk. The tea was still too hot to drink and, in a sudden fit of impatience, he added cold water from the tap although he wasn't quite sure against whom his exasperation was directed. Partly at Nina for going off on this wild-goose chase in the first place; partly at himself for not having succeeded in persuading her against it. But mostly at Danny, her bloody irresponsible younger brother, who had cleared off to France in March, having got himself into some indefinable trouble in Birmingham where he was working as a garage mechanic. His subsequent whereabouts were unknown, apart from a letter posted weeks ago, asking Nina to send him some money and giving as his address a hotel in Marseilles. Since then, Nina hadn't heard a word from him.

It had been Nina's idea to go looking for him. Finch had advised her against it, urging her to wait until he had some leave and could go with her. She spoke only schoolgirl French, enough to order a meal but certainly not adequate to make inquiries about a missing person, if Danny was indeed missing. Privately, Finch was of the opinion that he'd surface again when he was short of money. He also had his doubts about what Danny was up to in France. Knowing him, it was probably something on the shady side of the law. He'd already made his own discreet inquiries through a contact in the Birmingham police and had been told in confidence that Danny Webb was one of those iffy characters who they kept a quiet eye on. The garage where he had worked was also considered dodgy and had been turned over a couple of times by the local CID, looking for stolen spare parts and false number-plates. He had, of course, passed none of this information on to Nina.

It was typical of her to go rushing off without giving the decision enough thought in that warm, impulsive way which he found both endearing and infuriating. She had simply rung him up one evening to announce she was going to Marseilles to look for Danny and nothing he had said would dissuade her. She had booked the flight, the hotel, everything, she had told him. She couldn't cancel now. And anyway, she didn't want to. In the face of her obduracy, he had felt the least he could do was wangle a day off and drive her to Heathrow after picking her up in Hampstead.

With a mixture of affection, amusement and exasperation, he

remembered saying goodbye to her in the departure lounge at the airport. She was wearing slacks for the flight which didn't suit her and a blouse which was already parting company with the waistband. Her red hair, which she'd bundled back because of the heat, was beginning to come loose from its black ribbon bow. Little tendrils, damp with sweat, had fallen forward over her forehead.

But she was glowing with excitement and the adventure of it all, like a child at Christmas. As he had kissed her goodbye, she had nuzzled her face against his cheek and he had felt some of that warmth and glow transferred to him.

'Take care,' he had told her. He could have added, 'I love you, Nina.' It would have been so easy. But he hadn't said it.

And that was the trouble.

Did he love her? He wasn't sure. He only knew that, now she wasn't there, he missed her dreadfully.

He had first met her several years before during a murder investigation which had involved Max Gifford, an elderly artist with whom she was then living although they weren't, in fact, married. At the time, Finch had been attracted to her but nothing had come of it and, after Max's suicide, he had lost touch with her when she moved to London. He had met up with her again a few years later during another investigation and they had developed a kind of relationship, meeting occasionally in London for dinner or a day out together. He himself was wary of commitment. He'd already had his fingers burnt a couple of times in the past, once years ago when he'd fallen in love with a young woman called Kate who had married someone else instead. Occasionally, he heard news of her through his sister Dorothy who had kept in touch with her, exchanging Christmas and birthday cards. Through Dorothy, he learned that Kate now had three children and was living in Colchester. He doubted if he'd recognise her if he met her in the street.

His other relationship had been with a young woman pathologist, Marion Greave, who had also turned him down, preferring her career to marriage. She, too, had moved away to take up a hospital appointment in Leeds and he had no idea what had happened to her since. Perhaps she, too, was married although he doubted it.

Both experiences had left him wary of relationships, unwilling to take the plunge. Like a nervous swimmer dithering about on the edge of a pool, he thought wryly as he finished his tea and dumped the empty mug in the sink. And yet it only took a little courage and determination to jump in at the deep end.

Propping Nina's card against the tea-caddy, he let himself out of the house.

On the drive to the PM, it occurred to him again that his was a similar situation to Alex Bennet's. He, too, had been thrown over by a woman he had presumably loved which would, on the face of it, have given Bennet a strong motive for murder. But that was apparently ruled out by Bennet's alibi although there was still the uncertain business of the time of death which he hoped Pardoe would be able to sort out.

As Finch had expected, Pardoe hadn't yet left although the actual post-mortem examination was over, thank God, and Christa Wyatt's body had been filed away, like so much back correspondence, in a refrigerated drawer in the mortuary. Since the death of his wife, Stella, the year before from cancer, Pardoe seemed to spend most of his time at work, 'down among the dead men', as he sardonically termed it, preferring their company, Finch assumed, to going home to an empty house.

As he pushed open the swing doors, Finch felt that uneasy lurch to his stomach which he always experienced whenever he entered Pardoe's world. It smelt different, of chemicals and preservatives, overlaid with the sweetish odour of disinfectant, the smell of death itself, Finch always thought. Even the sounds were unfamiliar, hollow noises, harsh and metallic, accompanied by the rush of running water and the hiss of rubber tyres on plastic floors.

Pardoe was in his office, transferring on to paper his spoken comments from the little tape-recorder which he used while carrying out the PM, an opened bottle of whisky and a paper cup in front of him on the desk. Since Stella's death, he had started to drink more heavily.

As Finch knocked and entered, he looked up and grinned.

'So you've turned up at last,' he remarked. 'I thought you'd chickened out. Pull up a chair and have a dram.'

He indicated the whisky bottle and Finch said, 'Just a small one then. I'm driving.'

He didn't like to refuse although whisky wasn't his favourite tipple, especially on an almost-empty stomach. He'd had nothing to eat all day apart from the cheese sandwich for lunch.

Pardoe took another paper cup from the top drawer and poured a little whisky into the bottom of it, then leaned back in his chair, regarding the chief inspector with an amused, quizzical air.

He said, 'You won't need me to confirm death was by strangulation but that's official now. By the way, the tea-towel's bagged up along with the clothing.'

'I'll send Kyle round tomorrow to pick them up,' Finch said. 'Any other injuries?'

'Not a scratch on her. And nothing under the fingernails.'

So he'd been right in thinking Christa Wyatt hadn't put up a fight for her life, Finch told himself.

Out loud, he said, 'It's the time of death I'm mainly interested in, Reg. Any chance she could have been murdered as late as eleven o'clock?'

'Eleven?' Pardoe raised his eyebrows. 'I suppose you've got your reasons for picking that particular time but yes, it's certainly possible. I don't want to blind you with science, Jack, and it'll all be nicely written down in my report which I'll be sending on to you in the next couple of days. Briefly speaking, I made my examination this morning at ten past eleven and, at that time, rigor mortis was fully developed which means she'd been dead between twelve to seventeen hours. Unless my arithmetic is way out, that means she'd died between 6 p.m. and 11 p.m. yesterday evening. But that's only a rough estimate. The body temperature's a better guide although even that's not infallible. According to the rectal temperature, I'd put her death at nearer 8 or 9 p.m. On average a body loses about one degree Celsius every hour during the first twelve hours after death. After that, the heat loss slows down. But in the case of strangulation, the body temperature tends to rise at the time of death although this can vary according to the individual. Added to that, you've got to take into account the temperature of the surroundings. It was bloody hot in that hall this morning when I made the preliminary examination but it must have been cooler during the night and even during the evening after that rain-storm. So, yes, I suppose it's possible she died as late as eleven. As you know, the time of death can't usually be precisely fixed. I'm sending the stomach contents off for analysis anyway but unless you know what time she last ate, it's not going to be a lot of help in fixing the time more accurately.'

'I'll ask around,' Finch said.

Ruth Page might know when Christa Wyatt was in the habit of eating an evening meal although he suspected that even she wouldn't be able to give him an exact time. He was uneasy, too, about Pardoe's reservations concerning the time of death even though the pathologist seemed prepared to accept the time of 11 p.m. as feasible, taking into account those special factors he had mentioned.

Pardoe said, holding up the whisky bottle, 'Want a top up?'

'Not for me, thanks. I ought to be pushing off,' Finch replied. He hesitated before adding, 'Have you got your car, Reg, or can I give you a lift home?'

Pardoe, interpreting his hesitation, gave him a wry, sideways grin.

'It's all right, Jack. I'll take a taxi home later. I'm not fool enough to drive when I'm over the limit. So don't worry, although I appreciate the concern. Before you go, is there anything else you need to know?'

'I don't think so.'

'You don't want a last look at your *corpus delicti* before I lock her away for the night?'

It had been on the tip of Finch's tongue to invite Pardoe out for a meal one evening but the man's final remark and the caustic little laugh which accompanied it made him bite back the invitation at the last moment. Pardoe would not make a comfortable dinner companion, he decided. He was too bitter, too cynical and, worst of all perhaps, too tragic.

He held out his hand and tried to make his voice sound sincerely grateful.

'Thanks for the help, Reg. It's much appreciated.'

Pardoe waved a dismissive hand.

'Any time, old chap. You know me; I'm always open for business.'

At the door, the chief inspector took a last look back. Pardoe was bent again over his desk, a pen in one hand and his paper cup of whisky in the other. Quietly, Finch closed the door on him.

He had intended driving straight home but some of Pardoe's reluctance to face an empty house seemed to have rubbed off on him for, on the way, he changed his mind and drove instead to Bishop's Close, Ruth Page's home address. It had been on his mind anyway to have a look round the road where she lived, if only out of curiosity, and it was probably better to make the visit on his own, rather than in Boyce's company. Although he never let it deter him, the chief inspector was aware of the sergeant's disapproval of these little recces of his, during which he liked to take his time nosing around and sniffing up the atmosphere.

In the event, there wasn't much to see. Ruth Page was clearly at home. Her Peugeot was parked on the hard-stand outside her garage, the door of which was open. Inside, he caught a glimpse, as he drove past, of a lawn-mower and a woman's bike standing against the left-hand wall. But of the house itself, he could see nothing through the high hawthorn hedge which fronted it, except for an upstairs window and part of the red-tiled roof.

At the end of the cul-de-sac, he turned the car and drove back, concentrating this time on the general look of the area. There were other houses, about eight altogether, and all, like hers, were hidden away behind hedges or shrubbery. No one was about and the place might have been depopulated by some sudden catastrophe although the traffic still continued to run normally up and down Springfield Road.

As he turned into it, he made a mental note to ask Stapleton to extend the house-to-house inquiries to Bishop's Close; not that he expected anything useful would come out of it but at least he'd've covered every possible angle to this part of the inquiry. And it wouldn't take up too much precious police time. A couple of PCs could do it in a few hours.

And then there was the business of putting out an official statement. He'd get Latham, the press officer, to handle that tomorrow. Not too detailed at this early stage, he thought; he didn't want to stir up too much interest in the case before it was properly off the ground although the local paper, the *Gazette*, would probably run it as a front-page story however little was released.

His attitude to the press was ambivalent. He preferred to work well out of the glare of publicity but newspaper coverage had its advantages. Sometimes a witness came forward with useful information which might otherwise not have turned up.

On the way home, he stopped off at an Indian take-away for a chicken tikka masala with rice, even though the weather was too hot to enjoy a full-sized meal. But it would save him the trouble of preparing something for himself and anyway he had nothing much in the fridge except some cheese and tomatoes.

The rain had stopped but whatever freshness it had brought was only temporary. Although it was getting dusk, the air was already heavy again with heat. As he drove, he could feel his shirt sticking to his back.

At the house, he went round flinging open all the windows and then sat at the french doors with a tray on his lap, eating the curry and rereading Nina's postcard which he'd brought through from the kitchen.

Tomorrow, he thought, he'd have to get a telex to her at her hotel in Marseilles, warning her that it was unlikely he'd be able to meet her at Heathrow on her return and that she'd have to make her own way home.

And sometime, too, he'd have to find a spare half an hour and cut the bloody lawn.

14

Alex woke at six o'clock the following morning to find himself lying, still fully dressed, on the sofa, and with the hung-over feeling of having slept too long and too heavily. It was another sunny day and the heat had already begun to build up although it must have rained while he was asleep. The curtains at the open window were damp and the carpet beneath was soggy with water. He threw down a couple of towels to sop up the worst of it, intending to deal with it later after he'd showered and dressed.

Although Joyce Stanley had advised him to take the day off, he decided to go to work. It would be better than hanging about the flat all day with nothing to do and it was the last day of term, thank God. He supposed he'd get through it somehow.

Joyce Stanley must have been looking out for him for, as he parked the car and walked into the main building, she met him in the entrance.

'You should have stayed at home,' she said. 'Are you all right?'

'Not too bad,' he replied. He even managed a smile.

'Well, you don't look it,' she told him, regarding him critically. 'I've been checking your timetable in case you turned up today. You've got a double lesson first two periods with 9A, haven't you? And then you're free until a single just before lunch with 7C. I'll take that lesson for you. I'm free myself then. And I'll shove your ninth year in with mine. I've brought along a recording of *The Importance of Being Earnest*. They can listen to that.'

'It's kind of you –' he began.

'No, it's not. You can do something for me in return – check the book-store. You know how I hate doing that.'

The bell rang for registration and she smiled and patted his arm before walking away.

He went through the usual morning routine automatically, checking the register with his form, 8B, and then followed the pupils to assembly where he joined the other members of staff on the platform. No one else seemed aware of what had happened although one or two colleagues asked if he were better. He assumed Joyce Stanley had told them he'd been ill the day before to explain his absence. He thanked her silently for her discretion.

Afterwards, when the staff and pupils dispersed to their various lessons, he shut himself up in the English department's store, a small room lined with shelves, where he set about the job of sorting through and putting away the piles of textbooks collected in from each form which were piled up on the floor. It was one of those mindless tasks for which he was grateful, demanding little more than physical labour and the minimum of mental effort. Shakespeare here; lower school poetry there; novels and language course books on their own separate shelves. As he worked through the piles, he counted the numbers in each set of books, noting them down in the stock records. He was undisturbed apart from a few occasions when children arrived with odd copies found lurking in the corners of classrooms. Sod's law. It happened every year.

He worked on through the mid-morning break and also through the lunch hour, not stopping until five minutes before the bell rang for the afternoon session when he went to wash his hands before joining his class in their form-room.

It was almost over. A last registration. A final check in desks to make sure they were empty and then, when the bell rang again, the kids were free to go home. They poured out of the room like a flock of birds released from captivity. Alex watched them go, envying their joy and feeling of freedom.

After that, he should have gone down to the staff-room for the farewell party laid on for two members of staff who were leaving, a young woman from the French department who was taking maternity leave and the head of Geography who was moving on to a deputy headship of a London comprehensive. Alex had been dreading the occasion all morning – the need to be social over glasses of wine and bowls of crisps and peanuts and to laugh at the right moment at the head's speech when the farewell presents were handed out.

Joyce Stanley met him at the staff-room door.

'Clear off home, Alex,' she said briskly. 'I've told the head you're still not well and, quite frankly, you look ghastly.'

'Thanks, Joyce.' He gave her a wry smile as he handed over the key to the stockroom. 'I've sorted the books.'

'Bless you.' To his surprise, she stretched up and kissed him on the cheek. 'Take care, Alex.'

At the flat, he took another shower and slept again on the sofa until five o'clock, waking with a sudden start to find the sunlight pouring in through the window.

He got up reluctantly, aware of the hours which stretched ahead of him and which would have to be filled somehow. If none of this had happened, he and Christa might have been planning their tour of the Dordogne. They had spoken about leaving soon after the end of his term.

Thrusting the memory aside, he began to tidy up the flat, reconnecting the phone and picking up the damp towels which he threw into the washing-machine. He supposed he ought to make himself a meal; he had had nothing to eat all day but he felt no appetite for food. Instead, he made himself coffee which he carried into the sitting-room.

The phone rang almost immediately. It was Nick Duffield again, sounding accusatory.

'I've been trying to reach you for the last couple of hours,' he said.

'I'd unplugged the phone,' Alex told him.

'Well, listen. I've got some news for you. Remember that contact of mine I told you about? The one with the inside information?' From the conspiratorial tone in his voice, he might have been discussing international espionage. 'I got in touch with him today and he's come up with some interesting info I thought you'd like to know.'

'What is it?'

'Not over the bloody phone.' Nick sounded shocked. 'What about meeting up for a drink this evening?'

Why not? Alex thought. Knowing Nick's capacity for exaggeration, he doubted if he'd hear anything of great importance but it would at least be an excuse to get out of the flat.

'All right,' he said. 'Seven o'clock at the Bull?'

'You're on,' Nick said and rang off.

Alex walked there, taking the long route across the park. It was good to be out of doors. He spent too much time inside, he realised, in rooms or in the car, eating, teaching, sleeping, driving. Another world was out there which surprised him by its normality. People were walking about, feeding the ducks, playing football with their children on the grass. But there were couples, too, strolling hand in hand or lying under the trees, their arms about each other, their faces pressed together.

As he passed them, Alex averted his eyes, finding their intimacy too painful. The sight of them and the scent of the warm grass

124

reminded him of those occasions when he and Christa had also kissed under the trees.

He arrived early at the pub and took the opportunity to order a ham salad and a lager which he carried to a table in the far corner of the bar under an open window. Even though he still had little appetite for food, he supposed he ought to eat something. As the old cliché said, life had to go on. His, as well. And time was a great healer; another of those bloody banal statements people came out with at times of bereavement which were meant to console. But it was small comfort. It was the present he was facing and he had no idea yet how to cope with that.

Nick joined him soon afterwards, bursting with whatever news he had to tell and, so that he could postpone, if only for a few moments, the need to listen, Alex left him at the table to order him a drink. He had been a fool to come, he decided. He should have insisted Nick told him what he had to say over the phone. At least that way, he wouldn't have to put on a brave face, another bloody cliché, and pretend to be social for Nick's sake.

'So what's the news?' he asked, trying to look and sound casual as he put Nick's pint of bitter on the table and took his seat opposite him.

'First off, the police have put out a statement. It'll be in tomorrow's paper. It's not much at this stage, just a couple of sentences. A woman's body has been discovered at a house in Clifford Street. The police are regarding the circumstances as suspicious and are making further inquiries blah, blah. No name yet. They're evidently trying to contact next-of-kin first.'

'I'm not sure Christa had any,' Alex said. 'She never spoke of her family. I know both her parents are dead. Ruth Page told me.'

He was struck again by how little he knew about Christa. Although she had let him into her bed, she had deliberately excluded him from her private life. Sex without intimacy, he thought bitterly.

'Is that all?' he added, wondering if Nick had got him there under false pretences.

Nick leaned forward, lowering his voice conspiratorially.

'They're pretty sure it's not an intruder. According to my contact, they're looking for a man, someone who must have called on her later in the evening, after you left. She didn't happen to mention she was expecting someone else, did she?'

'No, she didn't,' Alex said shortly. 'I've already told the police that. I've no idea who else she might have been meeting.'

'A bit of a goer, wasn't she?' Nick hinted. 'Off with the old, on with the new. God, you never would've guessed it to look at her.'

'If that's all . . .' Alex began, getting up from his chair.

'Sorry, old son. I'm way out of order again. Subject closed,' Nick said. 'Anyway, to fill you in with the rest, I gather the police have set up an incident room in Divisional headquarters and they've started house-to-house inquiries in Clifford Street. I drove down there myself this morning with a photographer; got some nice shots of bobbies banging on front doors. There'll be a pic in the paper to go with the official statement.'

Alex sat down again. In the turmoil of events surrounding Christa's murder, he had forgotten these other aspects of the police investigation. Of course they'd make inquiries in Clifford Street. It was possible they'd already spoken to the elderly man with the dog whom he'd passed on his way to Christa's. This didn't worry him too much. Anything the man told them would only corroborate his own statement about the time he had arrived at Christa's on the evening she was murdered.

It was the thought of the woman which concerned him; the one who had come out to speak to him on that evening in June when he'd sat in the car watching Christa's house. He had a sudden vivid image of her face as she bent down to speak to him through the open driver's window. Thin, middle-aged features, tense with indignation, dark eyes which had looked into his with the intensity of someone eager for a confrontation.

She'd remember him, all right. She'd probably noted down the number of his car as well as the colour of the shirt he'd been wearing.

He felt a surge of panic which must have shown on his face because Nick asked anxiously, 'What's the matter?'

'It's hot in here,' he said, stumbling to his feet, afraid he might pass out or throw up before he could get to the door.

Nick came with him, holding him by the arm as he walked him into the car-park at the side of the pub where, sitting him down on the wall, he shoved his head between his knees.

Gradually, the sweat dried on his skin and the waves of nausea passed, leaving him feeling drained of all energy. It was as much as he could do to raise his head. When he did so, he was aware of the passers-by on the pavement beyond the car-park wall who had stopped to watch, their faces amused or disgusted. They must think he was drunk. But he was past caring beyond one thought which kept hammering in his head.

I've got to get away. I've got to bloody get away.

Nick was saying, 'I don't think you ought to drive.'

'I walked here,' Alex told him.

'Then I'll run you home.'

To give Nick his due, he couldn't have been more concerned, helping Alex tenderly into the passenger seat of his car as if he was an elderly invalid and opening all the windows. And he had the good sense to keep silent on the drive back to the flat.

But even his solicitude had a dramatic, over-blown quality to it. At the flat, he insisted on coming upstairs with him, despite Alex's protestations, and, once inside, clattered about in the kitchen making black coffee, calling out at intervals to ask where the sugar was kept and were there any aspirins? And when he finally carried the coffee through to the sitting-room, he seemed in no hurry to leave, installing himself in one of the armchairs with the air of a man settling in for the rest of the evening.

'Thanks. It's kind of you, Nick,' Alex said. He genuinely meant it. He only wished to God Nick would bloody well go home.

'Stress,' Nick announced as if trying to supply some explanation for Alex's behaviour. 'That's what's the matter with you. I mean, you've been through a lot recently. You ought to take it easy.'

'Yes, I will,' Alex assured him, thinking that the remark had the banality of all the other platitudes which people offer in such situations. 'I might try to get away for a few days.'

'It'd do you good.'

'That's what I thought.'

It was obvious to both of them that the conversation was winding down but still Nick wasn't apparently ready to leave. He was fidgeting in his chair, crossing and then recrossing his legs.

'You don't happen to know Ruth Page's home telephone number, do you?' he asked unexpectedly, making the question sound too obviously casual.

'Sorry, I don't,' Alex replied, lying instinctively. Knowing Nick, he doubted if his reasons were disinterested. 'Can't you phone her at her office? That's listed.'

'I've tried a couple of times. Her secretary keeps saying she's unavailable.'

'Why do you want to speak to her?'

Nick shuffled again in his chair.

'I'd like to get hold of a photograph of Christa. I could run it on the front page, once the story breaks properly. I might even manage to sell it to some of the nationals. It would make a good feature –

young woman artist, mysterious circumstances, possibility of an anonymous lover. It's the sort of stuff the *Sun* or the *Mirror* might go for.'

'I can't help you,' Alex said stiffly. He felt nausea churn again in his stomach, mixed this time with rage. It was directed not so much at Nick, who was only trying to do his job, but at the whole world of popular journalism which was capable of turning Christa's death into their form of a Roman holiday to entertain the masses. If they brought back public hanging, he thought disgustedly, there'd be no shortage of willing spectators. The idea enraged him.

Putting down his coffee mug, he stood up.

'I'm sorry, Nick . . .'

Nick took the hint.

'Yes, well; perhaps I ought to be pushing off.' He had the grace to look embarrassed but it wasn't enough to prevent him from adding, 'I don't suppose you have a photo? Even a snapshot?' Seeing the look on Alex's face, 'Sorry, old son, I shouldn't have asked.'

'No,' Alex agreed. 'You shouldn't.'

Whether or not Nick made his final remark as a kind of peace offering, as a child might offer one of its toys in an effort to make amends, or whether he merely wanted to show off his inside knowledge, Alex wasn't sure. But at the door, Nick paused to add, 'By the way, talking of the anonymous lover reminded me. I forgot to tell you earlier. The police are going to have a hell of a job finding him. Whoever he is, it seems he cleared off with Christa's address book. Bloody clever of him, wasn't it? Don't bother to come down. I'll see myself out.'

Alex closed the door at the top of the stairs and leaned against it, breathing deeply in an attempt to control the rising nausea. But it was no use. Dashing to the bathroom, he vomited into the lavatory, throwing up not only the contents of his stomach, it seemed to him, but all the grief and rage as well as the panic and fear which had been accumulating inside him like black, bitter bile.

Afterwards, he ran cold water into the basin and splashed it over his head and hands, before sitting down on the edge of the bath, the towel still held to his face.

The bout of nausea had left him trembling but oddly cold and empty. He felt he could think clearly for the first time since Christa's murder. All the extraneous concerns which had filled his mind had been flushed away with that other spewed-up waste, leaving only one behind.

Murray.

If he had had any doubts before, Alex was now quite certain. Murray was as guilty as hell. Who else would want to take Christa's address book except him? His motives for doing so were quite clear. It was because it contained his name, address and phone number, information which would lead the police straight to him.

There remained only one consideration which needed careful thought. How the hell could he bring Murray into the picture?

He could tell Ruth Page about the missing address book and let her inform the police about Murray. She had promised to do so when they had discussed the situation after Christa's murder. But he hesitated to involve her. It might get her into trouble and he didn't want that. She'd have to explain why she hadn't mentioned Murray before which might be awkward for her. Besides, she'd done enough to help him. He didn't want to lean on her again. He preferred to deal with Murray himself.

He could, of course, simply inform the police himself. It would take only a phone call to Finch at Divisional headquarters. But he'd have to be careful how he went about it. As Ruth had warned him, if he admitted knowledge of Murray's existence, the police would want to know how he'd found out and that would mean admitting to a whole lot more information which might throw suspicion on to himself. It wouldn't look too good if he had to tell them that he'd kept watch on Christa and followed her to Murray's house.

He could get round that by making the phone call anonymous which he could do simply by leaving a message for Finch with whoever first answered the phone and by refusing to give his name. But he shied away from this solution. It smacked too much of the coward, the police-state snooper who informed on others out of sheer spite. And it wasn't spite he felt for Murray; it wasn't even anger or jealousy any more. It was simply a need to bring the man to justice which he'd rather do face to face, so to speak, than anonymously behind his back.

But if that wasn't possible and the worst came to the worst, he might, after all, have to act as a nameless informer, however much it went against the grain.

Decide tomorrow, he told himself. Sleep on it.

He felt exhausted again, physically as well as emotionally. The muscles in his chest and stomach ached from the spasms of vomiting.

Getting stiffly to his feet, he went into the sitting-room to unplug the phone again before undressing and lying down on the sofa.

Sleep came quickly, like a blind coming down. But before it

closed completely, he had made one small decision. Before he took any positive action, he'd go back to Murray's house and take a last look at it. Tomorrow was Saturday. The chances were Murray might be at home. He might even catch a glimpse of the man himself. Not to gloat but to remind himself of what Murray looked like and to have, if only at a distance, a chance for some contact with him before he turned him over to the police.

15

On Saturday morning, Finch settled down to the task of going through the reports on the house-to-house inquiries which Stapleton had sent up to his office.

The rest of the investigation was temporarily on hold apart from routine matters. He himself had spent the previous day checking through the video-recording and the still photographs taken at the house in Clifford Street where the search was almost completed. All that remained was the garden and the attic, neither of which Finch expected to yield any worthwhile evidence.

He had better hopes of Stapleton's reports. Somebody must have witnessed something at the time Christa Wyatt was murdered. It was a warm summer evening, for God's sake. The rain didn't start until after ten past nine. People must have been out and about before that. They can't all have been stuffed indoors watching the telly. It was not so much Alex Bennet's movements which interested the chief inspector although a question mark still hung over the man. Bennet might appear to be in the clear as far as an alibi was concerned but, in Finch's book, that didn't rule him out entirely as a suspect. And while he seemed to have been perfectly truthful about the time he had arrived and left the house in Clifford Street, it would help the investigation if someone could be found who could corroborate the man's movements. Apart from Bennet's statement, Ruth Page's also needed verifying.

It was the likelihood that a second person had called on Christa Wyatt after Bennet had left which most intrigued the chief inspector; the new lover, as Boyce called him. The theory was, of course, purely speculative but the evidence, such as it was, tended to support the man's existence; the bottle of wine and the two glasses for a start. Finch was sure Bennet hadn't been lying when he'd said

Christa Wyatt hadn't offered him anything to drink. But someone had shared half a bottle of Chablis with her, presumably her murderer. Why else had he gone to the trouble of washing up the glasses and taking away the cork unless he was trying to remove fingerprint evidence? Then there was the missing address book. Bennet had no reason to take it. He had openly admitted his relationship with the victim so there was no need for him to try and hide his identity by stealing it.

And perhaps somewhere in the pile of reports which lay in front of him on the desk there might be a description of the man or his car or, if that was too much to hope for, some piece of evidence, however small, which might confirm the man really existed.

It was a temptation to turn first to the reports which covered Clifford Street. Instead, Finch picked up those for Bishop's Close and Moulsham Street. A bit like a kid at Christmas, he thought with a grin, who starts with the smallest present, saving the big one till last.

They made boring reading but at least there weren't many of them to plough through. Bishop's Close was short and the houses subsequently few. None of them were marked, he noticed, with the small pencilled star which Stapleton always used to indicate those reports which had any substance in them. All the same, Finch went through them dutifully. They amounted to damn all. Like the deaf and blind monkeys, no one had seen or heard anything. As far as her neighbours were concerned, Ruth Page might not have existed. She certainly hadn't been seen during the latter part of Wednesday evening and the only sighting of her was earlier, just before six o'clock, when her immediate neighbour, a Mrs Ferriby, had seen her car turning into the gateway, when Ruth Page was presumably returning home from work. The same witness had heard a car drive off later, a little while after ten o'clock, but she couldn't be sure who it belonged to.

The Moulsham Street inquiry had come up with more positive results. Finch had told Stapleton to concentrate initially on the pub which was almost directly opposite Ruth Page's office and he had found a couple of regulars who had been drinking in the Star and Garter on the Wednesday evening and who, when they left about ten twenty, had noticed lights burning downstairs in the building and a car parked outside. Although they had seen no one, their accounts seemed to back up part, at least, of Ruth Page's own statement that she had called at Personelle to pick up some notes on one of her clients.

The biggest pile of reports was the ones for Clifford Street. Finch shuffled quickly through it, putting aside those which Stapleton had starred. The unmarked ones, and they were by far the greater number, were as unproductive as those for Bishop's Close. It was another case of the monkeys: see no evil, hear no evil, and certainly do not speak any evil, not when you'd spent the crucial hours between half-past eight and half-past ten, the times to which Stapleton's men had been asked to confine their inquiries, cooking or eating an evening meal, having a bath or, inevitably, despite the heat of that summer evening, watching the television. A lot of it could be blamed on cricket. Essex had been playing Surrey at home that day and highlights of the match were shown on BBC2 between 8.30 and 9 p.m. And then, of course, the threat of the storm, which had been gathering as early as eight o'clock, had deterred a lot of people from setting foot out of doors.

Which left three starred reports, one of which was a statement from a Mr Beaumont who lived half-way up Clifford Street. On the night of the murder, he had been returning home from an evening at his girlfriend's when he had seen a woman standing at the top of the steps of number 47, talking to someone inside the house through the open door. Although he had seen her quite clearly in the security light over the porch of the architect's office next door, he couldn't give a detailed description as he hadn't paid that much attention. He thought she was short and dark-haired. Nor had he seen the person she was talking to. However, just as he passed the gate, the woman turned away and whoever it was inside the house had started to close the front door. The time had been roughly half-past ten.

Taken together, Beaumont's statement and those from the Moulsham Street witnesses seemed to corroborate Ruth Page's own account of her movements on the night of the murder and, while it was true Beaumont hadn't actually seen Christa Wyatt, the fact that the door had been closed by someone inside the house suggested that Christa Wyatt was still alive at half-past ten, as Ruth Page had stated.

Laying them aside, Finch turned to the last two statements which covered Clifford Street, the first from a Mr Fletcher. In it, Mr Fletcher reported that at about eight thirty on the Wednesday evening he had been taking his dog for a walk when he'd passed a man heading in the opposite direction towards the Henrietta Street end of Clifford Street, that is, as Finch noted for himself, towards Christa Wyatt's house. Although Mr Fletcher hadn't taken much notice of the man, his description of him – tall, youngish, dark-haired, clean-shaven – fitted Alex Bennet's physical appearance. The timing also agreed with Bennet's statement that he'd arrived at Christa Wyatt's house at about 8.35 p.m.

As Finch realised, it did nothing to forward the investigation but at least proved Bennet hadn't been lying about that particular fact.

The last report seemed at a cursory glance to belong to the heap of non-starters. It was from a Mrs Willard who lived at number 25 and, like the majority of the Clifford Street inhabitants, she'd seen nothing on the evening of July 26th. In fact, she wasn't even at home. She was out attending a meeting of the Ladies' Conservative Party, of which she was vice-chairperson, between 8 p.m. and 10 p.m. It was an incident which had happened several weeks earlier which caught Finch's attention as it obviously had Stapleton's as well for it was marked with a star.

It was to do with a minor parking dispute and, like the friction between Alex Bennet and the Milners over their car-parking, it still clearly rankled to the extent that she'd taken the opportunity to complain about it to the uniformed constables who'd doorstepped her with their inquiry sheet. Thank God she had and thank God, too, that Matthews, one of the PCs, had possessed not only enough patience to hear her out but enough gumption to make a note of what she'd had to say.

It concerned a man who had parked his car outside her house one evening in mid-June at six o'clock and had remained sitting in it for some considerable time. Mrs Willard, who was expecting her daughter to arrive with her baby, had been annoyed by this. Parking in Clifford Street was bad enough at the best of times and, while she acknowledged she had no rights over the road outside her house, she had thought it inconsiderate of the man to sit there in his car, doing nothing that she could see except take up valuable parking space which would be of better use to her daughter who had the baby's carry-cot to bring into the house.

Five minutes before her daughter was due to arrive at seven o'clock, she'd gone out to speak to the man who had, she admitted, been perfectly polite and, after apologising, had driven away.

No, she couldn't be sure of the date but she had got a good look at the man. He was in his late twenties, she imagined; good-looking; dark hair and eyes; rather thin features.

The car? A dark green Volkswagen. She was quite sure of the make. It was the same as her son's. But she had no idea of the registration number.

As for the direction in which it was parked, she'd noticed this because, strictly speaking, he was on the wrong side of the road, on the right instead of the left. Alongside this paragraph, Stapleton had added one of his neat little handwritten notes: 'i.e. facing east towards Henrietta Street', the scene of the crime, as Finch himself noted.

Finch sat back in his chair and contemplated Mrs Willard's statement, trying not to jump to too hasty a conclusion. But the inference was obvious. Bennet had been keeping watch on Christa Wyatt's house. Why else was he parked in Clifford Street between 6 and 7 p.m.? He couldn't have been waiting all that time to pick her up and take her out somewhere. And anyway, according to Bennet's own statement, which was corroborated by the date on the letter Christa Wyatt had sent him, breaking off their relationship, he hadn't seen or heard anything from her since May 22nd until Wednesday evening when she'd phoned and asked him to call on her.

It was a point he put to Boyce when he called him into the office.

'Looks iffy,' Boyce agreed. 'So what are you going to do about it?'

'Have another little chat with Bennet,' Finch replied, shoving the report into the file and making for the door.

In the event, they weren't to talk to Bennet that morning. As they were drawing up in Maynard's Avenue to park by the kerb, they saw his Volkswagen backing out of the forecourt in front of his house and driving off up the road.

'Follow him!' Finch ordered.

It was a spur-of-the-moment decision. For all he knew, Bennet might have been on his way to do the weekend shopping or get his hair cut. And God knew he had enough on his plate without tailing Bennet to the supermarket or the barber's. As it was, they nearly lost him on Parkway and only managed to catch up with him at the Army and Navy roundabout where he turned on to the A12.

'Where the hell's he making for?' Finch asked.

Boyce shrugged. He had tucked the car neatly in behind a Range Rover which gave them good cover and, by keeping well over to the nearside, allowed Finch to keep a watch on the Volkswagen's rear indicators.

They drove for about six miles before Finch saw one of the lights flash and announced, 'He's turning left.'

Boyce also indicated and dropped his speed down as they made the turn on to the Witham road where the traffic was much lighter.

At the junction a couple of miles from Witham, Bennet turned again, right this time on to a B road which was signposted to

Buckleigh Green. But the village was evidently not his destination for he drove through it, continuing along the same minor route past its outskirts where the road narrowed down to little more than a lane which looked as if it had been designed by someone the worse for drink.

They lost sight of him round the S bends but Finch consoled himself with the thought that Bennet must still be somewhere ahead of them. They had passed no turnings off the road which he might have taken.

And then, when they'd rounded a particularly sharp bend, there was his car drawn up on the left on a grass verge and Bennet himself in the act of opening the driver's door.

'Keep going,' Finch said, 'but turn round as soon as you can and drive back. I want to know what the hell he's up to.'

He was apparently not up to much at all, for when Boyce swung the car round at a crossroads further along and headed back in the direction from which they had come, Bennet was simply standing by a white-painted gate which seemed to lead into the driveway to a house.

Alex Bennet was vaguely aware a car had passed him as he was standing there but he was more concerned with who might see him from the house than from the road. However, the position he had chosen seemed safe enough. The shrubbery which fronted Rose-lands gave him cover, while allowing him a clear if oblique view of the front of the house over the top of the gate.

Someone was evidently at home. The windows as well as the front door were open and Murray's BMW was parked on the gra-velled forecourt. But there was no sign of anyone and this disap-pointed him. He had wanted to see Murray in the hope that, if only by catching a glimpse of the man, it would help him to make up his mind. For, despite thinking about it ever since he had woken up in the early hours of the morning, Alex was no nearer coming to a decision. On one level, it was all perfectly straightforward. Murray had murdered Christa and somehow the police had to be informed.

It was the 'somehow' which continued to concern him and he still hadn't found a solution. To inform on the man anonymously still struck him as discreditable. Even the words associated with such an action carried that same condemnation. To shop. To grass. To sneak.

He wasn't even sure any more why he had come, except out of some vague hope that Murray would make up his mind for him. God knows how. But something in the way he walked or held his head, some gesture of hand or arm, might convince him that the man deserved everything he was going to get and that he himself would be justified in turning him over to the police even if it meant acting as an informer.

But when Murray finally appeared, there was nothing about him which was in any way out of the ordinary. He came walking briskly down the porch steps, carrying a golf-bag which he put into the boot of the BMW. He was followed by Helen Murray and, for a few moments, the pair of them stood by the car, talking.

They were too far away for Alex to hear what they were saying or even to make out their features. At that distance, all he could see was a man and a woman, both tall, both casually dressed. And not only that. There was an intimacy about them which marked them out as husband and wife, a relationship which, seconds later, was confirmed. As Alex watched, Helen Murray leaned forward to kiss Murray on the cheek while he placed his hand on her bare arm. The next moment, he had moved away to get into the car and she had stepped back a few paces to stand at the bottom of the steps between the urns of pink geraniums.

Alex retreated hurriedly to his own car and shut himself inside it behind the wheel. There was no time to drive away. Before he could start the engine, Murray's BMW had turned out of the gateway and was heading up the road towards the village.

Alex waited until he was out of sight beyond the S bend and then drove on to the crossroads where he made a three-point turn before driving back along the same route. He guessed where Murray was making for – the golf-course at Tollford – but he had no desire to follow him any further. What was the point? What he had already seen should have been enough to make up his mind for him. But the truth was he was no nearer to coming to a decision. In fact, he was even less certain than he had been before. That glimpse of Murray with his wife had made him aware of a new aspect of the dilemma which had previously not occurred to him. By shopping Murray, if that's what in the end he intended doing, he would also in a sense be betraying Murray's wife, a totally innocent person. Without a doubt Murray, if found guilty, would go to prison for life, which usually meant fifteen years and, even if he got remission, he'd probably serve at least ten.

Ten years. It was a hell of a long time. And meanwhile, she would be left alone, trying to cope without him. Although he assumed there were no children – he had seen none nor any signs about the place such as a bike or toys which might suggest their existence – it was still not much of a future for her to face on her own.

When he came to weigh that against Christa's murder, he realised the decision was not as clear-cut as he might imagine. Could a death be set against ten years of a man's life, with his career inevitably in ruins, and his wife, the innocent party in all this, made to suffer her own form of punishment? He wasn't God to decide who deserved retribution, who forgiveness.

Christ! he thought furiously, bringing his fist down on the steering-wheel. If only he could make up his bloody mind!

Finch and Boyce watched his Volkswagen drive through the centre of Buckleigh Green from the vantage point of one of the front windows of the George and Dragon pub which overlooked the road and to which they'd retired after passing Bennet outside the gateway.

'There he goes,' Finch remarked with a satisfied nod. 'Drink up, Tom. It's time we got going.'

They drew up where Bennet had parked on the grass verge and where Finch got out of the car. With the air of a man who was merely stretching his legs, he strolled back to the gateway to reconnoitre briefly, noting the name on the gate and a few details of the house which lay beyond it.

A large house; attractive; well-kept, which suggested a man with money; someone in business, perhaps, or one of the professions. In fact, the whole area, he discovered, as he walked on a little further, had that same prosperous appearance.

Satisfied that he'd seen enough, he turned and walked back to the car.

'Roselands,' he informed Boyce as he climbed in beside him. 'I'll get Kyle to look up the owner in the electoral register and then, once we've got a name, we'll run a check on him through the police computer, make sure he hasn't got a record. And then we'll go and have a chat with him. Because one thing I'm certain of, Tom – without realising it, Alex Bennet's just led us to Christa Wyatt's new lover.'

16

There was a message from Ruth on the answer-phone when Alex got back to the flat.

'I just wondered how things were with you,' her recorded voice said. 'I'm in the office until half-past five. Please give me a ring.'

He phoned her more for the sake of returning her call than for any specific reason. What could he say to her? As he had decided to say nothing about the missing address book, he could hardly confide in her either that he'd been to look at Murray's house again. Or that he was thinking of shopping Murray to the police. He knew what her reaction would be. She'd advise him against it. And besides, he still hadn't decided what to do.

Their conversation was short. Ruth was expecting a client at any moment and they were both wary of saying too much in case Ruth's secretary overheard the conversation.

'Are you all right, Alex?' Ruth asked. 'I'm worried about you.'

'I'm okay,' he replied.

'You don't sound it.'

He wanted to say, What the hell do you expect? Instead, he remained silent and it was Ruth who filled in the pause.

'Listen, Alex. Come over to my place this evening for a meal. Please don't say no. I'm feeling pretty low myself and I'd like someone to talk to.'

'I don't know,' he said.

'Please, for my sake if not for yours. We needn't speak about her if you don't want to.'

Her. She meant Christa, of course.

Alex wasn't even sure about that. Did he want to talk about Christa or not? To revive his memories of her? To exorcise her ghost? To relive the time he had found her body? Or was it better to leave it stuffed away at the back of his mind along with all the rest that was dead and gone?

There were muffled voices at the end of the phone and then Ruth came back on the line.

'That was Janet. My client's just arrived. Will you please come this evening, Alex?'

'Yes, all right,' he agreed, letting her make the decision for him.

'Half-past seven,' she said and rang off.

After she had hung up, he disconnected the phone again in case Nick should call him, and then set about cleaning the flat, more out of a need for something to fill in the time than any real necessity. But while he was sorting through the papers on his desk, tearing up those which he no longer needed, he was aware that this urge to discard anything useless was taking on a symbolic quality of its own.

He was, so to speak, clearing the decks, he realised, but for what purpose he himself wasn't yet sure.

Ruth came out to meet him on the porch as she had done, he remembered, on the evening he had found Christa's body and, as on that occasion, too, she stretched up to kiss him on the cheek. And that, too, was symbolic. With that kiss, he felt that she was sealing some kind of pact with him. They were bonded together by Christa's death and, in that kiss, he knew she was telling him that, whatever happened, he could rely on her support. To signal his recognition of this, he kissed her cheek in return and then they walked together into the house.

On entering the sitting-room, he saw that, despite the fact that she hadn't left the office until half-past five, she had gone to considerable trouble to prepare for his visit. The patio doors into the garden were flung wide open and a low table was set out in front of it with glasses and a bottle of wine in an ice-bucket. In the dining-room end, the table was also prepared for supper with a lace cloth, more glasses, silver cutlery and a bowl of roses.

'You're looking tired, Alex,' Ruth remarked.

He could have said the same about her. Although she had prepared herself with as much care as the setting, her face looked drawn under her make-up and there were dark patches, like bruises, under her eyes.

'I keep waking up early and can't get back to sleep,' he admitted.

'Yes, I do, too,' she agreed. 'It's those hours before dawn which are the worst.'

She poured wine for them both and they sat looking out at the garden in silence for several long moments; a companionable silence which neither of them seemed to find oppressive although Alex had the impression that she was waiting for him to speak first and, as it were, set the tone for the rest of the evening.

'I'm glad I came,' he said at last. It was a simple statement but he meant it. 'I was finding it hard to cope with the guilt.'

'Guilt?' she asked. 'Why should you feel guilty?'

About Murray, he wanted to say but knew he mustn't. So despite their pact and that special bonding, there were still certain restraints between them, he thought wryly; taboo subjects which he couldn't discuss with her, like Murray and his own indecision concerning what to do about the man now that he had seen him again with his wife, much as he would have liked to ask Ruth for her advice.

Instead, he replied, 'Guilt about Christa.'

Which was also true.

'Why?'

Alex turned the cool glass of wine round and round in his hands.

'It's difficult to explain, Ruth. When she broke off our relationship, I felt so angry, I think I could have killed her. I didn't, simply because there wasn't an opportunity. But had she phoned me then and asked me round to her house, I might easily have murdered her myself. I feel . . .'

He wanted to say that, ridiculous though such an idea might seem, he felt Murray would understand his feelings and that was why he found it difficult to inform on him. The thought came to him suddenly, like a revelation, and he realised why he could not make up his mind what to do about the man. They had both loved Christa and both had lost her. God, why hadn't it occurred to him before? But, instead of making it easier to come to terms with his own indecision, it only made it worse. What the hell was he supposed to do now?

Getting up from his chair, he went to stand at the window with his back to Ruth, looking out at her green garden where a blackbird was singing its heart out from the top of a lilac tree.

'I must get away, Ruth, if only for a few days,' he said abruptly. 'I need to distance myself from it all, find some space.'

'Yes, I can understand that,' she replied. 'So why don't you? You could book yourself into an hotel somewhere.'

'No, not an hotel,' he said quickly, turning towards her. 'I need to be quite alone.'

'You and Christa were going away to the Dordogne, weren't you?' Ruth asked.

'She told you about it?'

Alex was surprised. It just hadn't occurred to him until then that Christa might have discussed their relationship with Ruth. But, on reflection, he realised that, of course, she would have done so. She and Ruth were close friends. A special bonding had existed between them, too.

'Yes, she was looking forward to it,' Ruth was saying.

'Was she?' he asked eagerly, glancing into her face.

'She loved the Dordogne. She'd been there once before.'

'With someone?'

How ridiculous, he thought, that even though Christa was dead, he should feel a stab of jealousy that she might have gone there with a former lover.

'With her father,' Ruth was explaining. 'It was the year before he died. I think she always loved that part of France. It was very special to her because of him.'

In a way, it was a comfort to know this. Christa must, after all, have cared enough for him to ask him to accompany her to a place which meant so much to her. Why then had she thrown him over? He could only conclude that her passion for Murray had been so strong that it had far outweighed any feelings she might have had for him. Ruth's remark had roused in him all those old longings for what might have been.

If only.

Hadn't someone once said they were the two saddest words in the whole of the English language?

He was relieved that, over the meal, they talked about other subjects – places they had both visited abroad, Rome, Florence, Paris. And food. Ruth had gone to considerable trouble over the meal, preparing gazpacho soup, poached salmon in dill sauce and wild strawberries with cream. Christa's name wasn't mentioned. Nor was Murray's.

It wasn't until after the meal that the conversation returned to the more personal subject which they had discussed earlier in the evening.

After Alex had helped her clear the table and she had loaded the dish-washer, she asked him to carry the tray of coffee things through to the sitting-room. While he was doing so, she went upstairs, returning shortly afterwards with something in her hand which she placed in front of him on the low table. It was a set of keys on a ring to which was attached a small piece of polished slate, on which had been painted in white a Celtic symbol in the shape of an intricate knot. He recognised the work as Christa's. The delicate, intertwined lines reminded him of the illustrations he had seen in the book of children's stories of the rose-covered tower and the women's long robes and hair.

'Take them,' Ruth said. 'They're the keys to a cottage I own in Cornwall. You said you wanted to get away to somewhere quiet. I think you'll find what you're looking for there. It's totally isolated so you'll be quite alone. In fact, if you're careful, no one need know you're there.'

'Careful?' he asked, surprised by the word.

'I mean about leaving the car outside or showing any lights. There's a farm further up the lane. I have an arrangement with the farmer's wife to keep an eye on the place for me and to get it ready if anyone's going down there to stay. She's reliable and she means well but she can be something of a nuisance, always calling in to know if everything's all right and if you want milk or eggs. I expect she's lonely and is looking for someone to talk to.'

'Yes, I expect so,' Alex said. He had picked up the key-ring and was swinging it slowly by its little painted fob.

'Take them,' Ruth urged him again. 'You can stay there as long as you like. You need a rest, Alex. You simply can't go on like this.'

He smiled at her, grateful for her concern.

'I think I will,' he said and slipped them into his pocket.

Ruth immediately became brisk and practical, fetching a large-scale map of Cornwall from the bookcase and tracing out the route for him which she copied down on a piece of paper. On another sheet, she jotted down details about the cottage, where the main electricity switch was located, where he could find bedding and towels.

He watched and listened, amused as well as touched by her new animation. She seemed suddenly transformed. As she bent over the paper, her hair shone in the lamplight, swinging down round her face, and she paused several times to push it back impatiently behind her ears. Her animation affected him and he felt his own spirits rise in response.

'And take whatever food you'll need with you,' she added as she passed the two sheets of paper to him. 'The fridge'll be empty and the nearest shop is in Tintagel and that's three or four miles away.'

Putting the notes in his pocket along with the keys, he stood up.

'Thanks, Ruth,' he said. 'I'm very grateful.'

'I only let close friends stay at the cottage,' she replied.

It was an oblique statement but one which served to strengthen the bond which was already established between them and, as if no further confirmation was needed, they did not kiss on parting. Instead, as she showed him out of the front door, her hand rested for a moment on his sleeve.

It was eleven o'clock before he got back to the flat but he immediately started packing for the trip to Cornwall before that warm feeling of animation could go cold on him. Leaving the phone unplugged, he threw some things quickly into a hold-all, clothes, his washing and shaving gear, a couple of books. As a last-minute decision, he picked up his briefcase as he made for the door. It contained a few items he might need, a new cheque book, a couple of biros and some file paper in case he wanted to write down something although God alone knew what. The rest he left just as it was.

142

At the door, he paused to look round before turning off the lights. The place already looked abandoned, like a hotel room he was leaving for the last time.

But he had no regrets, only an enormous relief that he had made up his mind at last about something. He was going and leaving everything behind – Finch, Murray, the police investigation. Perhaps even Christa. Or, at least, he thought, he might be able to distance himself from his memories of her.

He drove through the night, following the route Ruth had planned for him. Once he had turned off the M25 on to the M4, the traffic thinned out and he made good time, only stopping at an all-night motorway service station on the M5 somewhere outside Exeter for petrol and to stock up with food he'd need for the first few days at the cottage, basic provisions such as coffee, bread, milk, tinned ham and tomatoes. He also bought himself an early breakfast at the cafeteria.

It was still dark but it might have been any time of the day or night. The cafeteria was brilliantly lit and busy with people, the tables crowded with all-night lorry drivers and holiday-makers who had made an early start in order to avoid the daytime rush of traffic for the seaside resorts on the west coast. There was a festive air about the place. From his table at one of the windows, he watched the reflections of the brightly lit interior in the plate glass, more clearly defined than the dark void beyond, which had been reduced to the ghostly outlines of the trees in the picnic area and, in the distance, a continuous double row of headlamps and rear lights moving, as if in a dream, along the invisible motorway.

It was dawn when he passed through the village of Penherrick, a small collection of houses clustered either side of a red-brick chapel. Now that he had turned off the major roads, there was no traffic at all. The narrow road he was following was empty, enclosed on both sides with high hedges and stunted, wind-bent trees. Over to his left, he could see the sky brightening as the sun lifted above some unseen horizon.

And then a quarter of a mile further on, as he turned a corner, the hedges dropped away and the landscape was revealed, rolling out before him in a great semicircular vista of steeply sloping fields running down to a valley where the land lifted again, thrusting itself upwards into headlands and rocky promontories, beyond which lay the sea. It shone like copper in the reddish early morning light, its gleaming surface faintly wrinkled like a huge vat of molten metal moving gently towards the shoreline.

143

He found the turning just as Ruth had described it, on the left and a hundred yards past a signpost for Penherrick Farm. The turning, which was unmarked, was little more than a track, hardly wide enough to take even one car. Once again, the high, banked hedges closed in on him, shutting out the view although, through the open window, he could still smell and hear the sea.

The cottage stood on the right with its back to the sea, at an angle of the track where it swung round to join a slightly wider lane which led, he assumed, to the farm. It was a small, unpretentious building of stone with a low slate roof and with a single-storey addition to one side which served as a garage. Remembering Ruth's warning about not leaving the car parked outside, he unlocked the up-and-over door and drove the car inside, closing and locking the door behind him and carrying his luggage to the house, the keys still in his hand.

The front door, set in a white-painted wooden porch, led into a narrow hall from which three other doors opened, that on the left, he discovered, into a small but well-equipped kitchen, that on the right into a bathroom-cum-laundry. Venetian blinds were lowered over the windows to both rooms, making them dark. The air was close and smelt of warm stone and plaster, not unpleasant but he nevertheless felt a keen sense of disappointment. He had driven down there with such high expectations of finding light and free-dom and space only to discover the place was smaller and more claustrophobic than the flat.

He was therefore unprepared for what lay beyond the third door, the one which faced him at the end of the hall and which, when he pushed it open, led into one huge, open living area.

He stood for a moment on the threshold taking it in. It was, he assumed, converted from the original rooms of what had once been a pair of farm cottages from which all the interior walls had been stripped away as well as the bedroom floors, exposing the exterior stone-built shell and the rafters of the roof. Along one side, a huge fireplace had been installed, nothing more than a simple opening in the wall with a cast-iron fireback and a raised hearth of black, polished slate. The facing wall was lined with shelves filled with books and those objects which can be picked up from a beach – stones and shells and pieces of sea-bleached driftwood, bent, like modern sculptures, into strange, contorted shapes.

The floor was bare except for a couple of woven rugs and the furniture simple, just a couple of wicker armchairs and a large, shabby sofa, filled with cushions. At the far side stood a gate-legged table and four wheel-backed chairs, drawn up in front of the end wall which was one huge expanse of glass, like the east window in a church, covered, as were the other windows, with white venetian blinds through which thin slats of sunlight fell into the room. It was cut in half by a platform, not unlike a balcony, built of pine which was reached at one end by an open-tread staircase and which served, as he discovered when he climbed up to it, as a sleeping platform. Two single divan beds stood side by side, facing the window, the rails which extended along the front of the balcony forming a simple headboard. A curtain ran the length of it which, when closed, would cut the room off, like a stage in a theatre, from the living area below.

Two more doors opened off each end of this balcony-bedroom, one into a shower-room, the other into a walk-in wardrobe and linen room, fitted with hanging rails and shelves. Both rooms were built into the slope under the roof.

And beyond the window lay the sea. It burst in on him as he opened the blind, glittering silver now that the light had strengthened. It stretched out in all its magnificent splendour not more than twenty yards away across an open area of rough grass and small, wind-bent gorse bushes.

At the sight of it, he felt his spirits soar. He had come home.

And yet an uneasiness remained which he couldn't properly define and which he thrust to the back of his mind as he set about laying claim to the place. Having found the main switches and turned on the electricity and water, he stowed the food he had brought with him in the fridge in the little kitchen and filled a kettle which he put on to boil. While waiting for it, he unpacked his clothes and took a shower. That done, he made coffee and carried the mug outside where he sat on the grass looking at the sea, taking in through his eyes, his ears and, it seemed, even his pores, the sounds and scents of the place, the immensity of sky and water.

Compared to that, everything else seemed so far away as to be of no consequence at all.

Lying back on the grass, he fell asleep; a deep and untroubled sleep, undisturbed by dreams or that half-conscious awareness of some undefined danger which always seemed to lurk somewhere at the back of his mind.

He awoke about an hour later to find the sun fully risen and shining straight down on to his face and he scrambled quickly to his feet, remembering Ruth's warning about the farmer's wife who might come calling if she realised the cottage was occupied.

On re-entering the big living-room, that sense of uneasiness which he had felt earlier returned and this time, rested and refreshed, he was able at last to analyse it.

The place reminded him of Christa. There was nothing tangible he could lay his finger on, none of her drawings on the walls nor any personal possessions which he could positively identify as hers. And yet her essence was everywhere, in the plain white walls and the bare polished boards, in the shells and pieces of bleached driftwood displayed on the shelves. It was even in the air he breathed, that faint scent of pine and wood smoke and sun-drenched grass overlaid by the salty tang of the sea. Ruth might own the place as bricks and mortar but it belonged essentially to Christa. It was hers.

Alex ran a hand over the wall just inside the door. The stones of which the cottage was built were smooth and warm to the touch, like living flesh; like Christa's body as he remembered it when they made love.

So there was no escape after all, he thought wryly. Christa's ghost had followed him even here, like an unquiet soul which itself could find no rest.

17

On Monday morning, Kyle had completed his research in the electoral register in the central library and, like Alex Bennet before him, had come up with the name Robert Murray and his wife Helen, as well as their address in Buckleigh Green. To this information, Kyle had added Murray's phone number which he had gone to the trouble of looking up for the chief inspector's benefit.

Finch himself had spent part of the morning at the house in Clifford Street, leaving Boyce at Divisional headquarters to read through the report on the fingerprint evidence and to write up a short digest of its contents. It was a purely personal visit from which he expected to discover nothing of any tangible value to the investigation and, had he been pressed for a reason, he would have found it difficult to give a rational explanation.

It was, he supposed, a kind of silent communion with the dead.

The search was finally finished and the uniformed men and the SOCO team had gone, taking with them their plastic bags of evidence. The place was deserted.

Letting himself in through the front door, he strolled quietly from room to room, stopping occasionally to look out of a window or to examine some object which had caught his attention. The books on the shelves in the sitting-room came in for particular scrutiny. Among them he noticed a volume of the collected poems of Thomas Hardy. Remembering how, as a schoolboy at the grammar school, he had enjoyed Hardy's 'Snow in the Suburbs', he took the book down and flipped over the pages, stopping at one poem, the words of which struck him as specially poignant – Hardy's tribute to his dead wife, Emma.

Woman much missed, how you call to me, call to me,
Saying you are not once as you were.

Not as you were. The lines were apt, he thought. They could apply to Nina whom he certainly missed and usually thought about late at night, after he had returned to his empty house. But they were more applicable to Christa Wyatt whose unseen presence seemed to fill these abandoned rooms and whose appearance he knew only in death, not in life, and who was missed, too, he assumed, by those who had known her: by Ruth Page, for example, and Alex Bennet; perhaps even by the man who had strangled her.

The book was illustrated with a few black and white drawings of landscapes: a wood, a ploughed field in winter with rooks feeding along the furrows, a cottage half buried in foliage, a cliff viewed from the sea with a tiny figure which might have been a woman on horseback riding along its ridge, her hair blowing in the wind and a rainbow arching across the sky behind her.

There was something in the simple yet fluid lines of the drawings which struck him as familiar and, turning to the front of the book, Finch confirmed his supposition. The illustrations were by Christa Wyatt.

Putting the book back on the shelf, he unlocked the french windows and ambled out into the garden, his hands in his pockets, to look at the head of the goddess which stood in its little yew arbour at the far side. The lips seemed to smile at him but the stone eyes were dead, gazing blankly back at him and, after a few moments of silent contemplation, he turned and re-entered the house.

He stopped the longest in the hall, gazing down at the place where Christa Wyatt's body had been lying and remembering her face as he had seen it through the thin, transparent membrane of

147

the plastic bag or afterwards in the video and the still photographs taken not long after her body was found, her hair spread out and her eyes fixed and blank and expressing nothing, like those of the statue.

You are not as you were, he thought, recalling Hardy's words.

He left soon afterwards, locking the house up behind him with a sense of finality. That part of the inquiry was over and done with. Finis.

Finding Kyle's note with Robert Murray's name and address on it when he returned to his office gave him a sense of new beginnings.

He'd go later that evening with Boyce to interview the man, he decided. Murray would presumably be out at work during the day. And before they set out, he'd get the sergeant to run Murray's details through the police computer to check if he had a record.

Boyce's summary of the report of the fingerprint evidence, which was also lying on the chief inspector's desk, wasn't so straightforward but such evidence rarely was, in Finch's experience. Several sets of prints had been found throughout the Clifford Street house, not all of which could be identified. Of those which had, Alex Bennet's, Ruth Page's and Mrs Hunter's had been discovered in every room except the studio, not unexpectedly as all three of them were known to have visited the house when Christa Wyatt was alive. Inevitably, however, there were some unidentified prints, one set in the kitchen, mainly in the area round the gas central heating boiler, which probably belonged to a maintenance engineer. He'd get Kyle to check with Mrs Hunter whether the boiler had been recently serviced or repaired. It was the second set of unidentified prints which interested Finch the most. Like those belonging to Bennet and the others, they were scattered throughout the house, including, most significantly, the bedroom where they had been found on the headboard, on one of the bedside tables and on the switch which controlled the lamp on the right-hand side.

'Murray's?' Finch suggested to Boyce when the sergeant, hearing the chief inspector had returned, strolled into his office.

The sergeant grinned.

'They're not likely to be the milkman's, are they?' he replied. 'Not unless she was in the habit of having her gold-top delivered to her in bed.'

'Well, we'll see what happens when we talk to Murray this evening,' Finch said. 'And, while we're on the subject, check Murray on the computer.'

'I already have,' Boyce replied.

'And?'

'Nothing. No trace on him at all.'

They arrived at Murray's house at seven o'clock. The white-painted gate was open and they drove straight up to the house this time, parking at the foot of the porch steps behind a sleek, silver-grey BMW; Murray's, Finch assumed.

As they got out, Boyce stood for a moment, looking about him, and then raised one shoulder. It was a simple enough gesture and yet seemed to convey a wealth of meaning. In it was expressed admiration, touched perhaps with a little envy, at the garden and the rose beds, the house with its large bay windows, Murray's car, even the urns of geraniums.

The door was opened to them by a tall, attractive woman, slim and youthful-looking, who was dressed casually in grey linen slacks and a pink blouse.

'Mrs Murray?' Finch asked pleasantly, producing his ID card. 'I'm Detective Chief Inspector Finch and this is my detective sergeant, Boyce. I wonder if we could speak to your husband? I assume he's at home?'

'Yes, he is,' Mrs Murray replied. She hesitated for a moment and then stood aside to let them enter. 'He's upstairs making a phone call at the moment. I'll tell him you're here. If you'd like to wait . . .'

She showed them into a large drawing-room at the back of the house where she invited them to sit down.

'He shouldn't be long,' she added.

In the brighter light streaming in through large patio doors which overlooked the garden, Finch saw that she was not as young as he had first thought. The bone structure of her face was good and she had style which suggested she spent time and money on her appearance. Only a very good hairdresser could have produced that casual-seeming cut to her dark hair. The blouse she was wearing had the expensive sheen of pure silk and the long chain she wore round her neck, though simple, was heavy and had the look of 22-carat gold.

But there was an anxious air about her which was apparent as she turned as if to leave the room. It was well disguised although Finch was aware of her tension. At the door, she hesitated again.

'If you'd care to tell me what you've called about, I could let my husband know,' she said.

'Just inquiries,' Finch replied cheerfully.

149

She accepted the reply without any change of expression and left the room.

'Posh,' Boyce said as the door closed behind her.

It was a general remark intended to encompass not only Mrs Murray herself but also the room and the view beyond the windows. It was a fair summing up although 'elegant' might have been a better choice of word. Like Mrs Murray, the room showed a similar expensive but understated taste. The Murrays had clearly spent a great deal of care and money in not advertising their wealth. There were no displays of silver, no showy gilding. But the pale chintz covers on the sofas and chairs and the expanse of cream carpet must have cost a small fortune in dry-cleaning bills in order to maintain their pristine freshness. The garden had the same immaculate appearance. The lawn might have been a newly laid stretch of top-grade Wilton while the herbaceous borders looked as if they had been planted that very afternoon with the choicest flowering specimens from the very best nursery suppliers.

'I thought . . .' Finch began.

He was about to say that he wondered if Mrs Murray had some inkling of what they had come about when the door opened and Robert Murray came in.

He, too, shared that same expensive, well-maintained look but it was not so much his physical appearance which interested Finch as his carefully prepared air of charming unconcern which the chief inspector suspected had been assumed entirely for their benefit.

He came forward smiling and holding out his hand.

'Detective Chief Inspector Finch?' he inquired. 'I'm so sorry to have kept you waiting. Now how can I help you?'

'I'm investigating a murder,' Finch informed him with deliberate bluntness, hoping to force a crack in Murray's smiling insouciance.

'A murder?' Murray did indeed look and sound shocked but no more than might be expected from anyone confronted with such an uncompromising opening statement. 'Whose, may I ask? Oh, do please sit down.'

He waved them towards a pair of armchairs covered in pale blue chintz sprigged with white, he himself choosing a sofa opposite where he settled himself comfortably and crossed his legs.

'A young woman's,' Finch replied.

'I see.' Murray paused and although he continued to look only blandly interested, there was a harder, more watchful expression in his eyes. 'You must forgive me, Chief Inspector, if I ask you a few questions before answering any you put to me. I'm a solicitor, you see, and I'm afraid my legal training has taught me to establish the facts of a case first. Very much as you, too, must do, I imagine, when carrying out your own inquiries. Who is this young woman?'

Finch decided to try another approach. He'd get nowhere with Murray, he realised, by using shock tactics although he had a few legal cards of his own up his sleeve which, when the time came, he was prepared to produce with a flourish.

'Her name was Christa Wyatt.'

Murray didn't make the mistake of answering too quickly. Again, there was a small silence in which he frowned slightly as if searching for the name through a mental file.

Then he said, 'It means nothing at all to me. I don't think she was a client of mine. Perhaps one of my partners handled her case. Where did she live?'

'In Clifford Street.'

Once more, Murray paused to consider this fact before replying, 'I'm afraid that doesn't ring any bells either. What part of London is it in?'

'It's not in London,' Finch told him. 'It's in Chelmsford.'

'Oh, I see.' Murray recrossed his legs. 'In that case, Chief Inspector, she almost certainly wasn't one of our clients. We're a London-based firm – our offices are in the Strand – and it's very unusual for us to have any clients outside the London area unless their affairs are of special interest in which case, as senior partner, I'd probably handle it myself or at least have my attention drawn to it. What makes you think I have any connection with – Miss Wyatt, wasn't it?'

Finch played his first card. In his best, official, dead-pan voice, he said, 'I'm afraid I can't divulge the source of my information.'

'Then it looks like stale-mate, Chief Inspector. Until I know where you heard this information, I'm afraid I can't help you. I repeat, the name Wyatt means nothing to me. Nor does Clifford Street. If that's all . . .'

He had begun to rise from his chair but, seeing that the two men remained seated, he sat down again.

'Is there something else?' he asked.

'Yes, there is, Mr Murray,' Finch replied, playing his second card. 'I'd like to know what you were doing last Wednesday evening between eight o'clock and half-past ten?'

For the first time, Murray showed some sign of emotion. There was a visible stiffening of the muscles in his dark, good-looking

151

face, especially round the mouth, the corners of which tightened. But his voice remained controlled.

'I stayed the night in London,' he replied.

'In an hotel?'

'No; I – we, that is – have a flat just off Sloane Square. My wife uses it as well when she comes up to London shopping or we go to the theatre or opera together. I often stay there mid-week, particularly when I have a heavy case-load. I was in the flat working all Wednesday evening and didn't, in fact, return to Buckleigh Green until Thursday night.'

It was the first crack in Murray's defences. He was talking too much, adding too much detail, a sure sign he had something to hide.

'I see,' Finch said blandly. 'Could anyone corroborate this?'

Murray tried to retrieve the situation. In an attempt at jocularity, he said in an amused, urbane voice, 'If you mean, was I entertaining a mistress, then I'm afraid I shall have to disappoint you, Chief Inspector.'

'I was thinking more of telephone calls or a friend who might have called on you that evening,' Finch replied in his own suave manner.

It did his heart good to see the smile wiped off Murray's face.

'No, I had no visitors that evening and I usually switch the answer-phone on when I'm working,' he said stiffly. 'The whole purpose of my staying in the flat is so that I shan't be interrupted.'

'Quite,' said Finch with no change of expression. 'The address, Mr Murray?'

'Flat 2, 26 Lauriston Gardens, SW1.'

Boyce noted it down and then Finch nodded to the sergeant as if to indicate to him that the interview was over. It was only when the three of them were on their feet that he played his last card.

'Oh, by the way, Mr Murray,' he said, as if the idea had only just occurred to him, 'I'd be grateful if you called in at Divisional headquarters sometime in the near future to make a statement and to have your fingerprints taken. Ask for Detective Sergeant Craddock at the front desk. Thank you for your help. We'll see ourselves out.'

Outside, he took his time getting into the car. He could see Murray, who had followed them to the front door, standing a few feet inside the hall. He looked a disconsolate figure, Finch thought, although that didn't prevent him from remarking to Boyce as the car crunched down the drive over Murray's immaculate gravel, 'He knows something, Tom. I'm damn sure of that. And we've got him rattled. Stop in the village. I want to make a phone call.'

'Who to?'

'Alex Bennet. If he's home, we'll drop in on him on our way back and mention the name Murray to him; see if we can't rattle his cage as well.'

He was out of luck. When he finally emerged from the phone box outside the George and Dragon, he shrugged his shoulders at Boyce in a gesture of exasperation.

'The phone's disconnected. I got on to the engineer and it's definitely not a fault on the line. We'll call on him anyway on the off-chance he's at the flat.'

In the event, Bennet was not there. Neither was his car. All the same, Finch tried his bell and, having received no answer, rang the Milners' instead. After a few moments' delay, Mrs Milner came to the door.

'We were hoping to see Mr Bennet,' Finch said pleasantly, 'but it seems he's not at home. Have you any idea what time he'll be back?'

'He's gone away,' Mrs Milner informed him. 'We heard him leave the flat about a quarter to twelve last night and drive off. He hasn't been back since.'

'You've no idea where he's gone?'

'Sorry, I can't help you,' she said and closed the door.

'He's gone; God knows where,' Finch told Boyce briefly, climbing back into the car.

'Done a runner?' Boyce suggested.

'It could be,' Finch agreed. 'If he has, he's a damn fool. It only makes things look worse for him.'

'Worse than what?' Boyce asked, not unreasonably. 'I thought Bennet had an alibi which puts him in the clear. Perhaps he's just lost his bottle. So what now? Are we packing it in for the evening?'

'No; we'll drop in on Ruth Page instead,' Finch said, coming to a sudden decision, 'and try running the name Murray past her; see if we get any reaction.'

He didn't add that he was also curious to see her in her home background instead of in the more impersonal setting of her office.

She was at home and the room she showed them into was pleasant and comfortably furnished. Although it was now dusk, it was still warm and the patio doors were wide open, letting in the scents of warm earth and leaves from the shadowy garden.

153

Ruth Page herself looked more informal. Instead of the black suit, she was wearing jeans and a blue and white checked blouse, the neck open and the sleeves pushed up to her elbows.

'I'm sorry we've called so late,' Finch began.

'It's no problem,' Ruth Page replied easily. 'I don't usually go to bed until much later. Can I offer you anything? Tea? Coffee?'

'No, nothing, thank you.'

'Then what can I do for you?'

'A couple of things have come up which you may be able to help us with.'

'Of course, if I can.'

'Does the name Murray mean anything to you?'

He was watching her face closely and saw it change subtly. There was a sudden look of surprise, almost of shock, which was replaced immediately by a more guarded expression.

'Murray?' she repeated. 'I'm not sure. I used to know someone in London called Ann Murray. I shared a flat with her once but that was years ago. I assume this has something to do with Christa? I'm sorry but I don't see the connection. As far as I know, Christa and Ann only met a couple of times and hadn't been in touch recently. In fact, I haven't seen Ann myself for ages.'

'No; it's not Ann Murray,' Finch said. He felt he had lost the advantage. By introducing the subject of her former flat-mate, Ruth Page had successfully led him into a dead-end. Instead, he decided to approach the matter from a different angle.

'Do you know if Miss Wyatt had any friends in Buckleigh Green?'

'Not that I'm aware of.'

There was a matter-of-fact briskness in Ruth Page's voice which seemed to dismiss Buckleigh Green as well. She also seemed to have assumed the interview was over for she had half turned towards the door as if to show them out.

Finch followed her, waiting until he was standing beside her in the doorway before asking his final question.

'It seems Mr Bennet went away last night,' he said. 'Have you any idea where he's gone?'

He was so close to her that he could look directly into her eyes. Intelligent eyes, he noticed; a clear, bright brown but for all that not particularly expressive. They held the look which he'd seen in the eyes of other successful women as well as men, a quality of polite opaqueness assumed by someone who, in the course of the day, meets many people and who has learnt to veil her own regard from the scrutiny of strangers.

154

And yet something flickered there for an instant before it was gone.

'I'm sorry, I really don't know.'

'Then have you any idea why Mr Bennet should have left?'

'Perhaps he simply wanted to get away for a few days,' she suggested, her tone of voice implying that this conclusion was one which the chief inspector might easily have drawn for himself with a little imagination. It was an intended snub although it was said lightly and was accompanied by a smile.

'She bloody well knows something!' Finch asserted, slamming the passenger door behind him with more force than was needed. Ruth Page's parting remark still rankled.

Boyce, who seemed oblivious both of the snub and of Finch's reaction to it, merely shrugged, more intent on backing the car out of the gateway.

'Knows what?' he asked, when he had completed the manoeuvre. 'About Murray? Or where Bennet's gone?'

'Possibly both,' Finch replied although he didn't sound too sure.

They drove in silence down Springfield Road and then Finch announced suddenly, 'Drop me off at headquarters.'

'At this time? What the hell for?'

'There's something I want to check on,' Finch replied shortly. He seemed in no mood to go into details and, knowing the chief inspector, Boyce thought it prudent not to press him.

It was, in fact, a long shot and for that reason, Finch preferred not to discuss it with Boyce until he had had a chance to verify his hunch.

Alone in the office, Finch sent for the box of drawings and photographs which had been taken from the pin-up board in Christa Wyatt's studio. He went through them slowly, as if postponing the moment of inevitable disappointment. Most of them were no use but a few he set aside for more careful consideration after he'd sorted through the whole collection. Once that was done, he turned back to them.

They didn't amount to much, one water-colour of a seascape, showing a small, rocky beach backed by cliffs which reminded him of the illustration he'd seen that morning in the book of Hardy's poems of the figure on the clifftop.

He associated Hardy with Wessex and Wessex meant Dorset. It was a possibility, Finch thought. Christa Wyatt might well have visited Dorset to get ideas for illustrations for the book. It was worth considering even if, in his mind, he didn't immediately connect Dorset with cliffs.

He turned next to the two photographs of Ruth Page, one of her standing in front of a high bank, covered in what looked like wild flowers, a signpost just visible on the far side of the print. Part of the right arm of the post was cut off by the edge of the paper but the left-hand one was in the picture although the lettering on it was too small for him to make out with the naked eye and was partly obscured as well by the foliage of a tree which was also not in the frame. Even the magnifying glass which he got one of the uniformed PCs to find for him wasn't strong enough to bring the lettering into focus.

The second photograph, which he examined while Jeffreys was hunting up the magnifying lens, wasn't, at first glance, all that useful. It was the one of Ruth Page standing at the door of a house. Nothing in the snapshot gave any clues to its location although the door, with its little white-painted porch surmounted by a peaked roof, suggested a cottage which might, in turn, imply a rural setting.

Finch laid the two photographs out on the desk like a pair of cards and then, picking out one of them, slipped it into an envelope, across the front of which he wrote the name of McCullum, the police photographer, together with a few short instructions.

On his way out, he left the envelope at the front desk with orders that it was to be passed on to McCullum first thing in the morning.

18

Alex spent the first few days walking when he wasn't sleeping, leaving the cottage early in the morning and setting out across the cliffs. He walked without thinking, concentrating only on the physical need to keep moving and on the landscape about him. In that setting of rocks, sky and sea, Christa's murder and the police investigation seemed strangely distanced. Even Murray no longer had any significance. It was as if all of it had happened a long time ago in some faraway country to people whom he had heard about but had never met.

Although he kept clear of the tourist centres, it wasn't possible to avoid people altogether and from time to time, he would meet others, like him, walking the cliffs or in a village pub when, forced by hunger, he would strike out across the fields to find somewhere to eat. Even these casual encounters seemed remote, the people alien. He might have been alone in a foreign country, coming across strangers who spoke another language. He heard but did not register their speech.

In the evenings when the light was fading, he returned to the cottage, letting himself in through the back door into the silent living-room. With the exception of the blinds over the bedroom window, which he had adjusted so that they would let in a little light, he had left the rest of them closed. He liked coming back to this twilit world in which everything was reduced to mere shapes, too vague to remind him of Christa's presence. In the semi-darkness, he learned to find his way round the place, padding about in bare feet as he felt for the taps in the kitchen to fill the kettle to make coffee for himself or to shower in the little bathroom under the sloping eaves.

The nights were warm and he slept naked, listening to the sound of the sea as it came washing into the room through the big windows which he slid partly open before going to bed. He went to sleep to its rhythm which rose and fell in time to his own breathing. It was as if the sea had entered his body and had become part of him, bearing him away on its dark tide into dreamless sleep. And when he woke in the morning, it was to the same rhythmic pulse of the waves and the high-pitched cries of the gulls.

It wasn't until the third day that he thought about Murray. He was walking as usual along the cliffs towards Morwenstow when he met a couple coming in the opposite direction. The path was narrow and he stood aside to let them pass. The woman came first, smiling at him but saying nothing. It was the man who spoke, making some general remark about it being a beautiful day. There was nothing about his appearance to remind him of Murray. The man was gaunt, sun-burnt, grey-haired. It was his voice, that same casual, self-assured, slightly amused tone which Murray had assumed on that afternoon when Alex had called on him with the briefcase.

And there was that same urge to control. As they moved away from him, Alex heard the man call out to the woman to take care where the path ran close to the cliff edge.

'Mind how you go,' Alex heard him say. 'The grass is quite slippery. It could be dangerous.'

As if the woman were incapable of noticing this for herself.

As he watched them disappear from sight over the ridge, Alex remembered how Murray had come walking down the hall and had taken charge of the situation.

It was as if a shutter had suddenly snapped open in his mind, releasing a flood of other memories which came tumbling out so quickly that they were almost subliminal, like images flashed for a few seconds on to a screen in rapid succession.

Murray's face, smiling that half-smile of his; Finch's, listening, head cocked to one side; Ruth's, pale, grave, watching him from across the room. And Christa's. Again and again, Christa's. Christa alive, laughing, tendrils of her hair blowing in the wind through the open car window. Christa dead, her blank, blue stare and her hair spreading like pale water-weed across the polished boards.

Alex was not sure how long he stood there on the clifftop, looking out to sea but registering nothing. The present reality had retreated and it was the past which crowded close about him. When he finally returned to an awareness of his immediate surroundings, he was stunned by the vividness of it all, the glittering air, the restless, sparkling expanse of water, the grass itself shining as if every individual blade was stroked with light.

Turning away, he set off inland, walking rapidly, his mind made up although he had no clear idea where he was making for. Eventually he reached a village, a small scattering of cottages and houses, a church and a pub which he entered.

The dark, low-ceilinged bar was almost deserted apart from two old men, sitting silent in separate corners, staring into the middle distance, each with a glass on the table in front of him.

A door at the far side of the room was labelled 'Toilets' and 'Telephone'. Alex pushed through it into a narrow passage where a pay-telephone was squeezed in between the Ladies and Gents. Laying all the change he had in his pockets along the top of the ledge, he dialled Nick's office number.

A woman's voice answered him.

'I'd like to speak to Nick Duffield, please,' Alex said.

'I'll see if he's in,' the woman replied indifferently.

There followed a delay in which Alex fed the phone with money, anxious that he'd be cut off before Nick came on the line.

'Nick Duffield here,' he said at last in that professional voice he always used for business calls. 'How can I help . . . ?'

'It's Alex,' he told him.

'Alex? For Christ's sake, where the hell are you?' Nick demanded, reverting to his normal style. 'I've been trying to ring you for days but the phone's not connected. I've even called round to the flat –'

'Listen, Nick,' Alex broke in. 'I haven't much time. How's the investigation going? Have you heard any news from your contact?'

158

'There's a whisper going around. But I don't like discussing it over the phone . . .'

Alex came close to losing his temper.

'Don't mess me about, Nick. I bloody need to know.'

'Okay, okay.' Nick sounded conciliatory. His voice advanced, speaking so close to the receiver that Alex could feel it vibrating against his ear-drum. 'I gather they're on to someone – no name yet. They're keeping that under wraps. It's someone with clout, though; a London solicitor; lives the other side of Buckleigh Green, if the rumour's correct. That's all my little dicky-bird knows at the moment although, if the bloke's arrested, there'll be a hell of a story, front-page stuff in the London dailies, no less. I could make myself a nice little packet there –'

'Thanks, Nick,' Alex said hurriedly. 'That's all I wanted to know.'

He was about to ring off but Nick was too quick for him.

'Hang about,' he said, suddenly aware of the implication behind Alex's remark. 'You know about him, don't you? You might have bloody told me! What's his name? His address? Come on, Alex, you owe me one. Give me a handle on the man.'

'I can't. I don't know anything.'

'Bloody pull the other one!' Nick sounded outraged. 'Christ, and I thought you were a mate! Well, listen, old chum, I'll tell you something for nothing. You'd better get your arse back here double-quick before the police start putting you in the frame. My little bird tells me they're more than keen to find you. It'd make a super front-page story. I can even see the headline, "Police Hunt Missing Ex-Lover of Murder Victim".'

'You wouldn't,' Alex said flatly, trusting to Nick's good nature.

'Not yet. But remember, if the shit hits the fan and your name comes up on an official police hand-out, that's it, mate. You'll be dog's-meat as far as the press hounds are concerned, and that means me, too, so don't try pushing your luck too far.'

'Thanks for the warning, Nick,' Alex said, genuinely meaning it. 'I'm sorry I didn't come clean about everything. I'll explain why when I see you. I should be back . . .'

But the line went dead as the money ran out and, replacing the receiver, Alex went back to the bar where he ordered a pint of bitter and a cheese sandwich. Carrying the plate and glass over to a far table, he sat down to think over what Nick had told him.

The information had roused in him complex emotions, mainly relief that the police had at last got on to Murray without his having to shop the man. He wondered who had tipped them off. It had to be Ruth, he concluded. Apart from himself, no one else knew of Murray's existence. So Ruth must have changed her mind about the risk of telling Finch about Murray, a decision she must have made after he had left for Cornwall, otherwise she would have let him know what she was proposing to do.

He also wondered what had prompted her decision. She had been so adamant that Murray's name should not be mentioned for fear it strengthened the case against himself. It was possible something had happened during the past few days about which he knew nothing but which had led to her change of heart. He could phone her later, of course, but first he wanted to think through the ramifications of what Nick had told him.

The news that the police were looking for him caused him some alarm but this was lessened to a large extent by several other factors. Now that Murray was in the frame, to use Nick's words, the investigation would inevitably shift to him and away from himself although no doubt the police would want to talk to him about Murray and how much he knew about Christa's relationship with the man. And this, in turn, raised further complications. How much should he tell them? Or should he deny all knowledge of Murray's existence?

The latter course would save him a great deal of embarrassment. If he admitted knowing about Murray, it meant explaining how he had found out about the man and that would lead to his having to describe how he had kept watch on Christa's house and followed her to Murray's, as well as the occasion when he had called on him with the story about the briefcase.

Now that he had met Finch, either course had its own problems. Lying to the chief inspector wouldn't be easy. There was that quiet, watchful quality about him and Alex doubted if he could maintain such a deceit for the second time, especially as, despite any sympathy he might feel for Murray, or more particularly for his wife, deep down he wanted the man to be found guilty.

But to confess would be as bad as, if not worse than, lying about Murray. He could imagine Finch sitting there, that polite, bland expression on his face, while he stumbled through his account of waiting in the car in Clifford Street evening after evening, as well as all the rest of it. God, it would be so bloody humiliating!

And then there was Nick to consider as well. Because of his own damned stupidity, Nick now suspected he had known about Murray all along although, if the worst came to the worst, he supposed that situation could be retrieved. He could explain to Nick that he'd

160

only guessed Christa was meeting another man but had not known anything about him.

A sudden weary revulsion swept over him. Here he was, back in the same morass of lies and deceit which, by coming to Cornwall, he had hoped to escape from. What good had it done him? None, that he could see. He realised that he was being driven by the same cowardly instinct for self-preservation which had prompted him to run away from Christa's house on the evening he had discovered her body.

I should have phoned the police straight away, he thought in disgust. But I hadn't the courage.

So what the hell do I do now? Go back and tell them the truth? And would they believe me?

'Are you all right, sir?'

The voice cut across his thoughts and Alex looked up to see the pub landlord standing over him, a look of concern on his face.

'Yes; I'm okay,' Alex said quickly.

'Only you don't look well,' the man persisted.

The two old men seated at the other side of the bar were also staring at him.

'There's nothing wrong. I'm fine,' Alex replied more loudly, exasperated by their curiosity.

He stood up, leaving the rest of his beer unfinished but, as he crossed to the door, he was conscious of their eyes following him.

Outside, he set off towards Penherrick, walking quickly and with a new purpose. Although the encounter with the landlord had unsettled him, it had at least jolted him back into an awareness of the reality of his situation.

He would not return to Chelmsford just yet, he decided. Instead, he would stay on at the cottage for a few more days and give himself time to think things through properly.

Despite what Nick had said about the police looking for him, there was very little chance that Finch would find him. Ruth could be trusted not to give away his whereabouts. But he'd have to be far more careful about keeping his presence at the cottage secret. It would only take a little slip on his part and someone might notice something suspicious and report it to the local police who might call on him and, in turn, might check up on him with the CID in Chelmsford. He wanted to avoid that at all costs. When he went back, it had to be in his own time and on his own terms.

In the meantime, the situation with regard to Murray might well have been resolved. Alex hesitated to use the word 'arrested'. But now that the police had the man's name and address, Finch and the other CID officers involved with the case would surely be collecting up evidence which would prove the man's guilt: his fingerprints in Christa's house or perhaps even a witness who could prove Murray had been there on the evening Christa was murdered.

For the first time since the murder, it occurred to Alex to consider in any detail what had happened on that Wednesday evening. When Murray called on her, he had almost certainly left his car some distance from the house. His BMW was distinctive and he wouldn't have risked parking it in Clifford Street. He had then walked to Christa's, letting himself in by the back way through the garden door. That would explain why it had been left unlocked.

So far so good. What had happened afterwards was less easy to imagine. They must have quarrelled. Perhaps Christa had written a letter to Murray, similar to the one she had sent to him, breaking off the relationship, and Murray had simply turned up unexpectedly to confront her. Or had she been expecting him?

But whatever the circumstances, what had followed had about it its own terrible inevitability. Murray had lost his temper, prompted perhaps by Christa's cool, dismissive manner, and, in an excess of jealous rage, had strangled her. He had then left, probably through the back garden, and had driven home. Perhaps it was then that the garden door had been unlocked, not earlier, as he had first imagined.

The theory hung together, except it left out two important factors which he hadn't until that moment considered in any detail.

At a quarter past eight, when she had phoned him at the flat, Christa was still alive and yet by twenty-five to nine he had found her dead, leaving a time gap of only twenty minutes.

So when exactly had Murray arrived at her house? Before or after that eight fifteen phone call? And why in God's name had Christa phoned him anyway?

Alex halted. He was walking down a narrow lane, following the signs for Tintagel, the nearest large town to Penherrick, when he stopped abruptly in the centre of the road.

Someone had been with her. He suddenly remembered that, when she had spoken to him on that Wednesday evening, he had been aware of some quality about the call which, at the time, he hadn't been able to define and which, in the turmoil of events which had followed, had slipped his mind entirely. He realised only now what it was. It had been there in the tone of her voice,

162

a consciousness of another person's presence, as if what she was saying was intended to be heard by someone else as well as him.

It had to be Murray. No other explanation was possible. But why had Christa wanted him to call on her that evening, knowing Murray was in the house?

Not out of fear. She hadn't phoned him because she had wanted his protection. Her voice had sounded cold and contemptuous. She was angry with him, not with Murray. So it must follow that, at the time she had made the call, she had no reason either to fear Murray or to think that he was going to murder her.

Then why the anger directed at him? Why the need to get him to the house while Murray was there?

At the time, Alex had realised that the purpose behind her summons was to force some kind of confrontation between himself and her. Murray's presence as a third party added a new and unexpected twist to the situation. And, in view of that, there was only one possible explanation which made any sense at all.

Murray must have found out that he, Alex, was Christa's former lover and, for some reason, suspected wrongly that their relationship was still continuing. Murray might even have seen him waiting in the car in Clifford Street although this seemed unlikely. Had that been the case, Murray would have recognised him when he called at the house that Sunday with the briefcase. But there had been no sign on Murray's face, not even the smallest flicker, to suggest Murray had seen him before.

So there had to be some other explanation. It could be something quite simple, a chance remark on Christa's part which had aroused first Murray's suspicion and then his jealousy. Or had he found more tangible proof? Perhaps the letters which Alex had sent her? Had she kept them after all?

God knows they were passionate enough, the outpourings of his grief and despair. And was that why Christa had phoned him, in an attempt to defuse Murray's jealousy over the letters by bringing the two men face to face and by forcing Alex to acknowledge that his own affair with Christa was over?

If that were the explanation, and it seemed the most likely, then Alex realised he was faced by a new and horrifying truth about Christa's death. In a sense, it was not only Murray who was responsible. He was partly to blame as well. If he had not himself loved her so passionately, Murray might not have been tipped over the edge into murdering her.

163

19

Murray was on Finch's mind as well. On the Monday morning, he went to London alone to take a look at the man's flat in Lauriston Gardens, leaving Boyce behind. The trip was in the nature of a preliminary reconnoitre, an opportunity to inspect the lie of the land which wouldn't need the two of them. With no hard evidence yet against Murray, only suspicion, it was too early to start looking for any possible witnesses to Murray's movements on the evening of Christa Wyatt's murder. That would come later when the finger-prints found in the bedroom of the Clifford Street house had been checked against Murray's and proved to be his, as Finch had every confidence they would be.

He was held up, too, by the problem of enlarging the photograph of Ruth Page found in Christa Wyatt's studio, not an easy task, apparently. McCullum had already made three attempts to en-hance the lettering on the signpost so that the name of the place could be identified, but without success. The print had now been sent to a specialist firm in London and Finch was waiting for their report. In the meantime, the investigation was temporarily on hold.

Murray and Bennet. On the journey to London in the train, Finch thought about the two men. There had to be some connection. Why else had Bennet driven over to Murray's house on Saturday after-noon? Not to call on him, that was certain. He had merely stopped at the gate to look at the house as if to confirm it was still there.

The sod of it was, Bennet had chosen to clear off soon afterwards before he could be questioned about his knowledge of Murray. Find Bennet and he might find the answer to Christa Wyatt's mur-der. The two men were linked in some way.

London was stifling, the underground trains packed with people, late commuters and tourists and visitors who had come up to town to shop or for a day out. They stood pressed together, body to body, strangers in intimate contact, as far as Victoria where most of them got out and Finch was at last able to find a seat.

At Sloane Square, he, too, left the train and emerged into the open air which smelt of dust and exhaust fumes. He could taste their dry, corrosive odour on his lips.

On the walk to Lauriston Gardens, he thought about Nina. London was her place, not his. She would be used to the crowds, the glittering shop windows, the stationary traffic piling up at the lights before charging, like a herd of bison, towards the next set, where they halted once again, vibrating with angry frustration. He had sent a telex to her hotel in Marseilles, warning her that he'd probably not be able to meet her at Heathrow on Friday. At the rate the investigation was going, that now seemed a certainty.

Lauriston Gardens was lined with tall, imposing, five-storeyed houses, built, by the look of them, at the turn of the century for rich merchants or bankers, hard-headed businessmen who expected plenty to show for their money. Their façades of reddish-purple brick, the colour of beef, were decorated with bands of lighter and darker brick and tile, laid in patterns, the large, bulbous bay windows and the door faced with sandstone which was itself ornamented with incised diamond and trefoil shapes. Steps led down to deep basements, protected from the pavement by iron railings, spiked like medieval lances.

Number 26 was half-way down. Finch mounted the steps to the porch and peered at the panel with its entry-phone speaker and its rows of names and bell-buttons which was screwed to the wall by the front door. Mrs and Mrs R. Murray were listed for Flat 2, presumably on the first floor.

Retreating down the steps, Finch stood looking up at the first-floor bay window although there was nothing visible except the swags of curtains looped back at the edge of the glass. But he had seen enough to convince him that Murray could have left the flat unnoticed by any witnesses on the Wednesday evening Christa Wyatt was murdered and driven down to Buckleigh Green. Come to that, he needn't even have gone to the flat. He could have gone straight from his office in the Strand. The absence or presence of his BMW wouldn't have been noticed either in Lauriston Gardens or in the streets which led out of it, as Finch discovered when he strolled on a little further. They were all forested with parking meters, many of the spaces occupied by cars as expensive as Murray's. Even in that short walk, he counted two BMWs, a Bentley and a couple of Jaguars.

It would be a waste of time, he concluded, to try knocking on doors here, looking for witnesses. Far better to stick to the area round Clifford Street although, if the worst came to the worst, the investigation might have to be extended. And anyway, there was no point in involving the Metropolitan police until he'd got the report on Murray's fingerprints and those unidentified prints found in the bedroom of the Clifford Street house. But they'd match. Finch was certain about that.

He'd have to watch his step, though, with Murray. According to Craddock, when Murray had turned up at Divisional headquarters to make a statement and have his prints taken, he'd been accompanied by a London solicitor, a senior partner in a well-known City firm, specialising in criminal law, which even Craddock had heard of. While the two men had been perfectly polite, Murray, on his solicitor's advice, had refused to answer certain questions, as he had every right to do, of course. All the same, the man would need careful handling. Murray not only had clout, he knew about the law and, between them, he and his solicitor would be watching every move Finch made in Murray's direction.

It was almost lunchtime when he returned to his office to find the report from the photographic specialists in London waiting for him. Tearing the envelope open eagerly, he tipped the contents out on to his desk. Two prints came sliding out, the original snapshot of Ruth Page standing by the signpost, and the enhanced enlargement of the left-hand side cross-bar. Although the quality was still far from perfect, it was possible to pick out from the grainy texture and the dark blobs which he took to be leaves which had partly obscured the name, some individual letters or parts of letters. Finch jotted them down on a sheet of paper.

The first could be a 'P' or a 'B'. All that could be seen of it was part of its upper right-hand curve. The letters next to it were clearer and were definitely an 'E' and and 'N'. After these, there was a single upright stroke, a 'K' perhaps or an 'L' or an 'H'. After that came another 'E' and then an 'R'. The following letters, three in all, judging by the spacing, were lost behind a blob of foliage. But the last letter stood out clearly. It was a 'K'.

Turning to the report which accompanied the prints, Finch saw that whoever had drawn it up, an S. Morris, according to the signature, had come to exactly the same conclusions.

Finch was sitting back in his chair, contemplating the half-complete place-name, –EN–ER——K, when Boyce entered the room.

'So you're back,' the sergeant announced as if Finch himself were unaware of this fact. 'Any joy?'

'Not a lot,' Finch said distractedly. Tossing the sheet of paper over to the sergeant, he added, 'What do you make of that, Tom?'

'What is it? A crossword clue?'

'For God's sake!' Finch began and then realised that the sergeant wasn't aware of the significance of either the photograph or the name on the signpost. In the flurry of the day-to-day running of the investigation, it had slipped his mind to fill Boyce in about this particular inquiry of his own.

He gave Boyce a quick explanation, adding, 'I'm damn sure Ruth Page knows where Bennet's cleared off to and I'm also pretty damn sure it's got something to do with that snapshot.'

'Why? I don't see the connection,' Boyce objected, not unreasonably.

'Put it down to intuition,' Finch told him, grinning. 'I just *know*, Tom. And we have to find Bennet. He led us to Murray so he must have something on the man. I suppose he hasn't returned yet?'

'Not so far. Whittaker called at his flat again this morning. He's still not there.'

'And nothing yet on those prints found in the bedroom?'

Boyce shook his head.

'Palmer's still checking them against Murray's. He's hoping to come up with an answer later today.'

'Thank God for that,' Finch said. 'Perhaps the case'll start moving again. It's about bloody time it did.' Glancing down at the sheet of paper with its enigmatic group of letters, he added with apparent inconsequentiality, 'Who's likely to have a library ticket on him?'

'Library ticket? Well, Kyle, I suppose. Whenever I see him in the canteen, he's always got his head stuck in a book,' Boyce said with the dismissive air of someone who normally read nothing more than the *Daily Express* and the Ford Cortina handbook. 'Why do you ask?'

'Find Kyle and send him round to the central library to borrow these books,' Finch replied, jotting a couple of titles down in his notebook. Tearing off the sheet he handed it to the sergeant who read them out loud in the wooden tone of a rooky constable giving evidence for the first time in court. '*The Complete Poems of Thomas Hardy* and *The Life of Thomas Hardy*. Who's Thomas Hardy when he's at home?'

'A writer.'

'I don't get –' Boyce began.

'Just find Kyle and give him that bit of paper,' Finch said. He suddenly felt very weary and also hungry. In the rush to get off to London that morning, he hadn't bothered with breakfast. 'I'll explain later.'

The canteen was deserted. He sat at a table with a pork pie and a cup of tea, looking out at the roof-tops and chimney-pots, the view dissected in the middle distance by a train passing slowly over the

167

railway bridge, its windows flashing in the sun. He thought of Murray commuting by train to London and didn't envy the man his way of life even though it had, he supposed, its compensations in the way of the house, the BMW, the elegant wife. But he felt no animosity towards him even though eventually he'd have to arrest him. That went with the job.

The books were waiting for him on his desk by the time he returned to the office, two large volumes which Kyle had left piled up on top of one another, and he forgot Murray as he sat down to open them.

Out of sheer curiosity, Boyce put his head a couple of times inside the room during the next hour only to find the chief inspector seated at his desk, absorbed in reading. He didn't even look up when the door opened and, thinking it prudent not to disturb him, Boyce went quietly away.

It was nearly two hours before Finch found what he was looking for. He had given up on the biography almost at once. It was a large volume of closely printed text and, although it had an index, it wasn't much use, Finch realised, until he knew what it was he wanted to look up. He finally found it in one of the poems. It was entitled 'Beeny Cliff' and in it Hardy described a March day of 'irised rain' when he had walked on the clifftop accompanied by a woman riding a pony, her 'bright hair flapping free'.

Finch leaned back in his chair and stared out of the window. It was the same view he had looked at from the canteen only on a lower level. But he saw nothing. His mind was filled with the memory of one of Christa Wyatt's illustrations he had seen in the copy of Hardy's poems he had found in her sitting-room. The images in both the poem and the drawing matched each other almost exactly. The woman rider, her hair flying loose, even the rainbow, were present in both of them except Christa Wyatt had visualised the scene from below, as viewed from the sea, while, in the poem, Hardy had described it at closer quarters on the top of Beeny Cliff. But it had to be the same image, the one in the pen and ink drawing inspired by that in the poem.

Turning to the back of the biography, he looked up Beeny Cliff in the index, thinking that, knowing his luck, it probably wouldn't be listed. But it was, together with a page reference which he turned to quickly.

And there it was, in one of the earlier chapters which dealt with Hardy's life as a young man. He had been working then as a church architect for a firm in Dorchester and had been sent to St Juliot's, a small north Cornish village, to design the renovations for the local church which was when he had met Emma, the woman on the pony, Finch assumed, who was the sister of the vicar's wife and whom Hardy was later to marry.

Cornwall! Of course! He couldn't understand why he hadn't realised that for himself. The combination of cliffs and sea should have been obvious from the start.

As he sent for Boyce, he had a sense of jubilation, of events shifting into a higher gear. After the hours of waiting, something was happening at last.

Boyce was aware of Finch's heightened mood when he entered the office and, catching some of his excitement, didn't so much as raise an eyebrow when the chief inspector told him to get hold of Kyle again and send him out, this time to buy two large-scale maps of the north Cornwall coast p.d.q.

When Kyle returned with them, he and a WPC, whom Finch had caught in the corridor on her way back from the ladies' loo, were installed in one of the incident rooms where there was a table large enough on which to spread out the maps, given a copy each of the incomplete place-name and instructions to look for it on the maps, probably somewhere not far from the coast.

It was the WPC who came up with it. Finch, who had been in and out of the room during the half-hour it took to find it, like an anxious father waiting for the birth of his first child, beamed his delight, noticing for the first time that she wasn't bad-looking. She had pretty hair and a wonderful smile.

'I think it's Penherrick, sir,' she announced.

Finch bent over the map to look where her finger was planted, Boyce at his shoulder.

And there it was in tiny letters, marking a small village about a mile from the sea, with Tintagel the nearest large place to the south and Bude to the north.

'Right!' Finch said, turning to Boyce. 'Get on to someone at Bude – the local council office if they have one, or the police station. I want to know where someone living in the Penherrick area would pay their council tax.'

There followed one of those maddening delays in which the search for an apparently simple piece of information turns into a major enterprise.

Boyce rang directory inquiries which put him on to a recorded voice which announced that there was no listing for Bude Council, the name he had asked for. He rang directory inquiries again, asking instead for the local police station. This time he was given a number which he dialled. Whoever answered the phone wasn't sure of the answer to his question. His wife always dealt with the bills. Could he ring the sergeant back after he'd made some inquiries?

After ten minutes' wait, the man phoned with the name of the North Cornwall District Council in Wadebridge but not the telephone number. Boyce rang directory inquiries for the third time and, having obtained the number, dialled it. There followed another delay while his call was transferred to the right department.

It was at this point that Finch, who had been fretting with impatience at Boyce's side, grabbed the receiver, announced who he was and demanded to speak to someone in charge. A woman eventually came on the line.

'This is urgent,' Finch snapped, letting his exasperation come to the surface. 'I need to know if either a Miss Ruth Page or a Miss Christa Wyatt pays council tax on any property in the Penherrick area. If either of them does, I also want to know the address of that property.'

'How do you spell that last surname?' the woman inquired.

Finch spelt it out loudly and clearly, at the same time giving Boyce a God-help-us-all look, eyes raised to the ceiling.

'I'll have to ring you back after I've looked the names up,' the woman said severely. 'I shall need your name and telephone number, of course. We're obliged to check on this type of inquiry. We don't give such information to anyone, you understand.'

'Of course not,' Finch agreed, climbing down and sounding suitably chastened.

He repeated his name and added his phone number. 'And please,' he concluded, 'could you make this a priority? I need this information urgently.'

'I'll do my best,' the woman replied in a frosty tone.

To give the woman her due, she rang back in less than quarter of an hour. While he waited for her call, Finch gave Boyce a brief explanation of the connection between Thomas Hardy, Penherrick and Alex Bennet's present whereabouts.

'I'm pretty sure either Ruth Page or Christa Wyatt owns a cottage down there and that's where Bennet has gone to ground. Ruth Page must have given him the keys to the place. I had a gut feeling when I talked to her that she knew where he'd gone.'

At this point, the phone rang and Finch snatched up the receiver, listened, nodded and then scribbled something down on his note-pad before thanking the woman on the other end of the line. Hanging up, he turned to Boyce with a look of triumph.

'There it is, Tom,' he said, showing him the piece of paper. 'Cliff Cottage, Penherrick Farm Lane, Penherrick; owned by Ruth Page. Simple, isn't it, when you have the answer. It's bloody getting it which takes the time.'

After that, it was plain sailing. It took only one phone call to Divisional headquarters at Launceston and a demand to speak to a detective chief inspector who came on the line almost immediately and who listened, without interruption, to Finch's explanation and the request which followed it.

Yes, that was no problem, he said. He'd arrange for a couple of uniformed men to be sent to the address in question. He'd get that organised straight away. And yes, he'd make sure they went there fairly early in the morning to catch anyone who might be staying there at home. He'd phone the chief inspector back when he had any information.

'Bennet's there all right,' Finch told Boyce after he'd rung off. Leaning back in his chair, he stretched and yawned hugely, before adding with the air of a man well pleased with life, 'You know, Tom, I have that feeling that things are going our way at last. All we need now is confirmation that those are Murray's fingerprints in Christa Wyatt's bedroom and we're home and dry.'

As if Palmer had heard the chief inspector's remark, the man himself rang Finch's office about half an hour later. Boyce was in the middle of a story about an estimate he'd had from his garage for an oil-change which was, in his opinion, way over the odds and, if he had the time, he could do it himself for next to nothing, when the call came.

'Yes?' Finch said, picking up the receiver and flapping a hand at Boyce to shut up as soon as he recognised Palmer's voice.

'About those prints in Clifford Street,' Palmer began.

'Yes?' Finch repeated, sitting upright and preparing himself for good news.

Even before Finch replaced the receiver, Boyce knew the outcome wasn't at all what he had been expecting. The look of bright antici-pation had gone, wiped away in an instant.

'Well?' he asked as Finch remained silent, his hand still resting on the phone.

'They're not Murray's. They don't bloody match,' Finch said slowly in a voice of utter disbelief.

171

20

The following morning, Alex Bennet was jerked awake by a loud, metallic noise somewhere in the lane at the front of the cottage. For a few moments, he lay immobile, trying to identify the sound. Although he hadn't heard the vehicle arrive, he was sure it was a car door banging shut.

The next second, he was out of bed and had crossed to the window which was open. Sliding it shut, he then closed the slats of the venetian blind which were also partly open. In the semi-darkness, he went back to sit on the bed, listening intently.

There followed a moment or two of silence, broken eventually by a faint rattle as someone tried the front door and, finding it locked, opened the flap of the letterbox. Whoever it was wouldn't have seen anything. The inner door leading into the living-room was closed. Next, footsteps came tramping along the stone path to the back of the cottage where they paused and a man's voice said,

'I can't see into the garage so I don't know if there's a car there or not.'

Thank God, Alex thought, he'd had the sense to hang a sack he'd found there over the garage window which looked out over the cliff as a precaution in case the farmer's wife, who looked after the place for Ruth, decided to check up on it.

But this was the police. There was no doubt in his mind about that. Someone had sent them – Finch, he assumed – to find out if he was staying in the cottage although he couldn't think how the hell Finch had got hold of the address. He was too intent on listening to think about the implications of their arrival.

One of them tried the back door and then he heard a second voice say, 'I don't think anyone's here. The place's locked up. What do you think? Shall we try again later?'

His companion merely grunted in reply and then the footsteps retreated down the path. Shortly afterwards, Alex heard their car drive away.

He sat on the side of the bed, still naked, for ten minutes, waiting to give them time to get well clear of the place. At the same time, he thought over what he should do next although the decision had, in fact, been made for him. He would have to leave. There was no question of that; and soon, too, before they had time to come back, perhaps this time with a search warrant.

God knows what had happened in the time he had been away. Although Nick's contact had told Nick the police were looking for him, the man probably didn't know every detail about the investigation. After all, according to Nick, he was merely a civilian working on the clerical staff. It was possible Finch had found further evidence which pointed to his own guilt, at least in the chief inspector's eyes. Why else would he send a couple of policemen to the cottage in the early hours of the morning except to arrest him?

The problem was what to do next? Should he move on somewhere else, find a small hotel or boarding-house and go to ground there? But, as soon as the idea occurred to him, he dismissed it out of hand.

No, he couldn't do that. Not only would it be tantamount to admitting his guilt as far as the police were concerned, he knew he couldn't live like a hunted animal, waiting for the inevitable knock on the door. Because the police would eventually find him. Finch had his description, even the number of his car. Sooner or later, they'd catch up with him.

Which left him with only once choice – to return to Chelmsford and give himself up. If he told the truth, late though it was, he might be able to persuade Finch he was innocent of Christa's murder.

This left him with the question of Murray's guilt and for this he had no answer apart from an obvious inference. If the police were looking for him in Cornwall, it must mean Murray was in the clear as far as the inquiry was concerned, perhaps through lack of evidence or because he'd managed to concoct an alibi to cover himself for the time Christa was murdered. But again, with no exact information to rely on, he could only guess at what had happened.

Ring Nick on the way back, he told himself. His contact might have come up with some fresh information since his phone call to Nick the day before.

The question of how the police had found the address of the cottage seemed a minor matter compared to these other considerations. However, there appeared to be only two possible explanations. Either they'd found it in Christa's house when they'd searched it, although not in her address book which Murray had taken, and this seemed the more likely, or Ruth Page had told them. But he couldn't believe she would have betrayed him. Why should she? She had no reason to give him away.

173

Getting up from the bed, he dressed and began rapidly to gather together his possessions, stuffing them into the hold-all before turning off the electricity and water. Last of all, he picked up his briefcase and, resting it on the table downstairs, he opened it to look for his car keys and his wallet which he'd placed in there for safe-keeping, rather than carrying them about with him during the day when all he needed was enough ready money to pay for food and other minor expenses.

The car keys had slipped somewhere out of sight in the bottom of the case and he had to empty it before he could find them. Under his wallet and some sheets of unused paper, he came across another batch, fastened together with a paper clip, which had writing on them and which he couldn't identify in the semi-darkness. Wondering whether to dump them or keep them, he carried them over to the window and, lifting one of the slats a little to let in the light, he peered down at them.

There were about fifteen sheets of file paper altogether and each was headed with the words 'I know not seems', the title he remembered writing up on the board for the lower sixth class on the morning Ruth rang to tell him Mrs Hunter had discovered Christa's body. Below the title, under various sub-headings, 'Hamlet', 'Ophelia', 'Claudius', were the pupils' comments on each relationship. He remembered now taking them in and stuffing them into his briefcase just before the bell rang and Mrs Reynolds had come to tell him there was an urgent phone call for him. Since then, he'd forgotten all about them.

He shoved them back in the case, found his keys and took a last look round the cottage. The light was too dim for him to make out much detail of its interior, except the vague shapes of the furniture. But the odour of the place still pervaded the air, that scent of warm plaster and pine, of sea and grass. Christa's scent.

Quietly he let himself out of the front door, locking it behind him, shutting the fragrance inside, and, backing his car out of the garage, drove away down the lane.

For some extraordinary reason, however, he couldn't get out of his mind that title – 'I know not seems'. It kept coming back to him, evoking other thoughts. His seeming guilt. Christa's seeming love for him. Perhaps even her love for Murray, he thought, was just another form of seeming.

It was still on his mind when he stopped at a service station on the M5 for petrol and breakfast and to draw money from one of the cash-points. There were public telephones as well inside the entrance and he decided to ring Nick from there. It was gone half-past nine; too late to catch him at home but he should have arrived by now at the office. He only hoped to God Nick would be able to come up with some information, otherwise returning to Chelmsford would be like walking into a hidden trap.

This time there was no delay. As soon as he asked to speak to Nick Duffield, the same woman who had answered the phone the day before said immediately, 'He's not in the office. He's out on an assignment.'

'Do you know when he'll be back?' Alex asked.

'I've no idea,' the woman replied indifferently. 'He's asked me to take any messages so it seems likely he'll be out all day. Do you want to leave your name and number?'

'It doesn't matter,' Alex said and rang off.

'Seems', she had said. That bloody word again, applied this time to Nick.

It was only when Alex returned to the car and was in the act of putting the key into the ignition that he made the connection. It came to him out of the blue and yet was so blindingly obvious that he couldn't think why it hadn't occurred to him before.

Not daring to drive off, he sat behind the wheel, going over it point by point, to make sure he couldn't be wrong. But, now that the basic link had been made, all the rest of it fitted into place – his gut feeling that someone had been with Christa when she had phoned him that Wednesday evening; the missing address book; the fact that it had started to rain soon after he'd left the house after discovering Christa's body; even the head of Artemis standing at the end of the garden. He could see it now, the lips parted in that enigmatic smile.

God, what a fool he'd been!

At about the same time that Alex Bennet was sitting in his car in the motorway service station, Finch was seated at his desk, also thinking about Christa Wyatt's murder.

He had just received a phone call from the detective chief inspector at Launceston, informing him that two constables from Bude had called at the cottage in Penherrick but had found it locked up and apparently empty. It seemed Alex Bennet was not there although the officers would call again later in the day to make a second check. To add to his problems, Whittaker had also called in after checking on Bennet's flat to report that he wasn't there either.

So where the hell was he?

Now that the case against Murray had crumbled into nothing, only Bennet remained as a possible suspect unless someone else turned up which seemed unlikely at this late stage in the investigation.

As Boyce remarked after Whittaker had left the room, 'So where do we go from here?'

'We start again,' Finch said. 'Get the statements, Tom; Bennet's, Mrs Hunter's, the lot. I'm going over them with a fine-tooth comb. There must be something in them . . .'

He didn't complete the sentence. It seemed challenging fate to add '. . . which we missed the first time.' He'd read the bloody things at least five times already and he was damned sure he hadn't overlooked anything of significance.

As Boyce made for the door, he remarked, almost as an after-thought, 'And while you're at it, bring Christa Wyatt's correspond-ence as well; the stuff that was in her filing cabinet.'

He'd been through that lot, too, and found nothing useful there either. There was no personal correspondence, not even the letters which Bennet had said he'd sent her and which she had presum-ably destroyed after she'd broken off her affair with him. All that it contained were receipts, copies of contracts, letters and statements from her publishers; damn all, in short, that might shed any light on her private life.

Boyce dumped the lot on Finch's desk and then went off, at the chief inspector's request, with the two library books which he wanted Kyle to return. There was no point in keeping them any longer. That hunch about Bennet being in Cornwall had turned out a dead loss as well. It was also a ploy to get Boyce out of the office. Finch was in no mood to tolerate anybody else's presence, a reac-tion which Boyce, thank God, was apparently aware of for he cleared off for the next few hours.

Left alone, Finch rolled up his sleeves and moved his chair so that it had its back to the window. He also switched on his answer-phone. With this kind of tedious, nit-picking work, he wanted no distractions.

He began with those statements which contained the least controversial material, Mrs Hunter's first, although he already knew there was nothing useful in it to the investigation. Al-though she had found the body, Christa Wyatt's cleaning lady had known nothing about her employer's private affairs, nothing about her habits, nothing either on whom she might have been meeting.

176

The next statement from Mr Fletcher, who had been walking his dog in Clifford Street at the time Alex Bennet called on Christa Wyatt, added nothing new either. Bennet hadn't denied meeting Christa Wyatt on that Wednesday evening. All Fletcher's statement did was corroborate the time which Bennet had given for his arrival at the house.

The Milners' statements came into the same category, merely corroborating the time Bennet had returned to his flat, and, as such, proved nothing about the man's movements between 8.35 p.m. and 10.25 p.m.

The statement given by Mrs Willard, the woman who had spoken to Bennet in June when he had been parked outside her house and the last one in this little batch, seemed more relevant. Finch was still convinced in his own mind that Bennet had been keeping watch on Christa Wyatt's house, a suspicion which might have formed the basis for a case against the man if it hadn't been for Ruth Page's statement that she'd spoken to Christa Wyatt at half-past ten on the evening she was murdered. And that, in turn, was backed up by the witness Beaumont who'd seen a woman talking to someone inside Christa Wyatt's house at that crucial time; presumably Christa Wyatt herself.

Take that evidence away, he thought, and Bennet was placed bang in the middle of the picture as prime suspect.

So let's do just that, he told himself. For the moment, let's ignore Beaumont's and Ruth Page's statements and see what we're left with.

Bennet goes to see Christa Wyatt, perhaps after she'd phoned asking to see him although this wasn't definitely established. He only had Bennet's word on that and he could be lying. It was possible he simply turned up without prior warning at 8.35 p.m. as he had stated. It had to be then; the timing was corroborated by Fletcher's statement.

The first part of their meeting is amicable. Christa Wyatt opens a bottle of wine which they share. But, after that, the situation gets out of hand. There's a quarrel, almost certainly about Murray whom Bennet suspects Christa Wyatt is having an affair with. She goes into the hall, perhaps to make a call or to answer the phone. He comes up behind her and strangles her with the tea-towel from the kitchen. It could have been then, after the murder, that he took the glasses and bottle into the kitchen, or just before, which might account for the tea-towel being used as a ligature. Bennet had grabbed up the nearest object to hand.

177

Having strangled her, Bennet then washes up the glasses and pockets the cork, in order to remove any fingerprint evidence.

So far so good.

What happened next was less certain for it depended on what time Bennet left the house and that, in turn, depended on how long he and Christa Wyatt had been talking. There were three possible scenarios. Either Bennet went straight home from Clifford Street, arriving just before half-past ten, a timing corroborated by the Milners. This would place the murder at an earlier time; say between 9.45 p.m. and 10 p.m. which gave Bennet time to wash the glasses and remove the cork before driving back to his flat in Maynard's Avenue. Alternatively, the murder occurred even earlier in the evening, soon after Bennet's arrival, and Bennet had spent the intervening hour or so simply driving about, trying to calm himself down.

Or, thirdly, he went to see Ruth Page, as he had stated, and confessed to Christa Wyatt's murder which was when they concocted the alibi between them.

The scenario made sense up to a point. The only trouble was, there were two major flaws in it. Why the hell had Bennet taken Christa Wyatt's address book? As far as Finch could see, Bennet had no reason to remove it. There could, of course, be some quite simple explanation. Although it hadn't turned up anywhere in the house or her car, it was possible she'd taken it out with her for some reason and had lost it.

The second objection, and the more important of the two, concerned Ruth Page and his theory about a concocted alibi. She and Christa were friends. Why in God's name then would she agree to cover up for Bennet, knowing he'd murdered Christa? There was no way round that as far as he could see. Bennet and Ruth Page weren't particularly close; at least, that was his impression.

And what about Beaumont's evidence? He couldn't be lying. But could he have been mistaken? Supposing he'd only thought he'd seen the front door being closed from the inside?

Finch leaned back in his chair, trying to visualise the front door of Christa Wyatt's house. There was a mortice lock, he remembered, to the right and below it, in the centre of the door, a brass letterbox with a large, round knob, also of brass, a few inches above it, set at about waist height. Would it have been possible for someone standing on the doorstep and in the act of turning away to walk down the steps to stretch one hand backwards and pull the door shut?

Getting up from his chair, he went out into the corridor and, half opening his office door, tried it out for himself. Yes, it would work, he

178

decided. His body would have effectively shielded the movement of his hand and arm. To a casual passer-by, it could well seem that the door had been closed by someone inside the house.

The theory, and it was still only a theory, as he himself admitted, presupposed one fact – that Ruth Page must possess keys to Christa Wyatt's house. Mrs Hunter, her cleaning lady, might know. He'd have to check with her later.

But the theory still failed to answer his basic objection – why the hell should Ruth Page want to provide Alex Bennet with an alibi? Was she in love with Bennet herself? Or did he have some hold over her? And where did Murray fit into all this?

Unless he could find an answer to that fundamental problem, the whole theory amounted to damn all.

Leave it for the time being, he told himself. Go back to what you have – Bennet's and Ruth Page's original statements. If there's an answer, it could be in those.

He was half-way through them when he came upon it. It was one of those trivial-seeming sentences which he must have read half a dozen times already and which, because it was so unimportant, he had passed over time and time again.

On this occasion, it seemed to stare at him from the page.

'Check it!' he said out loud, as if there were two of him in the room, one sitting at the desk, the other standing at his shoulder, monitoring his every move.

Obeying his own instructions, he turned to the file containing Christa Wyatt's correspondence, making himself slow down so that he wouldn't be tempted to skip through it too quickly. Bent over his desk with his head between his hands, he read each letter, each contract, each financial statement word by word, paying particular attention to the dates.

It was five minutes to four when he finally finished and sent for Boyce. Sitting him down at the desk, he took the sergeant through the evidence, adding as he finished, 'It makes sense, doesn't it, Tom? It all hangs together?'

Although he was damn sure he was right, there was a note of appeal in his voice. But surely there were no holes in the case this time, no hidden flaws which he hadn't taken into account?

'It hangs together,' Boyce agreed.

'Thank God for that!' Finch exclaimed. He glanced at his watch. It was now 4.35 p.m.

'Right!' he said. 'Let's call on Beaumont and Mrs Hunter. And then we'll get over to Murray's place!'

Alex Bennet arrived at his flat at four twenty, just missing Whittaker who'd called again ten minutes earlier to check the house, although Alex wasn't aware of this. Seeing Bennet's car wasn't on the forecourt and receiving no answer when he rang the bell, Whittaker had returned to Divisional headquarters to report that Bennet still wasn't there and, in his turn, missed the chief inspector by quarter of an hour. On being told that both Finch and Boyce had already left, Whittaker wrote out a short memo about Bennet which he left on the chief inspector's desk before going off duty.

Alex Bennet's first action on re-entering the flat was to fling open all the windows to air the place off. The heat trapped inside it was unbearable. He then showered, changed and made himself coffee, deliberately taking his time. Like Finch, he wanted to avoid acting too quickly. Before he made his move, he needed to think it all through one more time just to make sure, although he knew he was right. Nothing else made sense.

The coffee finished, he reconnected the phone and, having dialled the number for Divisional headquarters, he asked to speak to Detective Chief Inspector Finch.

The detective chief inspector was out of his office, the woman at the other end of the line informed him. And no, she was sorry, she had no idea when he would return.

Alex replaced the receiver slowly. He had counted on Finch being there.

So what should he do now? Wait for Finch to get back? But that might take hours. He might not even return until the following day.

He couldn't wait that long. He wanted it over and done with now, to have finished once and for all with all the lies and deceptions.

Looking at his watch, he saw it was a quarter to six.

Time to go, he told himself.

Without even stopping to pick up his jacket, he let himself out of the flat.

21

She was at home, as he had expected, but hadn't yet had time to change out of her business suit.

'Alex, you're back!' she said as she opened the door. She seemed genuinely pleased to see him. As she led the way into the hall, she added over her shoulder, 'What made you decide to leave?'

'The police came looking for me,' he said roughly.

They had reached the sitting-room where the patio doors were open on to her leafy garden and in the evening sunlight which came pouring in, he saw her expression change from one of welcome to a look which was openly startled at the tone of his voice.

'I didn't tell them where you were,' she said quickly.

'It doesn't matter how they found out,' he replied. He wondered how the hell he was going to express what he had to say. But, in the event, it was easier than he had imagined. The rage he had felt on the drive there had died down, leaving him with a cold, contained anger out of which the words seemed to come without any effort on his part.

'I know about you and Christa,' he said. 'And I also know what happened on the night Christa was murdered.'

To give Ruth her due, she made no attempt at denial. She was too intelligent for that. And also perhaps, crazy though such an idea might seem given her deception which had fooled him for so long, too honest to lie now that she was confronted with the truth.

For a long moment, her gaze held his and then she said quite calmly, with a little challenging lift to her head, 'You're right, of course. What made you suspect me?'

He answered her directly, countering her honesty with his own.

'Several things. The cottage for one. Although it was yours, Christa was everywhere. It was she who dominated the place, not you. And then this morning, when I was packing up to leave, I found some pupils' work in my briefcase on a quotation from *Hamlet*, how things seem different to what they really are. It struck me later that nothing was as it seemed, not Christa and me, nor her and Murray, and certainly not you and Christa. It was you who were with her when she phoned me, wasn't it? Not Murray. And once I'd realised that, the rest of it made sense. I knew why Christa was angry with me –'

He was interrupted by the sound of the front door bell and, as Ruth Page made a small movement as if to go and answer it, he gripped her fiercely by the wrist.

'Leave it!' he said harshly. 'Whoever it is will go away.'

Still grasping her by the wrist, he continued. 'You'd told her,

181

hadn't you, that I'd followed her to Murray's house? That's why she was angry and wanted to see me. But it wasn't Murray she'd fallen in love with, was it? It was Murray's wife. I was a fool to jump to the wrong conclusion but the mistake was easily made. They're both tall and dark and, seen at a distance, with her short hair and jeans, she looked like a man. But you realised the truth, didn't you, Ruth? You were in love with Christa yourself and you couldn't bear the thought of her with another woman. What I still don't understand is why you weren't jealous of me.'

Ruth pulled away from him, forcing him to loosen his grip. Stepping back a few paces, she stood confronting him, her eyes still fixed on his face as though she were trying to stare him down.

'How bloody arrogant of you, Alex!' she retorted. 'Why should I be jealous of you? You meant nothing to Christa. To her, your affair was sexual, that's all; just a physical release. But like all the other men she'd slept with, you wanted to possess her and, in the end, that bored her. Do you want to know what we did with the letters you sent her? We set fire to them in the garden and then scattered the ashes over the head of the statue I'd given her, like a burnt offering.'

'To Artemis, goddess of hunting,' Alex put in with a wry grimace.

'Who hated the company of men,' Ruth countered quickly, giving him a smile which was oddly companionable, as if, despite all that had happened, there was still that ease of communication between them.

'And afterwards, we went into the house and made love,' she continued, her voice harder and more triumphant. 'No, Alex, you never possessed Christa. No man ever could.'

'And what about you?' he struck back. 'Did you possess her?'

He saw the smile vanish from her face.

'No,' she admitted sadly. 'I never possessed her either; not properly. There was only one person who ever did.'

'Her lover in London, the one who threw her over? It was a woman, I assume?'

'You're learning quickly,' Ruth said with an ironic twist to her mouth. 'Yes, Esther Durrant was Christa's first and probably her only love. She was one of her teachers at the Royal College of Art. Their relationship lasted for several years. It was like a marriage, a total commitment; or so Christa thought. And then Esther met someone else – another, younger student, a woman, of course, and it was all over. That was when she came back to me. But, if you

182

think about it, I never once said Christa's lover was a man. It was you who jumped to the wrong conclusion.'

As you intended I should, Alex thought. But to be fair, Ruth was right. Thinking back to that conversation, he realised she hadn't lied to him; not directly. It was he himself who'd made the wrong assumption as he had done with so much else.

Out loud, he said, 'And what about Helen Murray?'

'Oh, Helen. That was different. I took a leaf out of your book, Alex, and when you told me Christa was meeting someone else in Buckleigh Green, I followed her whenever I could. I knew it couldn't be a man; Christa would have told me about him as she had all the others. As soon as I saw her and Helen together, I knew Christa must be in love with her. Helen was like Esther, older than Christa, and beautiful and elegant; everything that Christa admired.'

'And so you decided to murder her,' Alex said bluntly.

'It wasn't like that!' Ruth protested, her voice rising. 'I didn't go there intending to kill her. I simply wanted to see her. She opened a bottle of wine and we sat together talking. We were thinking of going to London on the following Monday to see an exhibition at the Tate. Then she said, sorry, she couldn't make it after all. She had another arrangement which she couldn't cancel. And I said, "With Helen, I suppose?" I should have kept quiet, pretended I didn't know. Christa asked how I'd found out about her. And then after that everything went to pieces. I told her how you'd followed her, thinking it was Murray she was having an affair with. Christa was very angry with both of us. She said I was as bad as you, spying on her, trying to possess her. She wanted nothing more to do with me. It was all over.

'She went into the hall to phone you and demand you came to see her. I knew what she intended. She wanted to confront you with what I'd told her. I was going to leave; I didn't want to be there when it happened. But I'd left my bag in the kitchen with the keys to the house in it and, while she was on the phone, I went to get it.

'The kitchen door into the hall was open and, after she'd rung off, she saw me looking at her. She was standing by the little table and she gave me this smile. Oh God, Alex, it was devastating! I'd never seen Christa smile like that before. It was utterly contemptuous. I knew then she meant what she'd said about never wanting to see me again. And then she turned her back on me deliberately, as if I meant nothing to her at all.

'There was a tea-towel hanging by the sink. I don't remember exactly what happened next. It was over so quickly and it all seemed so far off, as if it was happening to other people, not to Christa and me. Oh God, Alex, I loved her so much!'

Her features seemed suddenly to fall to pieces, as if the muscles supporting the skin and flesh had collapsed. Turning away, she put both hands over her face to hide it from him.

He could hear her weeping with those same harsh intakes of breath he had heard over the phone when he had called to tell her Christa was dead. There was so much pain in her voice that, absurdly, he wanted to comfort her, to put his arms round her as she had done to him that same evening.

But the impulse was swept away by a much more urgent need to come at last to the truth and be done for ever with the lies and the deception.

He said, 'When I rang you, you'd only just got home, hadn't you, Ruth? You'd cycled over to Christa's and left your bike in the garden. That explains why the garden door was unlocked. And on the way back, you got caught in that storm. Your hair was still damp from the rain. That's why you said you'd had a shower and why you didn't want me to phone the police or say anything about Murray. If I did, the truth about Christa and Helen Murray would have come out and they'd have been suspicious of you. It was you who took Christa's address book because it had Helen Murray's name and phone number in it.

'No wonder you were so eager to provide me with an alibi. That was bloody clever of you, Ruth. I'll give you that. By covering for me, you put yourself in the clear. If I couldn't have murdered Christa, then you couldn't have killed her either. If she was still alive at half-past ten, then someone must have murdered her after you'd left, the person you said you thought was with her. What would you have done if I hadn't rung you but called the police instead? You knew I'd find Christa's body. Would you have let them think I was guilty of her murder?'

'I didn't mean that to happen,' Ruth said with a flash of her old spirit. She had taken her hands from her face and was looking straight into his eyes again with that challenging lift to her head.

'Didn't you, Miss Page?' a voice said unexpectedly behind them. They both turned with a shared sense of shock to see Finch standing at the open patio doors, looking into the room. Behind him were Boyce, whom both of them recognised, and two unfamiliar figures, a uniformed constable and a woman police officer.

'I'm sorry to make such an unorthodox entrance,' Finch continued, stepping into the room over the low threshold. 'I rang the bell but no one answered so I decided to come round the back. I noticed your car outside, Mr Bennet.' He nodded briefly at Alex, acknowledging his presence, although almost immediately his gaze switched back to Ruth Page.

Alex was astonished how quickly she had recovered from the shock of Finch's unexpected appearance. But perhaps it wasn't, after all, so surprising. He had always admired her courage and that cool intelligence of hers.

Holding her head high, she said quickly, 'How much did you overhear?'

'Enough to confirm what I already knew,' Finch replied, his voice and features expressionless. 'I spoke to Mrs Murray earlier this evening. She'll shortly be making a statement about her relationship with Miss Wyatt.'

Taking his eyes off her, he looked across at Alex.

'If you'll go outside with the constable, Mr Bennet, a police car will take you to headquarters where you'll be questioned. I'd be grateful, also, if you'd give the keys of your own car to the driver. They'll be returned to you once you've made a statement.'

It was said in the same impersonal manner and, as if the scene had already been rehearsed several times so that each person involved in it knew his or her movements, the uniformed PC came forward to conduct Alex from the room by the more conventional route through the hall and the front door, while the WPC came to take her place beside Ruth Page.

In the doorway, Alex looked back. For several seconds, his glance met Ruth's. Although she was looking directly at him, he found it difficult to read her expression except it reminded him of the child's in Christa's portrait hanging above the fireplace. It had that same wide, startled look of mute appeal. The next moment, he turned his back on her, as Christa had done that evening when Ruth had murdered her, and left the room. There was nothing he could do to help her.

Outside, events moved so quickly that he had little time to think about them. He was asked for his car keys and, as soon as he handed them over, he was escorted to one of the police cars which were parked in Bishop's Close. As he got into the back seat, he was aware that the normally quiet cul-de-sac was full of people, some standing on the pavements, some even watching from their upstairs windows. He could see their heads turned in his direction and hear their low, excited voices which soon were drowned by the sound of the car's engine as it drew away from the kerb and turned into Springfield Road where people were going about their ordinary affairs, waiting at pedestrian crossings, walking along the pavements, going into pubs.

At Divisional headquarters he was taken upstairs to an anonymous room, very like the one in which he had given his original statement; the same cream emulsion on the walls, the same nondescript furniture and carpet. Here he was given a chair and offered a cup of tea by a young, fresh-faced constable who seated himself on the other side of the room and, producing a copy of the *Evening Standard* from his pocket, proceeded to read it.

The tea came, brought by a WPC, and Alex drank it and looked out of the window at the roof-tops, watching the shadows slowly creeping across them.

It was ten past eight before Finch finally arrived, accompanied by Boyce. As they entered, the constable folded up his paper and left.

Turning a couple of chairs towards him, Finch and Boyce sat down. The chief inspector looked exhausted, his face grey and pouched with fatigue.

The last few hours had taken their toll of him, leaving him feeling raw, as if the upper layers of skin had been stripped away, exposing the nerve endings.

The process had begun earlier in the afternoon when he and Boyce had driven over to Buckleigh Green to interview Mrs Murray. It had been a distressing experience. Although she had admitted her relationship with Christa Wyatt, the interview, which should have been straightforward, had turned into a confession in which she had broken down and told him about other matters which Finch hadn't wanted or needed to know. Weeping inconsolably, she had spoken about her marriage to Robert Murray which, he gathered, was not happy, each of them leading their own lives although, for appearances' sake, they continued to live together.

He still felt guilty at witnessing her grief over Christa Wyatt's murder, which she'd read about in the local paper, and her own guilt and shame that she hadn't had the courage to come forward and admit to the relationship.

On returning to Divisional headquarters after arresting Ruth Page, he had seen her again, accompanied this time by her husband, leaving the building. She had called there, he assumed, as he had requested, to make a statement and have her prints taken so that they could be matched against those found in Christa Wyatt's bedroom.

186

To anyone who didn't know, they seemed a perfect couple, both tall, good-looking, well dressed and successful. And apparently happy. Murray, the ideal husband, was holding his wife tenderly by the elbow as he escorted her towards the exit.

Although Finch could only guess at Murray's sexual preferences, he had a strong suspicion that on those Wednesday evenings that Murray stayed in London, ostensibly working at the flat in Lauriston Gardens, he was engaged on quite another activity; visiting a mistress, perhaps, or a male lover; whatever he needed to turn him on.

The interview with Ruth Page had disturbed him for an entirely different reason. Unlike Mrs Murray, she hadn't wept. Sitting dry-eyed and straight-backed, she had replied to all his questions, even those her solicitor had advised her not to answer, frankly and without any overt emotion, agreeing to plead guilty at her trial. Afterwards, Boyce had remarked that it had been a push-over. And so it had been in some respects, but Finch had come away from the interview with the uncomfortable feeling that one day that steely self-control would split wide open. He could only thank God he wouldn't be around to witness it.

And then there was Bennet. As he entered the room where Bennet was waiting, Finch thought the man looked as exhausted as he felt. He was aware of a sudden upsurge of compassion although it didn't prompt him to soften the official rebuke which had to be made.

'Mr Bennet,' he began, his voice officially neutral, 'before we begin, I should warn you that proceedings may be taken against you on several serious charges which include withholding evidence, making a false statement and wasting police time. The decision, however, is not in my hands. That will be made at a higher level. You will be informed in due course what action, if any, will be taken. Do you understand?'

'Yes,' Alex replied. It was so long since he had last spoken that his voice sounded rough from lack of use and he cleared his throat. Despite Finch's warning, he felt a strange and unexpected relaxation of tension. Without being fully aware of it himself, he realised that, ever since Finch's arrival at Ruth Page's house, he had been holding himself in readiness for this interview with the chief inspector while at the same time closing his mind off from its inevitability. Now that it had come, he welcomed it with an overwhelming sense of relief. The lies and deceit were over and done with. The time for truth had at last, thank God, arrived.

He said, matching his own tone of voice to Finch's, 'I'd like to apologise for what I've done. I realise I have no excuse for my actions. I should have phoned the police as soon as I found Christa's body. I'm sorry about that. I'm afraid I panicked. I suppose you'll want me to tell you exactly what happened?'

'If you would, Mr Bennet,' Finch said.

Alex spoke slowly and with no emotion. It was all so distanced now anyway, like describing events which he had witnessed but not participated in, except as an observer.

Later, when he reached that part of his statement which dealt with his trip to Cornwall, the chief inspector, who had listened to his account without interruption, spoke for the first time.

'Was it your intention, Mr Bennet, to stay there permanently? I'd like that point clarified.'

'No,' Alex replied truthfully. 'I simply wanted to get away for a few days, that's all. I would have come back at some point although I admit I hadn't decided exactly when.'

After that, he gave a brief account of his return to Chelmsford, including his attempt to contact Finch and his decision to confront Ruth Page, in which he also explained, in as simple terms as he could, his reasons for suspecting her of Christa's murder.

And then it was all over. Finch rounded off the interview by glancing at the clock on the wall. Following his gaze, Alex saw to his astonishment that it was nearly quarter-past nine.

Finch was saying, 'You're free to go, Mr Bennet, although I'd like you to return at four o'clock tomorrow afternoon when you'll be informed what charges, if any, will be brought against you. A constable is waiting downstairs to take you to your car and give you back your keys. There's something else?' he added, seeing the man hesitate.

'I wondered how you found out Ruth Page was guilty,' Alex said. 'You obviously didn't arrive at the truth in the same way I did.'

'We used our own methods,' Finch said enigmatically. He had intended leaving it there but something about the man's frankness prompted him to add, 'It was a small point, Mr Bennet. In her statement, Miss Page said that Miss Wyatt had received a letter from her agent offering her a commission which Miss Wyatt wasn't sure whether or not to accept. But when I went through Miss Wyatt's correspondence, there was no such letter. So it occurred to me that if she hadn't told the truth about that, then perhaps she'd lied about seeing Miss Wyatt alive at half-past ten. It made me

188

wonder why she'd go to so much trouble to give you an alibi. Or was she trying to cover up for herself? The rest followed from that. If it's any consolation,' he continued, 'Miss Page has stated she'd had no intention of letting you be arrested for Miss Wyatt's murder. If it'd come to that, she insists she would've confessed. I think this time she was speaking the truth.'

'Thank you, Chief Inspector,' Alex said, grateful for this small crumb of comfort.

'So what do you intend doing now?' Finch asked more informally as they shook hands. 'I suppose you'll go back to your job; try to pick up the pieces?'

He was genuinely interested in the man's future.

Bennet smiled wryly.

'I suppose so; at least for the time being although I might try to get a job abroad. I don't know. I haven't decided.'

'It's not going to be easy,' Finch suggested.

'No,' Bennet agreed simply and turned to go. There was nothing more to be said.

After Bennet had left the room, Boyce asked, 'So what d'you think's going to happen to him? Will the Super decide to press charges?'

'Not if I can help it,' Finch replied. 'The man's made a full confession and that'll go in his favour. When I see Davies tomorrow, I'll recommend Bennet gets off with an official bollocking. I think he's been through enough already.'

There were other matters which would need dealing with the following day besides the four o'clock appointment with Bennet – statements to file, his own report to write, a further interview with Ruth Page, making sure all the loose ends were tied off, only they never were, of course; not properly, except on paper.

To hell with it all! he thought suddenly. He'd had enough for one day. It was about bloody time he started putting himself first for a change.

During the past few hours, he'd thought on and off about Nina who was due back from Marseilles that evening, telling himself that now she'd be packing, now setting off for the airport, now boarding the plane.

Her flight was due in at eleven twenty-five. If he left now and got a move on, he'd be in time to meet her at Heathrow.

And for God's sake why not? he asked himself. The rest could be left until tomorrow.

189

Boyce was asking, 'Do you fancy a quick jar before we pack it in for the night?'

'Sorry, can't make it. I promised my sister I'd call on her this evening,' Finch said, lying cheerfully.

Grabbing up his jacket, he made for the stairs which, in a sudden sense of release and jubilation, he took two at a time.